ENCOUNTERS
with
ENOCH COFFIN

W. H. Pugmire
&
Jeffrey Thomas

DRP

Dark Regions Press
2016

SECOND TRADE PAPERBACK EDITION

TEXT © 2013
BY W. H. PUGMIRE & JEFFREY THOMAS

FRONT & BACK COVER ART © 2013
BY SANTIAGO CARUSO
INTERIOR ART & FOIL STAMP © 2013
BY CHRIS LEDUC

EDITOR AND PUBLISHER, CHRIS MOREY

ISBN: 978-1-62641-158-6

FRONT COVER DESIGN BY X

BACK COVER AND INTERIOR DESIGN BY
F.J. BERGMANN
WWW.FIBITZ.COM

DARK REGIONS PRESS, LLC
6635 N. BALTIMORE AVE. STE. 245
PORTLAND, OR 97203
WWW.DARKREGIONS.COM

Dedication

Wilum dedicates this book to his magnificent friend, J. D. Worthington.

Jeffrey dedicates this book to his late father, the artist Robert Thomas.

Table of Contents

Ye Unkempt Thing

I.

I met my friend in front of the large green door of the Providence Art Club on Thomas Street, and she led me into the building and to its spacious exhibition room, where a new showing was being set up.

"We're just waiting for my other two acquaintances who will be joining us," said Candice. "They should be here—oh, they've arrived!"

I turned and greeted the rather ravishing black woman and her tall, handsome companion. "Do you two know each other?"

The black woman said, "No, we have just met out front. But I am acquainted with the work and reputation of this artist." The fellow stooped slightly in response and then winked at me, and I sensed that he might be a bit of a rogue. But as he was a friend of a friend, I would suspend judgment until I knew him better. The woman, whose tight yellow dress was really too low-cut and exposed her breasts rather alarmingly, held out a hand, which I took timidly. "And you are the Reverend Henry St. Clair, author of *Midnight Din and Other Weird Stories*?"

I confessed that I was. The artist, as he was referred to, introduced himself, and then Candice bade us follow her out of the building and down the inclined street to number 7, the Fleur-de-Lys Building, which I was especially interested in investigating, as an ancestor of mine had had a small studio there from 1930 until his suicide in 1951. We stopped to admire the fantastic façade of the old building, with its queer design and gargoyles and small paned windows, and then we were let inside. I loved everything about it, its delicious evocation of the past, the stairways and antique paneled doors. One spacious room was crowded with work tables and various paintings, mostly unframed, leaning here and there or hung carelessly on walls. We then followed our hostess to the upper regions and into smaller rooms, and I was certain that I recognized one of them from family photos of my poor deceased relation. As I entered the room, I fancied that the atmosphere subtly chilled, and I hugged myself protectively while the beauteous black woman offered me her strange smile.

"The past is alive here, is it not? One can feel it on this air breathed in and see it reflected on the windows where modern light is oddly muted." Her words bewildered me, as they seemed meant to have significance especially for me—which was absurd, of course; none of these people knew of my family's past relationship with the building; it was not something I confided to others, nor had I expressed its story in any of my fiction. I watched as the dark woman stepped to a windowsill that was half in shadow and upon which a cluster of dust had settled. I watched, as she bent to that dust and shadow, pursed her lips, and exhaled. Her eyes, as I watched the woman's face, darkened, as if suddenly overcast with storm clouds. The afternoon light dimmed on the other side of the room so that we stood in dusky gloom, but my attention was caught by the movement of the dust onto which the woman had blown—that dust that lifted and shaped itself weirdly as it seemed to conjoin with coils of shadow that rose with it. I watched the pygmy shape cavort in its corner on the sill, as if it were engaged in crazy dancing. And then the sun came out from behind clouds and light spilled into the room once more, and where I had imagined I had seen a fantastic shape there was nothing but some few particles of dust that fell so as to gather on the floor. I glanced at the Negress as she reached into the black leather bag that hung from its long two handles that rested on the woman's shoulder. She removed a white cloth and dabbed at her moist mouth.

We were shown other sections of the building for another half hour, and then returned to the steep hilly street, where we bade Candice goodbye and climbed up to Benefit Street. "There's a great sandwich shop a few blocks down," the artist chimed. "My treat, if y'all are hungry. I have a hankering to visit the churchyard at St. John's, where Poe used to court Sarah Helen Whitman, or so legend says. You two interested?"

I was rather hungry. "I have no appetite," the woman informed us, "but a visit to the churchyard would enchant me. I'm Marceline Dubois, of Sesqua Valley. You're from Florida, yes?" I replied that I was. "Then New England must seem almost a foreign land, yes? Such richness of history, such sensation of past things."

I turned to the artist. "And you?"

"Boston, so this is just like home, creepy burying grounds and all. Come on, I'm famished. This sandwich joint is good. I'm staying at an old bed-and-breakfast inn near it and had the best corned beef sandwich ever

2

last night."

A ten-minute stroll took us to the café, and their corned beef sandwich was quite excellent. We walked, we gents, with Miss Dubois between us as we chomped on our food and sipped from our bottled juices. Eventually we came to the steps that took us to the long winding brick pathway that led into the hidden churchyard. We had our old cemeteries in Florida, dating to the early 1800s, but there was certainly a different feel to the one we entered at that moment. The walkway took us toward the back of the venerable church, to a spot of land where we approached some few tabletop tombs that were entirely black with age. The artist leaped onto one of the slabs and danced irreverently.

"You're a merry fellow, Mr. Coffin," the black woman addressed him. "Would you court a woman in such a place?"

He stopped his silly capering and looked around. "I'd bring her here on a moody moonlit night and tell her such a ghastly tale that she would flee in horror, that would be fun."

"I fear you are not a romantic soul, Mr. Coffin," the woman scolded.

"I'm a beast, m'lady," he rejoined, bowing to her and then leaping off the opposite side of the tomb, toward the church. "Pah, what the hell is this?" We walked to where he stood and saw the curious pile of soiled clothing and bits of bone and other less recognizable debris that lay bundled on the earth. "Gawd, it stinks. Somebody meant to bury their pet or mother and changed their mind. Look at that hat, it's been gnawed on by graveyard rats, by the look of it. Ever seen anything so filthy? Pah!"

"It certainly reeks," I expressed, as Miss Dubois left my side and knelt before the pile with the strangest smile on her enchanting face. I watched as she picked up the grimy hat and sniffed at it. "You don't want to touch that stuff, my dear. It's coated with heaven knows what." Without answering me, she placed the hat onto the pile and leaned a little closer to the rubble. Subtly, she blew upon the heap, and as she did so the sunset grew a little darker. I watched her eyes as they caught and reflected the gold and amethyst shades of sundown.

"Well, this has been an enchanting afternoon. I have enjoyed your company," the lady informed us, standing and obviously signifying that our exploit was at an end. "It was wonderful to meet you, Mr. St. Clair. I hope we may look forward to a new collection of tales soon?"

I bowed to her and shook her hand. "My publisher has been making encouraging noises in that direction."

She turned to the artist. "Good day, Mr. Coffin." The handsome man refused her outstretched hand, strode to her and took her into his arms.

3

"The pleasure has been all mine," he sang as he lowered his head and pressed his mouth to her exposed bosom. "Let's come here alone some night before you leave and I'll spin you a macabre story."

"I think not, sirrah," she returned as she gently pushed him from her.

What curious creatures, I thought, as I walked with them up the red brick path to Benefit Street. I followed Miss Dubois up some steps, and then stopped as, holding onto the black metal handrail, the woman turned to gaze one last time at the ancient church. I turned as well, and saw the impish figure that watched us from where it stood near one of the flat tombs. Was it a child, perhaps, dressed in outlandish garb? As I watched, it raised one arm and seemed to wave to us, but something about its appearance disconcerted me and I did not return its gesture. The lady standing just before me did, however, lifting her handsome hand and moving it peculiarly, as twilight engulfed the sky.

II.

I accompanied the peculiar Enoch Coffin to his B&B on Benefit Street and accepted his invitation to his room, a spacious chamber on the first floor in which there was a large bed and choice pieces of good furniture. We sat in comfortable chairs before curtained windows and talked of Poe, weird literature, and other things. He asked why I had come to the city of seven hills.

"My publisher has sent me on a small book-signing tour of New England and New York, a short three-week affair. It's rather nice, I've never been one for doing much traveling. I'm anxious about New York—not much for crowds and such. Providence has been delightful, and the signing last night was well-attended."

He asked the name of the bookstore where I had signed, and nodded when I told him. "Yes, a charming little shop. I'll go there tonight and pick up your book. Interesting idea, a religious fellow writing horror. Being Christian, you naturally believe in evil. Yes, I thought you would. Have you ever confronted it, Reverend?"

"I've seen its manifestations, in crime and debauchery, certainly."

"Manifestations, yes." His voice was very quiet. "Personification? No? That's something I try to evoke with my art, you see—the essence of malignant evil. Not an ordinary every day iniquity, but the malevolence that one may detect, if one is keenly attuned, in secret places. *Old* places."

"But places of human habitation nonetheless, I think. Our conception of 'evil' is, these days, aligned with human crime, wouldn't you say?"

4

"That is a potent wickedness, certainly. But I was thinking of a different kind of—sin, let us say—that although implemented by human corruption has aspects of, um, *otherness,* something beyond mortality and—not quite human."

"Ah, yes, I try to suggest such things in my weird fiction. It's all fantasy, of course, but it can make for a powerful imaginative effect. It's a seeing beyond the veil, I tell my friends who criticize my penchant for writing horror. It's a lifting of shadow so as to peer, if one has the nerve, to that which lurks beyond."

Coffin clapped his hands together and nodded his head. "The great Outside, beyond the rim of time and dimension. The secrets of the grave, or beneath the grave. Gawd, how I adore it! How I love to conjure it with my art and give it aesthetic *life.* I love how it triggers things in the fools who react to my canvases and criticize them. They may not like what I paint, but they cannot deny its *effect.*"

I had had enough of the fellow's ego and eccentricity, and so I made my excuses, explaining that the next day would be my last in Providence and I needed to prepare for my trek to Salem. I had forgotten that it was late, and the darkness outside rather disconcerted me. Something in Coffin's energetic enthusiasm for 'the secrets of the grave' had gotten to me, which was amusing being that I was, after all, a horror author. I was at first uncertain as to where to walk so as to reach my room on College Hill, and so I crossed the street and walked toward the sandwich shop, which was about one block from where Coffin was staying. Right next to the old building that housed the café and some ascending apartments there was what looked like a large vacant parking lot, which was empty of everything except a large dumpster. I was still carrying my plastic bottle of apple juice, which I drained as I stood before the lot, and I decided to pop the empty bottle into the dumpster. The night was very quiet, deadly still. Going to the dumpster, I lifted its lid and dropped the bottle inside. The bin reeked, and something in the rancid odor seemed disturbingly familiar. It was as I lowered the lid that I noticed the shadowed figure, the dwarf in darkness, that stood against the cement wall just beside the dumpster. I thought, at first, that the figure was merely some flat silhouette that had been spray-painted onto the high cement wall, but then I saw the thing shiver and lift the head that wore the large round hat. The nighted area was too obscure for me to see any semblance of face or concrete form—the thing was just a shape that shivered momentarily and then lifted an arm, as if requesting alms. Saying nothing, barely breathing, I backed away and hurried out of the lot.

5

I climbed a steep street that took me to a cement staircase, and I grabbed onto its railing as I ascended to the area that took me to the neighborhood near Brown University where I was renting a room. Interestingly, I had felt a sudden itch to write, and so I walked to the bookshop where I had sat signing my collection the previous evening. The friendly proprietor smiled at me and indicated the table on which my book was being featured, and I was happy to see that there were far fewer copies than had been there when I finished signing. The book was selling well. I told the lady that I wanted to buy a couple of notebooks in which to scribble, and thus she led me to a section of the shop that featured a variety of types of notebooks and personal journals. I bought two thick notebooks of lined paper and this journal in which I am writing now. It came to me that I might be able to create an effective little tale concerning my experience in the parking lot, although I would have to expand on the horror. The idea came to me that my narrator could be a homeless hobo who had gone in search of food and found edible garbage in a dumpster, and so he climbed into the cozy den of compost and began to partake, and then he would fall asleep in the safety of the small confined area, until awakened by *something else,* something ravenous, that came in search of sustenance. I played with an outline but was suddenly too weary to write, although it was not yet late enough to sleep. My room looked out on a busy street that was active with college nightlife, and I opened my window so as to let the sound of youthful chatter and distant rock music filter into my little world. I welcomed the din of humanity, the buzz of mortal activity; for I had been touched by an aura of implacable menace ever since my meeting with the strange dark woman and the weird fellow from Boston.

I must have fallen asleep in my chair, for I awakened with a start. The activity outside my window had ceased, but music sounded still. I thought at first that one of my neighbors was either playing some exotic recording or that some foreign chap in a neighboring room was experimenting inexpertly on some flute or horn—at least, I assumed it was the playing of an instrument, for I don't think that a human mechanism could produce such a peculiar high wail; and yet, the more I listened, there did seem to be a kind of *articulation* in the sound. My chair was near to the window that I had opened, and I shifted my head a little so as to peer into the gulf of night, outside. That word—why did it send a tingle through my flesh? *Outside.* There, in night's gloom, where I saw no stars, I could but dimly discern one black globe that drifted ominously in an abyss of pitch. The midnight disc then opened two diamond-shaped stars in which sunset colors frolicked. Sparkling beams from those twin points of unearthly illumination drifted to me through the stillness of air and spilled into one corner of my room. It stood there, suddenly revealed— the dwarfish creature that wore its wretched rumpled clothing and from which a nauseating stench assailed. It lifted the malformed head that wore the tattered hat, and some void within what masqueraded as a face split so as to issue a high wailing that corresponded with the noise from the adjoining room. I saw the thin slits that served as nostrils and the pits that were vacant of eyes. The thing lifted an arm, as it had when I encountered it at the dumpster; but now I understood that it was not asking for alms but rather meant to *take* some kind of offering from me. I blinked as chilly exhalation froze my features, and I sensed the nearness of the black cosmic sphere that, having entered my little room, puffed upon my face. It brushed my countenance, an unholy gust, and my eyeball, inexplicably loosened, escaped its socket. The wretched imp, now very near me, caught my orb with its hand held out.

I awakened a second time, in my silent little room, with the wind of evening pouring to me from the opened window next to which I had slumbered.

III.

It was my last day in bewitching Providence, and I wanted to drink my fill of it before I boarded the late afternoon bus to Salem. I was rather annoyed, therefore, to run into Enoch Coffin soon after leaving my little room so as to walk the city lanes. He hadn't shaved and was dressed rather carelessly, I thought. He smiled at me in such a way that it seemed almost a condescending leer.

"Reverend St. Clair, how amazing of you to look so immaculate so early in the day. I have your little book and was hoping to run into you. Please, if you will." He held to me my book and a fountain pen, and I inscribed my name. "Excellent. I've read a few of the stories. You have a nice little style and a lively imagination. I like the one story set in Florida— it is a real achievement to evoke horror in such a dominion of sunshine."

"Evil may lurk during the brightest of days, Mr. Coffin," I rejoined.

"Indeed. Well, I don't want to abuse you if you're occupied. I was just on my way to Prospect Terrace on Congdon Street—such a wonderful view. You haven't seen it? Tag along if you like, the view of downtown and other westward regions is really spectacular. I've got some postcards in my valise, as I like to sit on one of the benches and jot wee notes to chums. You'll come? Delightful."

We walked together without speaking, and I grew suspicious when at last we entered the small park, as a familiar figure was seated on one of the benches and gazing toward the city spread below. Her bright red hair, which had been piled upon her head the previous day, now hung past her shoulders. She was attired in the same yellow dress, over which she wore a bright red coat that reached to her ankles. I almost wanted to make an excuse and depart, because I didn't want to be a part of any game they might have planned to play with me. It simply couldn't be coincidence, my being there with both of them. I decided I would be cordial for a little while and then be off. The woman stood as we approached her, and I tried not to gaze at her bosom, which seemed more exposed than it had previously, shockingly so. Coffin leered brutishly and let an obscene whistle escape his lips.

"Gentlemen, good day. I was just about to make my way down to Benefit Street. There's a forlorn little plot of wooded land just there." She pointed to an area below us. "It has a charming path that turns into wooden steps adjacent to a shunned house of ill repute. It would make an excellent little scene for some eerie horror story." She smiled at me. "Will you let me show you?"

"Um, I actually have some things I need to do before I catch my bus to Salem."

"Ah, certainly. Mr. Coffin? You will find the spot exceedingly atmospheric. You may want to sketch it. I'll pose for you, if you like."

"I'm all yours, wench. Nice knowing you, Reverend."

He held to her his arm and they prepared to walk away; and I was suddenly angered at being so easily dismissed, and so I cleared my throat and muttered something about joining them for the briefest moment. We walked, we three, down an extremely steep hill, and then along a rather rough road until we came to a path that took us into a little wooded region. We walked down the inclined path into a patch of gloom from which the light of day was held in abeyance, stopping just before a rather stout tree.

"Oh, look—our familiar friend."

I did not understand what Miss Dubois was alluding to until I drew nearer to the tree and saw the heap of clothing next to the base of the tree, on top of which rested the squalid hat. My anger increased.

"I don't know what kind of game you two are playing, but I am not amused."

"I think this would be a perfect pose," the Negress laughed as she leaned against the tree and unbuttoned more of her dress, so that her breasts spilled out. "What say you, Reverend?"

"Most inappropriate," I scolded, not looking away from the alluring sight.

Coffin raised his head and scanned the area. "It's a delicious atmosphere, don't you think, St. Clair? Triggers the imagination, don't you find? Come on, don't be so stuffy. Good grief, you write weird fiction! This is the clime that you at times skillfully stir up with your delicate prose. You really have an engaging style. How wonderful, to find the beauty of the beast, the wondrous secrets of the darkened realm. But you could see it more clearly, if you only tried. We can help you there, partner. Would you enjoy *really* seeing into the darkness, into the Outside? Would you?"

"I have no idea what you're babbling about."

"Let us conjure darkness for you, Henry," the woman sighed. "Let us show you what lurks therein, and help you to retain the taste of terror so that you can transfer it to your text. You have a splendid talent already— you just need a little assistance." I watched as she bent down and picked up the ruined hat, and I protested as she placed the wretched thing upon my head. "Nay, don't resist, my pet. Enjoy one new sensation."

She bent again, so as to dig her black hand into the debris of dirt and ash and bits of bone; and as she did so, Coffin pressed his lips together and began to whistle, and my blood froze as the sound that issued from his pursed lips was exactly the tune that I had heard, in dream or delirium I do not know, in my rented room the previous evening, that impish air, that fiendish melody. The Negress rose before me, her face a black sphere in which her eyes fantastically transformed and took on a diamond hue. I lifted my hand, wanting so to touch her eyes, as she brought forth her own hand and the pile of death that sat upon her palm. She blew the stuff into my eyes, and I blinked and blinked again as my vision altered, as I was able to see the darkness as never before, and that which lurks therein, as the cosmos whistled and shrieked idiotically all around me, and something, some dark thing, kissed at last my eye.

Matter of Truth and Death

I.

The cry of the beast was the combined final roar of every last dinosaur at the moment of mass extinction. The forlorn moan of a pod of sperm whales dying on the floor of the ocean. The howl of a hurricane at its vertex of strength, before its long diminishment. The long, single cry of the beast was all of these sounds at once, and yet even those comparisons could not capture its haunting resonance, its unearthly essence.

He had no idea how large the creature was, but it must be colossal, and yet there was something skeletal, wasted, in its aspect. It rested on all four weirdly bent, bony limbs, its emaciated body the same color as the rock upon which it was perched; a grayish-green, as if it were a chameleon that had changed its hue to blend in. The only other color was a white cloth or gauze wrapped around its hairless head, completely concealing its face. But as it called out, the depression of its elongated open mouth could be seen through the material that bound and blinded it.

The roughly-shaped block of green stone the beast squatted upon was the last in a string of similar blocks of varying sizes. He was not sure how many of these crude blocks there were, but all of them hung in the sky in defiance of earthly law, like fragments of an exploded moon in orbit around a globe. Yet above and below, instead of the blackness of space, there was only churning white mist. Against all this formlessness, only these hovering blocks. Maybe they were not fragments of something destroyed, however, so much as pieces yet to be assembled. Assembled into what, though?

So then, could it also be that the beast was not so much wasted away, as yet to be given its substance? Not crying out in impending death, but wailing in despair for not knowing what its final form must be?

As he gazed upon the floating chain of blocks, he noticed that there were odd symbols engraved into their surfaces, marks he had at first taken to be natural fissures. He could not decipher their meaning, but he sensed a potency in the carvings. What beings had incised these vast symbols, and how had they managed it with the rocks hanging in the void as they did? How gigantic must these entities be? Larger, perhaps, even than the wretched titan that crouched on the very last of the suspended fragments?

As if in answer to his question, he saw two immense arms emerge from the boiling, glowing mists. Two impossibly gigantic arms reaching toward the first in the string of suspended greenish blocks. His heart thudded in awe, for this being did indeed dwarf the enormous howling beast. It must be a god, with the powers of destruction and creation in those ten spread fingers.

And as he breathlessly watched, those hands took hold of the first hovering rock. They gripped it with such strength that the fingers dug deeply into the substance of the block. That substance proved malleable in the god-like entity's grasp. The two clutching hands squeezed, squeezed tighter, until the gray-green block was squashed and lost its form. Consequently, the odd glyphs carved into the surface lost their form as well.

With the symbols thus obliterated, a spell was broken and the vision faded from view, swallowed in the mists. But in the final moments before even that luminous fog lifted from his eyes and Enoch Coffin returned to himself, he realized that the two gigantic hands that had crushed the block of clay had been his own.

II.

Enoch Coffin roused from the self-induced trance of his waking dream to find himself again in his artist's studio, seated at a heavy wooden worktable much spattered with old paint. His hands rested on the tabletop in front of him, and in them he had crushed a large blob of oil-based greenish clay, extra-pliable from the warmth of his skin. He smiled in satisfaction, and still holding the mass of clay he rose from the table and turned toward a raised cement base he had molded in the center of the attic's floor.

Upon this makeshift pedestal crouched an odd figure, as large as himself. It was a bent-backed thing, with weird crooked limbs like those of a dog—a dog with human hands and feet. But the figure was merely an outline suggested by lengths of copper wire, its curved spine a bent piece of rebar, rooted in the cement block to support the wire skeleton. The head was merely suggested by several loops of the wire, a cloth draped over it.

The artist knelt down as if genuflecting and began pressing the clay around the right foot and lower leg of the framework. With sensuous strokes his thumbs smoothed the warm clay, which had the feel of human skin. And still he was smiling. Looking up at the veiled head, Enoch said in an arch, satisfied tone, "One obstacle removed. One step closer to you. When I finally stand before you on your pedestal, I'll tear that mask from your face—and know you."

Still shaping the artificial flesh with his skillful fingers, Enoch glanced behind him at the large package of clay resting atop the table. Tomorrow he would sit and concentrate on the vision again, focus on that image of the beast perched upon the last in a whole archipelago of clay blocks. Once more his dream self would slip through the weave of the curtain that separated this world from that other, and the mere vision would be replaced with awesome reality. At least, as much of a representation of that *other* reality as his human mind could process. But he had never let his human mind limit him in the pursuit of his art.

Each hovering block was etched with a binding spell, to keep the wailing prisoner isolated. But one by one he would eliminate those obstacles that separated him from his model. And with each block he destroyed in that world, when he returned he would add another mass of clay to the barren skeleton. The beast was the feral avatar of a Faceless God—a wild aspect of that god, which the god itself had imprisoned. Yet Enoch Coffin felt like a god himself, making Adam from the "dust of the ground."

He did not believe that this entity had no face, but only a hidden face. He was determined to see it—and reproduce it.

III.

With his concerns now returned to purely terrestrial matters, Enoch was prepared to leave his abode to take dinner and perhaps some carnal dessert at the apartment of a lady friend who ran a gallery on Newbury Street, and had even set upon his head his floppy-brimmed slouch hat so as to embark, when a figure stepped across the threshold of his attic studio unannounced. Enoch had witnessed—had conjured, both in his art and literally—many sinister things, and so he did not startle easily. His reaction to seeing this figure admit itself into his private sanctuary, then, was not one of fear but of anger.

"Will Ashman!" he exclaimed. "What the hell do you think you're doing, letting yourself into my home this way?"

The uninvited guest was an attractive young man with a tall, slender build, who looked as though he should move with a dancer's grace. Instead, he nearly collided with a small table by the door holding a lamp and a stack of sketchbooks. Ashman corrected himself with a little chuckle, but almost tipped back on his heels in so doing. He caught himself, staggered, and replied, "Sorry, my friend, very sorry. I did ring the bell, you know."

"The bell hasn't worked in decades."

"I knocked, too." Ashman had caught sight of a large unframed canvas leaning against a wall, and stumbled toward it to bend down and take a closer look. His expression twisted with confusion, then disgust. "It's perverse, your obsession with capturing ugliness so beautifully."

"If I didn't hear your knocks, that doesn't give you the right to let yourself in here."

Ashman straightened up again, grinning. "That will teach you not to lock your door in Boston."

"So it shall. Now if you'll excuse me, I have somewhere to be."

"Oh! So rude! But I know, shh, I know—it's I who am rude. Yes. So terrible, am I."

"So drunk, are you."

"Forgive me, Enoch," Ashman replied, with his smile now twitching almost imperceptibly. "I suppose I'm still mourning."

Enoch was mindful of a row of steel sculpting implements close by his hand, some with arrow-like tips and others with little hooks like dental probes. He had known that their exchange would soon turn to this matter, and he was wary. In a calmer tone, he said, "I'm sorry about your wife, Will."

"Sorry? Sorry, are you? What are you sorry for, exactly, Enoch?"

"I'm sorry that she killed herself, of course."

"Did you love Shoshana?"

"Will, don't talk foolishly. She was only a model to me."

"Oh! And did she know that? But of course she did. Maybe that sad knowledge prompted her decision, eh?"

Enoch lost his calm tone when he replied, "I'm sure your own difficulties had a lot more to do with her decision, Will, and your difficulties existed long before I met the two of you, so I won't have you laying Shoshana's suicide at my door."

Ashman cackled wildly, then clamped his hand over his mouth. "Sorry … sorry … but what an image you just put into my head! Me laying Shoshana's dead body at your doorstep. You should paint that, don't you think? Better yet, let me exhume her for you, maybe in a few years when she's more like the rest of the things you paint, and she can model for you once more!"

"You must leave this instant, Will," Enoch said in his most composed tone of voice. It was also his darkest, grimmest tone of voice.

Ashman ignored him, moving—as Enoch had feared—to the skeletal framework upon its crude pedestal. He didn't touch it, however, and didn't even remark upon it. To his layman's eyes, it was too insubstantial a form as yet to register as anything. Instead, the man went on, "As further proof of your perversity, in the painting of my dear wife I commissioned—yes, I introduced you to her myself, didn't I?—in that painting you made the beautiful Shoshana appear ugly, haunted, close to madness."

"I painted what I saw in her."

"It was a mirror she couldn't handle. Do you know she slashed your canvas to ribbons before she slashed her own flesh?"

Enoch made an involuntary sound of pain.

"Ah! But did you groan that way when you found out Shoshana was dead, or is it only your painting you mourn?" Ashman held his arms out wide. "Why not me, Enoch?"

"Why not you, what?"

"Why haven't you asked to paint me?"

"I didn't ask to paint your wife; you paid me, as you just stated."

"Why not paint me now? All right, I'll pay you, then! Paint me … paint me as you see me, too!"

"You wouldn't like what I see."

Ashman had already begun opening the front of his shirt. A button tore free and clattered across the attic's ancient floorboards. "Why won't you paint me?" the man sobbed the words now, undoing his belt and the front of his trousers.

As Enoch watched the young man remove the remainder of his clothing, and once again spread wide his arms as if crucified to an invisible cross, the truth dawned on him at last. How could he have missed it before? Will Ashman wasn't jealous that the artist had taken his wife as a lover. He was jealous that Enoch hadn't taken *him* as his lover, instead.

At the same time he took in this truth, he took in Ashman's wasted form. Had he always been this emaciated, or was it a result of his anguish? The man standing before him, wracked with sobs, was little more than a skeleton himself. The handsome features of his face had belied his actual condition. "Hideous, aren't I?" Ashman blubbered. "Do I repulse you?"

"No," Enoch stated, and he meant his words. "I find you terribly beautiful, actually."

The nude figure dropped to his knees, and now held his arms toward

15

the artist in supplication. "Then make me your model! Me … make *me*!"

Enoch acted on inspiration then, upon the artist's instincts he trusted more than he trusted conscious thought. After all, though of course much purposeful decision-making was part of each artwork he produced, Enoch Coffin also believed very much in intuition, and in the providence of the "happy accident." Such gifts as seemed to be given him by unknown powers he could almost credit as his collaborators.

What Enoch did was dig his hands into the open package of clay on his worktable, soften and warm a glob of it between his squeezing palms, and then approach his kneeling visitor. He reached out and smeared the greenish clay upon Will Ashman's face. Ashman closed his eyes and smiled rapturously, letting out a little sigh at the contact of the other's hands.

"My poor, poor golem," Enoch cooed, next smearing the clay down Ashman's neck, his shoulders, across his hairless chest.

"Yes," Ashman whimpered. "Yes!"

Before he had approached Ashman, and unknown to him, Enoch had pocketed one of his steel sculpting tools, one of those with a sharp little hook at its tip. With Ashman's eyes still closed and partially sealed by the sticky membrane of clay across his face, he didn't see Enoch raise this implement now and poise its tip over his forehead. Ashman gasped loudly when the tip bit into his flesh. As Enoch carved through the clay and into Ashman's flesh, he was reminded of the binding spells engraved on the archipelago of floating blocks in that other realm. The three symbols he inscribed, however, spelled out the Hebrew word *emet,* or "truth."

Ashman groaned in pleasure, not pain, as thin trickles of blood oozed from his new clay skin where it had been wounded. He lowered himself onto his back on the bare floorboards. And Enoch Coffin lowered over him, forgetting his dinner plans, forgetting his former disgust for his visitor. Happy accidents, and all that.

IV.

That howl, more lonely than the bleat of a foghorn turned to a deafening volume, cut through the swirling white masses of fog that filled this world. Enoch stood upon one of the hovering blocks of stone and smiled with satisfaction at how much closer he was drawing to that beast on the final block, each time he willed himself into this realm. And each time he came here now, he felt more in control of his abilities, no longer becoming overwhelmed and forgetting himself.

He could see, this time, that the bandages that blinded and masked the semi-human crouching beast were stained through with spots of blood. Was this a new development, or had he been too distant previously to make out this detail?

No longer suffering disorientation, he was not surprised when he directed his gaze to the block upon which he stood, and soon saw two vast hands reach out to take hold of it. These were his hands, his godly appendages, and he watched them crush the malleable block between them. One more stone removed from the barrier between him and his prize. One step nearer to what lay behind that gauze, like a corpse's winding sheet hiding his model from him.

V.

Much of the sculpture's body was complete now, though its copper skeleton was just barely concealed beneath its gaunt form. All that remained, really, was its shoulders and head, which was still only a series of wire hoops. Enoch felt exultant in his work; he could sense the power of the clay as he shaped it in his hands, caressed it smooth with his fingertips. It was the *blood* that had made the clay more potent. For after he had removed the bloodied material from Ashman's face and upper body, he had returned it to the batch of clay on his worktable.

For several days now Enoch hadn't heard anything from Will Ashman. He was relieved, as he had feared the man would cling to him like an orphaned child after that one feverish night in this loft. On the other hand, he found it odd, and finally a bit worrisome. He hadn't wanted to acknowledge that he might have played any kind of part in the suicide of Shoshana Ashman, but if her husband were to do himself in likewise, Enoch wouldn't be able to deny his contribution. And so, reluctant as he was to do so, when he wrapped up work on the sculpture he broke down and phoned Ashman's office. His secretary, however, informed Enoch that the man had called in sick for three days straight. Enoch next called Ashman's home, but there was no answer. More reluctant than ever, nevertheless he left his house in the early evening to look in on his former patron.

VI.

Enoch Coffin's house was located toward the bottom of the hill on Charter Street in Boston's North End, three stories tall including the attic that contained his studio, fronted in weathered dark shingles that looked like bark, and wedged tightly between taller brick row houses. Directly across the street was the extreme tip of Copp's Hill Burying Ground, the resting place of Cotton Mather. Enoch enjoyed having quiet neighbors, and wished they were all dead on his side of the street as well.

He had never liked automobiles, and one of the benefits of city life was the public transportation, but as it happened the Ashmans owned a condominium in one of the brick row houses on narrow, one-way Sheafe Street, only a few blocks away. Thus, Enoch thrust his hands into the pockets of his brown suede jacket, the brim of his hat pulled low as if to shade his eyes though it was already dusk, and set forth on foot.

When Enoch arrived at the building he rang the bell, which he heard distantly inside, and when no reply came he knocked loudly. Again his efforts went unrewarded, so he tried the door and found it locked. Irritated that Ashman followed his own advice, and feeling that he had at least made an effort to look in on the man, Enoch had started to turn away when he heard the door crack open behind him. He looked back and saw Ashman's eye at the opening, glittering at him in the darkness that had filled this thin alley-like street. Ashman recognized him from his hat, if not the face it shaded, and held the door wider, gesturing for Enoch to enter. If he spoke, it was too faintly for the artist to hear.

Ashman escorted Enoch into a parlor, and right away the artist could see that his painting of Shoshana was gone from the wall where it had hung. The light in the room was low. Ashman wore a silk kimono-style robe, but its front was open and he wore nothing underneath. It was not just the shadowed lighting, Enoch was sure, that made the man's ribs stand out like rungs in a ladder, his pelvis jut as if to tear through his dry yellow skin. The man's cheeks were sunken shockingly, his sockets pools of ink, and whatever good looks he had retained mere days ago had dissipated. The Hebrew word for truth still showed on his forehead, black with crusted blood.

"Your office said you were sick," Enoch said. "Get thee to a doctor, man."

"A doctor?" When Ashman spoke, it was in a cracked wheeze. "It isn't illness at work in me, or even grief, and you know that, Enoch; I can see it in your face. It's your black magic at work in me."

"I performed no black magic on you. I took pity on you with a little nonsense—no more."

"You pity me, do you?" Ashman sounded like he wanted to sob but hadn't the strength. "Everything is just material for your art, isn't it? Love. Blood. The soul. Just things you take and use without regard for their source."

"What can I do to help you?"

"It's that statue in your den of sin, isn't it?"

"You didn't mention it before."

"But I understand now. I see that wire figure in my dreams. It turns its empty head toward me, and looks at me without a face, and reaches out to me. I know what it wants. It wants my flesh."

Enoch could say nothing to deny Ashman's words.

Ashman continued, "What can you do for me, you ask? You can destroy that monstrosity."

"I can't."

"Can't, or you refuse?"

"I refuse to destroy my art."

"Then you'll destroy me."

"Nonsense. I'll take you to a doctor myself. Come and stay with me until you're well. Sleep and food will do you good, and I'll keep you away from the drink that's turning your mind to mush."

Ashman chuckled, a sound like broken bones clattering in his throat. "Ah, good doctor Enoch. Always the best of friends!" He gestured to the wounds on his forehead. "I'm Jewish, so I know that a golem is brought to life with this inscription. But do you also know how to shut the golem down? You erase one of these symbols and change the word 'truth' to the word 'death.' Did you know that part, too, Enoch? Did you?"

"I told you, it was only meant as play."

"Play, hm?" Ashman dipped into the shadows beside a sofa, and when he straightened he held a shotgun in both hands.

Enoch took a step back. "Will, don't be crude—this is beneath you."

"Home defense," Ashman explained. "To protect my art collection, of course."

"You know I can't destroy my artwork, but I'll help you in any way I can."

"Well, I admire your dedication to your craft. I guess you not only value it above the lives of your friends, but above your own life as well. Then the only other way you can help me is to get out. Get out, Enoch. You've cursed me enough."

"Will ..."

"*Go!*" Ashman rasped, thrusting the shotgun barrel toward him.

So Enoch Coffin backed out of the room, and Ashman didn't follow. Before he let himself out into the narrow brick chasm of Sheafe Street, Enoch heard a pitiful wailing sound come from within the depths of Will

Ashman's home, and its strange familiarity made him shudder.

VII.

The creature poised in the center of the attic studio, thin as a weirdly anthropomorphic greyhound and crouched as if to spring upon its prey, was now fully clothed in its meager flesh of clay. Except, of course, for the face. Even the back of the misshapen, hairless head was covered, but where a face should have been there was still only a gaping, empty hole. A void.

Yet last night, Enoch had stood upon and crushed the penultimate block; the last block before the one to which this untamed aspect of the Faceless God had been exiled, stranded as if on a lonely island in that former archipelago of clay.

Tonight, Enoch Coffin was determined, when he sent his consciousness, his vital essence—his very spirit -- into that realm of mist, he would join the avatar on the same block it perched upon. Surely it couldn't deny him. In that imprisoning pocket universe he had demonstrated the power of a god himself. It had nowhere to flee when he reached out to unveil the howling thing's visage.

As he sat at his worktable with a blood-impregnated lump of clay resting before him, however, and began the mental exercises for sending his astral self into the beyond, he found himself distracted as if an insect buzzed at his ear. That nagging insect was Will Ashman. He hadn't heard from Ashman since he had gone to his home several days earlier, and he had made no further effort to contact the man himself, either. Enoch had tried to help the poor fool, and Ashman had rejected him. What more could he do for him -- aside from destroying his art, which again was out of the question?

Irritated, Enoch tried to put the man out of his thoughts, and then to put irritation out of his thoughts as well. He must obtain a clarity of focus, a purity of concentration and purpose. Distraction wouldn't do, not when the object of his quest was so close he could almost touch it.

VIII.

Mist billowed around him, so thick it was as if he were blindfolded, and he felt that he shouldn't move an inch lest he step off the platform upon which he had found himself and plummet. But plummet where? What lay below him? Perhaps only a yawning infinity of nothingness. Nothing but this white ethereal fog.

Then came that howl, that despairing wail of unfathomable pain, and even though it shocked Enoch—particularly since it originated from directly in front of him—at the same time it oriented and grounded him. The terrible cry even seemed to dispel the mist that separated him from its source. As the fog parted like ectoplasmic curtains, the creature was revealed hunkering just a few paces in front of him.

The avatar was not colossal after all, but only the size of a man. Or was he the size of a god, himself? It rested on all fours, the bony tips of its long fingers curled into the very material of the greenish-gray block they shared.

The thing's cry was sustained in a single ear-shattering, mind-blasting note of suffering. Under the bandages that completely obscured the front of its ovoid head, there was an elongated depression that was possibly a mouth gaping impossibly wide. The gauze was stretched across this opening like the skin of a drum, and it vibrated with the beast's noise. Furthermore, whereas on his most recent visits the gauze had only been splotched with blood, now the entire front of the bandages had been soaked through with dark red ichor.

Enoch had been riding on increasing waves of confidence each time he ventured into this little oblivion that had been created to hold the beast, but now that he was only steps away from it he felt as close to a feeling of fear as he would ever admit to. Who was to say the entity would indeed be as cowed and humbled as he had imagined it would be, once he stood directly before it, as if it might view him as its new master?

And now, too, hadn't he thoroughly freed it from its bonds? If it didn't destroy him, might it at the very least spring past him, finally liberated, and plunge through the mist into a different plane? Perhaps even the plane in which Enoch's own reality existed? If the beast escaped now because of him, would the Faceless God that had caged it here seek to punish him? Imprison him, next, in his own little oblivion?

He had come too far to worry about that now; the time for doubt had gone, back when he crushed that first block engraved with its binding spell. And the best way to deal with his fear of the creature was to ignore that fear altogether. So before his nervousness could increase, and his resolve waver, Enoch Coffin strode boldly forward, reached out his hand toward the bandage wound around the head of the skeletal being, and wrenched it away in one sharp motion.

With the blood-saturated bandages drooping from his hand like a flayed skin, Enoch Coffin stared at the visage revealed before him and cried out, "No! *No!*"

But it wasn't horror that had made him cry out, cry out so that the creature's own howl abruptly ceased and his took its place. No, it was anger he felt. Fury at being cheated of his prize.

He had hoped to prove that the Faceless God, at least in this bastard incarnation, did indeed possess a face but that no mortal had ever glimpsed it before. So, it was a face he had anticipated uncovering. But not *this* face.

Back in his studio he had been distracted. His focus had been compromised. He had polluted the manifestation of this realm with his distorted vision, just as his friend's blood had polluted the clay and not enhanced it after all.

For the countenance that he had revealed, staring back at him with hopeless eyes in a shockingly skeletal yet still recognizable face, a face with the Hebrew word for "death" inscribed on its forehead, was that of his friend Will Ashman.

IX.

Enoch Coffin was wrenched so abruptly from the fog-filled purgatory that he had to sit at his worktable for a while until he felt less feeble and nauseated. From the corner of his eye, the nearly finished sculpture appeared to twist toward him slightly on its pedestal, but when he looked at it directly it was still, of course.

When he had his strength back he rose, but with uncertainty. Should he try calling? And if there were no answer, go to Sheafe Street in person? It was too late to call his friend's place of work. At last, Enoch decided to give an innocent-sounding call to the police.

"I'm concerned about my friend, Will Ashman," he explained to a detective he was finally transferred to. "I know he's been despondent over the recent suicide of his wife, and he hasn't answered my calls in days."

"Yeah, Ashman—on Sheafe Street, right?"

"Yes, that's him." Enoch was not surprised that the detective knew Will Ashman's name, or where he lived, and yet he had to *know* …

"I'm sorry to tell you, sir, but your friend committed suicide too, a couple nights ago."

The phone to his ear, Enoch turned his body to face toward the clay gargoyle again. "Oh Will. Poor, poor Will." He sighed. "How did he do it?"

"You really want to know?" said the policeman. "It was a shotgun. Must've put the barrel under his chin. The guys who responded to the call said he blew his whole face right off."

Enoch nodded, staring into the abyss that was the visage of the unfinished statue, and knowing that it would never be finished. In fact, just moments after he completed his phone call, Enoch Coffin set about destroying the tainted piece of artwork altogether.

W. H. PUGMIRE

Beneath Arkham

I.

(From the journal of Mona Malais)

We walked through the queer New England fog that had descended over Hangman's Hill and entered the forlorn area of Old Wooded Graveyard. It's funny, the way that fog can illuminate objects rather than conceal them—or maybe it's just Arkham fog that has such capability. Various pale tombstones almost shimmered as we passed them, although most were so ancient that the names of those buried beneath had been erased by time and the elements. I loved the place and dreamed of it always, and I had made arrangements with some sinister chums that my ashes would be interred here illegally, but I rarely came here at night because it was a place of danger. I watched Enoch as he drifted through the fog like some solid manifestation of a dream—he never looked like he belonged completely to the realm of reality. He moved differently than other people, in a way that is impossible to explain, and here he moved like smoke among the tombs, his eyes shining.

"Is it as you dreamed it?" I asked.

"No, in my dream there was an intense ... *yearning* in the air—or maybe it oozed from underground, an unwholesome hunger." I watched as he held out his arms and moved his large hands through the air as if they were implements of detection with which he could sense unseen things. "It was the appetite of the *Other,* but I can't feel it now. We own senses in dream-life that aren't within us in this mundane reality."

"I don't believe that," I countered as I raised my hands and tried to grasp the thing we sought. "The waking brain may function differently, but it still holds the elements it may possess in dreaming. I've had this recurring dream, although it feels more like a compulsion really, to come to this place and dig into the ground. In my dream I lift something from

25

a tiny cavity in the earth, but I always wake up before I can see what it is I've found. And now you tell me that since you've been in Arkham you've had a similar dream, even though you're entirely ignorant of Arkham's dark sites. So here we are, in search of the unknown."

He stood suddenly before me, very close. "We need to pool our resources, my dear." His heavy breath was sour, like the fog, and a new light had infested his eyes. I studied the face in which those blue eyes were set, the features of which were very masculine, except for the womanly mouth. To have him so close and breathing on me was thrilling, but more exciting still was the arcane power that I could sense pumping in his blood, a contagion with which I was intimate. Turning away from him, I raised my hands over the graveyard ground and spilled my mind into that sod. I sensed the buried thing. I fell to the earth, and Enoch fell with me, and together our frantic hands clawed into the dirt and formed a pit, until my hand touched the small metal box. Enoch wanted to disinter the object, but I pushed his hands away and clutched the box alone as I told my companion to erect himself. He rose in the fog, his eyes shimmering. I lifted the container out of our pit and placed it into Enoch's anxious hands. I actually thought he was going to drool as he made an uncouth sound that might have been a chortle.

"Let's violate this mystery and debauch this box with our hot hands." His eyes blazed with a kind of madness, and his lips were moist. Rising, I took hold of the ornamental box and watched his eyes as Enoch worked at the stiff latch, and after much swearing the fastener moved. Strangely, at that same moment the fog lifted and moonlight illuminated Enoch's sinister face. He sucked in the evening air as if it were an element of marvelous bouquet and lifted the necklace out of the box, and then he held it before me. I didn't move as his other hand combed my hair and began to unbutton my blouse. Cool evening air touched my breasts, as did his mouth. I laughed at his cunning smile as he erected himself and did not shut my eyes when he took the necklace in both hands and placed it over my head, guiding it onto my neck until its amulet nestled at my bosom. He moved a few steps away and regarded me with his artist's eyes. "Yes, it's quite superb, certainly worthy of the midnight visions it evokes. Why I've dreamed of it so curiously is a thing I do not yet understand. Why have those visions been planted into my brain—by whom?"

I heard his words but had trouble concentrating on them because my psyche was trying to decipher the effect that tainted my core being, an effect that impregnated me when the amulet touched my breasts. I imagined that I could still feel Enoch's cold mouth and rancid breath on my skin, although he was far from me; and as my senses drank in the weird sensation the air before me blurred a bit as if something from another dimension was stretching toward the necklace around my neck. That chill breath moved upward, kissed my eyes, until my vision smudged, an effect that allowed me to *see* more distinctly the phantom before me, a woman who gradually disintegrated and disappeared. I peered into Enoch's eyes to see if he had shared my vision, but he continued to concentrate on the necklace until, at last, he wafted to me and handled the ornament around my neck.

"Will she like it," I pondered.

"That's immaterial. It will add an esoteric touch to the painting because it's unusual and compelling. People will ponder its origin and significance. It will enhance her mystery."

I chuckled. "Her mystery needs no augmentation, as she is never without her veil. It wouldn't surprise me if she wears it always in the mansion." His enigmatic smile was his only reply. "Will she and her crippled brother really attend the opening?"

"Of course they will, that was one of my demands when they engaged me. They'll stay one hour exactly, and then they'll return to their secret lives." His smile was laced with cruelty.

"The real mystery is why she wanted to be painted."

"No," he spoke in his low-toned voice, "it was he who requested the canvas." His lips twitched, and I took this as a sign that he was tempted to tell me more but wanted secrets of his own. His cool hands caressed my breasts as he brought his face near to the necklace, and I thought perhaps he was studying his reflection on the smooth surface of the polished glass amulet. Then I felt him shudder and heave a little moan. I moaned with him, as his mouth moved away from the necklace and found my flesh.

II.

Having been erected in 1905, the manor house in which Randolph and Rebecca Lorne existed was not old by Arkham standards; but it was certainly an establishment of rich witch-town mystery and myth, legend that had reached its epitome with its current inhabitants. Enoch Coffin swung open the gate of the black wrought-iron fence and passed through onto the private land, but rather than going straight into the mansion he stopped and peered about, and then he stepped to a place that caught his weird sensibilities. He saw the circle of diseased ground and knew this it was the spot where the tree of legend had once towered, the tree from which Randolph Lorne had fallen as a child, an accident that necessitated the removal of a dead leg so as to save the boy's life. Oscar Lorne, the boy's bizarre father, had felled the tree and used portions of its wood to construct a series of artificial limbs that allowed his child the ability to stand and walk, and Enoch had heard the whispered lore of the arcane symbols that had been etched onto those imitation limbs. He raised one hand and moved his fingers strangely in an attempt to touch the magick and madness of the place. An influence pulled his hand toward the house, and to that edifice he stalked. The building was certainly innocuous in appearance, with its clean cream-colored wood and small-paned windows, its balconies and widow's walk. It looked a perfectly peaceful habitation from the outside, and it wasn't until one walked into the house that its sinister aspects became discernible. One passed the threshold and walked into a dark domain, a place that breathed of the past with its antique furnishings, its old oak paneling, its dead silence. The muted light kept things in semi-dusk, but as Enoch climbed the stairway he stopped to study some few of the large framed portraits that hung on the ascending wall in the poor light. It humored the artist that this family celebrated their sinister nature in the way they clothed themselves and the attitude expressed in crafty physiognomies. Each portrait had a small plaque fastened to it with the name of the person portrayed, but none had dates so as to provide the era in which the painted figure had existed; and the clothes donned by each individual were often so bizarre and inimitable in style that they offered no clue as to the decade in which a certain portrait had been executed. Enoch considered the defiance in the painted eyes and the subtle perversion expressed with curling lips, and then he touched a pair of frozen lips as if the smiling portrait might whisper some secret word into his hand. Yet the lips before him remained sealed, and so Enoch whispered an arcane word himself, an utterance that seemed to shape itself as darker air that sighed from out his mouth and floated upward, to the top of the stairs where another portrait peered at him with darksome eyes.

"Master Coffin, have you been absent all night?" The speaker looked little more than a fair-haired child, and although he shared some suggestion of features with the persons in the framed portraits, he looked almost too innocent to be one of the clan. The boy floated down the stairs and stood near the older man, and then he tilted toward the artist and pressed his face against Enoch's clothes. "Ah, you've been at the graveyard on the other side of town. Its clay has a distinctive smell, I find, which may have to do with the ghouls who are whispered to tunnel beneath it. Rather curious, the way a burying ground can infest your imagination and seem to be a place of *appetite*. It calls for the yet-living flesh that it would have burrow itself into its depths and find a habitat." Reaching for one of Enoch's hands, the boy lifted it to his face and studied the particles of silt that stained the artist's fingernails; and then he pressed the fellow's hand to his face and ran his moist lips over its tissue as swift air pushed out of the lad's nostrils.

Enoch moved his hand behind the young man's head and wound his fingers into the lad's thick hair, bending nearer so that their noses touched. "You smell so sanitary, dear boy. Let's find a plot of earth in which to sully you, and then I'll lick ye clean."

Randolph Lorne pushed the artist away. "It must get tiresome, having to live up to your legend of debauchery."

"You're far more a creature of legend than I'll ever be," the artist countered as he touched a hand to Lorne's stiff leg. The younger chap pouted for one moment, and then he moved away and limped into the spacious drawing room, where he fell onto a sofa and began to roll up his trouser leg enough so that the lower portion of his faux limb was revealed to the room's soft light. Silently, Enoch entered into the room and knelt before the boy, and then his hand ran along the surface of the wooden leg in which odd symbols had been etched.

"This is the second one I've had at this age. The one before got ruined when Rebecca attacked it with a hatchet during a moment of violent play. Father had a series of them fashioned which were fitted as my body expanded with growth—but I think I've reached my final height, so the others will stay in their little box."

Enoch's breath issued as a low-toned whistle. "I have seen these symbols in some few esoteric tomes—and yet there is something unique about these. Were all of your faux limbs constructed from the tree on which your ancestor was hanged?"

"Hanged herself. She wasn't executed. It's just a legend, anyway. The sigils are queer, aren't they? I used to fantasize, when I was a kid, that if I learned their true meaning their magick would transform my dummy leg into a limb of flesh and bone. But Rebecca and I discovered, as we aged, that we didn't have any deep interest in the old ancestral ways, no taste for alchemy or murder. It all seemed a bit stupid, you know, spells and philters and dancing nude in moonlight. It wasn't intellectual. It lacked the kind of art that interested us. And it's so exhausting, our ancestral ways, roaming the globe in search of keener arcane capacity. We wanted to stay here, within our fortress, with our books and dreams."

"What dull ideas you have had. So you lived within your safe and silent world of books, and literature lured you enough so that you began to write poetry of your own, such strange evocative verse?"

Randolph smiled a little. "That's a recent development. I do enjoy it, though, and I loved working on the design of the book, choosing the soft velvety binding, paper stock, a unique shade of ink, all of that. I wanted the construction of the actual book to be as aesthetic a thing as the writing of my little poems. I should have thought of you when I was contemplating the author's photograph. We had the photographer age the thing so that it resembled a faded portrait of the past—but how appropriate it would have been had you painted an actual portrait to be reproduced in the book."

"We can still do that."

"No, I'm not having any further editions printed. Three hundred copies is quite enough. I can't believe they all sold. Anyway, I didn't know about you until the write-up in the paper about your exhibition. That gallery has such a sordid reputation that no respectable artist will exhibit there, but their shows always get a little mention in the paper. We don't get the paper, of course, but some 'kind' anonymous person sent a clipping of your write-up with its photograph of your painting. That's when I decided to attend the opening."

"You were impressed enough to hire me to paint your sister's portrait, although the idea you have for the painting is grotesque and unimaginative. Do you not see that it would be cruel to transform your sibling into a fake resemblance of yourself? For that is what you seem to want from me, a painting in which her fascinating bestial distortion is smoothed into a boring replication of your ordinary beauty. You would turn her into another faux extension of yourself. Bah."

The young man did not reply with his mouth, but his eyes were expressive and malevolent. Enoch appreciated seeing the youth's true nature, if only for a moment. Randolph began to prepare to roll down his pants leg, but Enoch stopped him and bent to further investigate the leg with his fingers. He could tell by touching that some of the sigils were quite old, yet there were other etchings that were fresh. Whatever ritual the symbols were a part of, it was obviously ongoing.

"You will do the portrait you've been hired to produce, certainly."

Enoch frowned. "No. I will paint your sister as she is. Get someone else to do your other idea, I can't be bothered."

"You're bloody insolent. You may remove your hand from me now. Your roguish handsomeness does not allure me."

Enoch slapped his hand against the fellow's other leg of flesh and bone and rose as Randolph rolled down his pants leg. The lad followed Enoch out of the room and to the staircase with its portraits.

"Look at them, your unholy forebears. You think that you can ignore the sinister nature of your line? Bosh. It is your perverse and wicked nature that led you to me and made you whisper your request for your sister's portrait."

"No, it was your awful painting that brought me out, when I saw it in the article that announced your showing. That was a moment of nightmare, I can tell you. How you knew what the thing looked like—for it was destroyed years ago—I cannot guess."

"An Arkham resident sent me a photograph of the tree from which you fell as a child, the tree that has supplied your ersatz limb. The photograph wasn't clear, of course, so I couldn't quite make out the symbols that had been carved into the thing's bark—those esoteric etchings that now decorate your appendage. My friend was familiar with the tree and had made a copy of its symbols before the tree was destroyed; but of course she didn't need to do so, for I was familiar with the formulae with which your father—I assume it was he—had marked the tree."

"No, the tree's markings had been carved into it before we took hold of the property. Your friend is this Mona something, who then did a series of paintings of the tree? I've never seen them, although I hear they were exhibited in Boston. "

"Yes, Mona. She was so young when she did those paintings, and she wasn't quite able to capture the creature's ambiance as I sensed it from the photograph. Photography can sometimes capture things that elude ink and oil."

"Well, what I want from you is pure art. Now, be a good fellow and heed my request. Paint my sister as if she were beautiful. Give her a face like mine own."

"There is something rather cruel in your request. I've noted a touch of malice in your verse, and I see it darkening your petulant eyes now. What, I'll paint your sister as she can never be, and my canvas will be a tool with which you'll taunt her?"

"Oh, she's tough."

"Well, I again refuse. I'll pack tonight and be gone in the morning. Really, you're too insulting. I can make her magnificent as she is, I have that artistic power. I will not debauch her brutal fate by making her prosaically pretty, as you are."

"God, you're so superior, judging me as you do. I have my own depths and enigmas. I have this, damn you." He tapped his knuckles against the surface of his artificial leg. "You're smiling? Ah, this is a game, and you've played me. You desired an emotional rise, and you've gotten it. All right,

31

do as you wish. Paint Rebecca as you will, if you think you can study her face and not be tainted by her nature. You know so little. You'll find her a challenge as you have never known. Good day, Master Coffin."

Enoch watched the young man limp into the drawing room and close its doors. Then he turned and climbed the stairs that took him to his room, watched by the frozen eyes of those portraits that he passed.

III.

The face within the web watched him from its place in upper darkness. It was a visage almost immaterial, a residue of revenant that hungered for one last gasp of mortal breath. The face moved behind its covering and made a little sound, and Enoch fully awakened to discover that his patch of dream had substance in reality. She stood with her back to the antique upright mirror where her image, silhouetted by the slight slice of moonlight that filtered through thin curtains, was a nebulous blur. She brought a smell with her, like that of upturned old earth, and he breathed deeply as he sat up in bed and drank her strange allure.

The sound of soft laughter came from behind her layers of veil, and then she gasped as he pushed away the bedclothes with his legs and revealed that he was nude. Flowing toward him like hungry shadow, she stood above him and inhaled deeply. Again, she laughed, and something in the sound hinted of insanity. Enoch raised a knee and clasped his hands around it. "I have something for you," he said in his low sensual voice. Rebecca gasped softly and backed away as he pushed out of bed and walked to a bureau on which the embellished metal box sat. "Open the curtains there," he told her, "so that more moonlight can ooze into the room. Excellent. What a wonderful effect of light and gloom, and you look so proper in that duskiness, with your somber attire and air of mystery. Look at the way the design on the container is enhanced by lunar radiance, so lovely. Come here, I'll just undo this little latch and then we can open it together. Do you always wear gloves?"

"Never without my armor," she sighed, in a voice that wasn't much more than whisper.

"Does it protect you from the world, or just your brother?"

"We are rarely in your world, Mr. Coffin, and I have next to nothing to do with him. Do you want to know my sibling's great misfortune? He has no real imagination, he cannot think beyond his little self. His little book is nothing but a pathetic personal wail, for which it seems there is some small audience. He doesn't understand me or the reason that I dress as I do—he thinks it's a symbol of shame. I feel no ignominy in being bestial, or in the occult madness that created me."

"Do you like the dress I brought for you to pose in?"

"It's beautiful, such a dark red, like mingled blood and shadow. It fits superbly. Am I sitting for you in the morning?"

"Do not wear your masks. This is to be a portrait."

Her hands went to her veils and smoothed them. "Is that what you call them, my masks? No, I adore the way reality looks through their fabric. They complement my fashion, my mystique. I am a thing of shadow, that's what Randolph sometimes calls me. 'O thing of shadow, come kiss me sweet and twenty.' To be a thing of shadow gives one immense freedom, I find. I enjoy being kindred of darkness." She exuded a little laugh and then, kneeling before him, touched the container. "So what is this object?"

"Come," he said, taking her hand and guiding it to the hinged lid. Together, they lifted the lid, and she wheezed her little gasp as he took up the necklace and spilled it into her gloved palm.

"The amulet is so cold. God, look at its shape, like some poor creature's atrophied heart. The small black pearls look metallic, don't they? It's lovely, in an unholy kind of way. I've seen it before, I think." There was a kind of excitement in her chatter, but then it suddenly ceased and she grew still. Enoch took the necklace from her hand and raised it before her chest, and the young lady bent low so that he could slip the necklace around her. He was again aware of her smell, and he wondered why her scent reminded him of the upturned earth of the burying ground in which he and his whore had found the amulet. "Who was she?"

"She?"

"The previous owner. Your lover? Mother?"

"No, it's none of mine."

"But she's followed you here, can't you smell her? She reeks like moist cold clay. I thought it was you, but your only stench is your nasty breath. She's here, tugging."

"Why are *you* here?" His question came suddenly from him and surprised her. She shook her head and moved away, going to gaze out the window at the moon. "What brought you to my room tonight?"

"I have a little yen for danger and thought maybe I'd find it here. God, I'm bored. My brother likes to pretend that it was his idea to bring you into our realm, but the inspiration was all mine. He described your painting of our ancestral tree, and I'm curious as to what inspired your interest."

"A friend in Arkham did some paintings of it when she was very young, and they caught my fancy when she showed some few of them in Boston. She explained the legend of your family, the legend that you seem not to want to be conjoined to. After hearing your intriguing myth, it was startling to find Randolph at my Boston opening. And then he came to me, with his queer request." His smile, when he offered it to her, was a wicked thing. "Danger, if that's what you require, is easily applied. Rise, Rebecca, and sit here on my bed as I move to kneel before you. No, don't resist me as I lift your length of dress. There. Ah, your legs are smooth."

Her sudden laughter was strident. "You were expecting me to be some kind of missing link? The servants have told me some of the stupid legends concerning me in town, of how I'm bent and brutalized and bestial, a hobgoblin who hides from society. No, my face is my one 'misfortune.' Are you satisfied with my legs?" She moved one leg slightly toward him so as to allow her toes to frolic with his prick.

"They're nice, but I don't want to admire them. I'm going to mar them. Do you enjoy pain?"

"I've rarely experienced physical pain, if that's what you mean."

"Ah, but mental anguish is another matter."

"No. I'm too complacent to care what people think of me, and we are now so secluded that the other world rarely touches us. My life isn't hot or cold—just very bland and safe. What's that?"

"It's my exacto knife—an artistic implement. Yes, it's deadly sharp, don't press your finger too keenly against the blade. The aluminum handle is quite solid and I work it deftly, as you see. Ready? Let me just recall your brother's limb." The artist closed his eyes and conjured an image in his brain, and it always thrilled him that his memory was so keen and its images so lucid. Enoch pressed the blade's point against the skin of the woman's leg and, with eyes still shut, began to etch. Rebecca made no sound but watched the sigil that began to form in her flesh, a replica of one of the esoteric symbols that had been carved into her brother's faux leg. She watched, as Enoch took a handkerchief from his shirt pocket and dabbed at the blood that began to spill down her limb, and then he kissed the aesthetic wound and licked the residue of blood away, revealing the symbolic white scar. "Grab some of those Kleenexes or whatever they are from that sachet and press one here while I work."

The artist continued his labor until there were three nice scars etched into the woman's leg. Rebecca ran one hand over the pale etchings and then lifted both hands to her veils and smoothed them. "What are you laughing about?" she queried.

"You and your brother pretend to have no interest in your sinister ancestry, and yet you are both so infested by it. Why do you pretend to disown it?"

"I don't, that's him, and he's so boring about it. He's grown conceited since his book was published. I think he secretly wants to go into the world and 'be' someone, but then the idea frightens him, we've been so *out* of the world our entire lives." She strolled past him and went to a bell pull, which she yanked, and soon an elderly man crept into the room, looking surprised to find his mistress in the nude stranger's boudoir. "Prepare the lighting in the grotto, Upton. That's all." The gentleman genuflected and escaped the room. "Put some clothes on, I'm going to take you on a little journey." Then she, too, stepped out of the room and haunted the hallway as he quickly dressed. Stepping from the room, he stopped and gazed at the strange woman in her black attire and veils. She did not look at him as she raised her hand and motioned like some eerie harbinger that ached to announce some secret thing. He followed her quietly down the stairs and through a dusty hallway, and then through a doorway that led to a flight of rough stone steps that took them into a place beneath Arkham's earth. Enoch noticed the odd blue lights that had, here and there, been embedded into the rough-hewn walls of rock, supplying feeble light. The place to which he was led was indeed a small grotto, but instead of being filled with religious icons he saw that it contained a number of very ancient-looking spinning wheels, all of which were coated with filigrees of dusty webs. The dirt floor looked smooth, but some portion of it must have been recently dislodged, for Enoch smelled a nasty residue of upturned earth. He listened as, standing close behind him, the young woman inhaled the stench as well.

"What is this place?" he asked her, placing a hand upon the gritty surface of the spinning wheel that was nearest him.

"I come from a family of weavers, witches who made their own clothing into which they embedded signs and sigils." She floated to one wheel that looked less antique than the others. "My mother used this to make my gowns, lots and lots of them that would see me into maturity, gowns into which she sewed protective charms. She must have been plotting her suicide even then. It was she, you see, who—but that's not important. Funny, she didn't teach me the art of the wheel, as has been our ancestral tradition. But I taught myself a bit of it."

Enoch watched as she sat at the wheel and began to work it, but he couldn't see any material with which she labored. And then he noticed the shadow on the floor of earth—or, rather, the shadow that seemed to swim just beneath the surface of hard sod. And he smelled the increasing

35

stench of death's debris that accompanied the moving form, the silhouette that wound around Rebecca's form and touched what might have been a phantom's head to the charm that Enoch had given the young woman. Ghastly laughter, soft and low, issued from the face concealed behind its veils as Rebecca shuddered and rose, and he tried to ascertain the thing that she held onto so delicately, her work of weaving. As she held it before him he thought it was a curious mask composed of cobwebs and shadow, and he did not move as Rebecca pressed the topmost portion of it to his temple and let the ghostly fabric fall so that it covered his face. No, he did not move, except to shudder slightly as the monster moved her hands to her own veils, which she lifted so as to reveal her face, the unholy mouth of which she pressed against Enoch's own.

IV.

They scuttled to him through web of dreaming, the denizens of the portraits on the stairway of the great house; and they seemed to split their mouths as if in calling, yet it was not the artist they sought. Pale fog, spilled from phantom mouths, filled his dream with rotten reek. The phantom portraits sank from sight as Enoch rose from slumber. He slipped into stained work clothes and strolled down to the lower level, to the neglected and unfinished conservatory near the back of the manse. It was there that Enoch had wanted to paint the lady's portrait, for the light was very good, and the inoperative fountain in the middle of the room would serve as a baroque background before which Rebecca could pose. Dirt and cobwebs were everywhere, and the room's floor was smooth packed earth onto which the artist had set up his easel and stool. The morning light was a soft haze that filtered through the many windows and gently warmed him; he raised his face to it, smiled and shut his eyes as an aged servant crept into the room with a tray of tea and buttered scones. The raisins and cinnamon in the scones proved a pleasant counter to the room's rancid air and odious smells. The stale, lifeless odors of the place reminded Enoch of his fantastic dream and gave him pause. When at last he opened his eyes his gaze met that of Randolph's.

"I hate this place," the young man whispered as he limped to the tray and took up half a scone. "Haven't been in here since that final leg was adjusted."

"What?" The artist watched as the lad lumbered to an oblong box, coffin-shaped, that sat on the floor of dust and dirt. Undoing a latch, Randolph opened the container's lid, and going to stand beside the boy

Enoch saw the assembly of artificial limbs of various sizes. Enoch's large hand took up one prosthesis and held it to the room's good light, and he ran his other hand over the symbols chiseled thereon; and then, strangely, he tilted his head to the limb, kissed it and uttered weird words. The boy beside him gasped. "What?"

Randolph had gone very white, but his eyes were dark and troubled. "I—thought I felt something—on my limb. Something tugged it…" He then seemed to hear what he was saying and laughed unconvincingly. "I think the wretched ventilation of this lair is getting to me." But then his eyes looked startled again as a figure glided silently into the conservatory. She was dressed in the maroon gown that Enoch had brought for her to pose in, and her face was unconcealed. The ruddy relic that had been found beneath cemetery sod was worn so that it rested at her bosom. Enoch's eyes slid to observe the brother, and it was obvious that Randolph had not seen his sister unveiled for a very long time, if ever, his expression of horror was so intense.

Rebecca laughed at the expression on her brother's face. "Behold the beast," she sang as Enoch stepped to her and took up her naked hand to kiss. The flesh he pressed against his lips was soft and firm, and he smiled as he turned that hand over so as to play a finger through the fur that sprouted from its palm. Yet the artist could not keep his gaze from rising so as to linger over the creature's monstrous pate, and yet to observe it was to experience an overwhelming vertigo and sharp pain behind the eyes. The contour of her enlarged square head was not fixed but rather subtly altered in outline, shrinking and expanding. The wide mouth could not comfortably fit over the enlarged flat teeth and portions of the lips had been continually chewed into. The black eyes were liquid pools sunk into pits of blue and purple flesh. The mouth exhaled thick breath. "Come, sirrah," the fiend commanded. "Come kiss me sweet and twenty." Enoch made a monstrous sound as he took Rebecca into his arm and smashed their mouths together. When he moved his lips away he could taste the blood that spilled from where they had been bitten. He tried to gaze at the grotesque face before him, but the way its shape seemed to seethe with subtle reshaping hurt his eyes. "I've forgotten my effect," she whispered. "Does it give you pain to look on me?"

"Yes, delectable pain. My eyes, mostly. Looking on you is like peeping past some preposterous alien dimension into which one might plunder. You're ghastly."

The young creature howled merriment. "It will be a challenge, then, to paint me. You were going to do just a charcoal outline this morning,

yes?" She looked away from him to her brother and the crate beside him.
"Ah, brother—your remnants. I don't see the one I damaged not too long
ago, when I came at you with that little hatchet, remember? You were
taunting me by placing a shawl over your head and aping my veils. I cured
your cruelty that day, brother." She turned her sable eyes to Enoch. "Do
you understand this gift you've given me?"

"I realized that the sigils had been first applied to a sentient limb, the
living tree. This is where your sire's divorce from dark arts did him an
injustice. But of course he wasn't your father in fact, as you are an element
of the Goat with a Thousand Young. Perhaps that's what initially triggered
his antipathy toward alchemy, pathetic mortal jealousy. He recognized the
potency of the sigil's magick and followed an ancestral instinct that led
him to carving them on his son's artificial limbs, not understanding they
would be impotent."

Rebecca sighed happily. "They are potent indeed."

"What the hell are you two babbling about?"

"No, no, young Master," Enoch remonstrated. "There is no confusion
in our discourse. We know the power of esoteric language, and its purpose.
We comprehend the power of occult sigils etched onto a living surface,
such as the daemon tree from which your false limbs have been fabricated.
And yet your pappy was not completely mistaken—for alchemy can often
transform one thing into another. Water becomes wine. Copper shines as
gold. Extinction rises as existence."

"Your slices into my skin have spilled ability to my clumsy tongue,"
the young mistress sighed. "I felt the tugging in my brain earlier, you
must have spoken the sigils for one brief moment. Let me utter them
now, at length." She opened her mouth and began to chant, and as she
did so she lifted the hem of her gown so as to expose the etchings on her
leg, those living symbols that pulsed as conscious scars. She ignored her
brother's sudden screams as he tumbled to the ground and writhed. Enoch
watched as the objects inside the oblong box next to which Randolph
collapsed began to tremble. The boy did not seem to notice, for he was
too occupied with ripping his ersatz appendage from where it was fastened
to his form. Randolph finally freed his false leg and threw it from him,
and Enoch chortled as he watched the surface of the wooden leg ripple
and grow supple. The crate finally exploded as its contents, pulsing with
resurrection, crept toward the boy's discarded leg. Randolph stifled his
screams as he watched in horror at the transformed legs that began to
conjoin and spread roots into the earth. Unable to stand, he pushed away
along the dirty ground, toward the young woman who cooed at him and

held out her sisterly arms. Weeping and confused, the boy dragged himself to her and buried his face into the folds of her gown. Rebecca wove her fingers into his hair and then closed them, tightly.

"Water into wine," the woman sighed and shuddered. "Extinction writhes."

The smell came then, powerfully, from beneath the Arkham earth. Phantom cracks seemed to split sections of the ground, and from those crevices obscure forms began to lift, dark ambiguous fiends. A sound of buried rhythm pulsed from some deep place, and Enoch watched as the relic worn at the young woman's breast shimmered faintly in time to daemonic pulsation. The shadows rose and shaped themselves playfully into the portraits that lined the stairway of the mansion, the phantoms that had visited Enoch in vision. Rebecca laughed as her wide malformed nostrils sucked in the fetid aroma of ancient upturned sod in which rank things had been interred. One specter especially caught Enoch's attention, a woman who shared Randolph's beauty yet whose face was scarred with sorrow, a woman who wore at her bosom a relic identical to that which now adorned her daughter.

Enoch watched as the apparitions drifted around the entity of conjoined limbs that had now rooted into the earth and lifted as single entity, its symbols pulsing as sentient white scars upon its husk. He glanced at the magnificent woman as her claws continued to dig into her brother's scalp, from which minute streams of blood began to leak. And then the diabolic artist lay upon his stomach and began to sketch Rebecca's portrait in the dust.

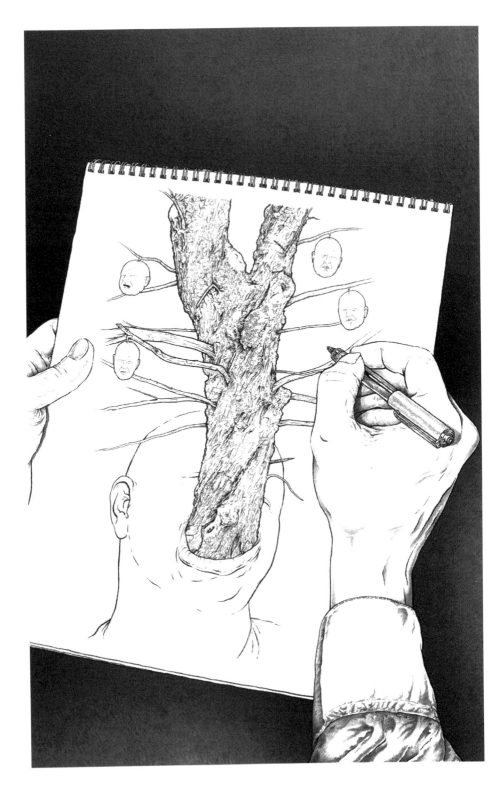

Spectral Evidence

I.

Enoch Coffin disliked two things about the "Witch City," as Salem, Massachusetts referred to itself for the sake of tourism. One was that the city had indeed made witchcraft a source of fame, when that fame was built upon the execution of twenty innocent people. The other thing that soured him was that in more recent times Salem had become infested with people only too eager to identify themselves as witches, who were to Enoch's mind no more witches than those innocents had been. Fakers, posers, goths, eccentrics. Even earnest and devoted pagans, whom he had more respect for, didn't seem to understand the sorts of witchcraft he himself had become familiar with, and even utilized, in his travels and in his art. But it wasn't that he found no charm in the city's year-round Halloween atmosphere, however tacky it might be. How could someone with his aesthetics be totally unmoved by a city that festooned and bedecked itself with images of death, the macabre, the supernatural? No, things were not always black or white. Not even when it came to magic.

Enoch didn't care for cars and avoided driving when he could. North Station was an acceptable distance on foot from his home in the North End of Boston, and from North Station it was only a thirty-minute ride by train to Salem. Along the way, he sketched with a technical pen on a pad open across his knees. His model was an obese man, head shaved entirely bald, seated across the aisle from him, asleep with his head tilted back and mouth gaping wide. Enoch portrayed a monstrous old tree growing from the man's mouth, from which hung a crop of fruit, each one of them a miniature version of the sleeping man's face.

Bah—uninspired, but maybe he could add it to his selection of pieces on display at his destination today; an art show in Salem limited to the month of October, called *Gallery of the Grotesque*. He hadn't visited this place again since he had delivered his pieces to be included in the exhibit, and upon that occasion he had been sorry to even set foot a single time within its rented space. A series of linked rooms, their walls covered with dragons and vampires, zombies and more vampires. At first glance he had felt humiliated to be associated with it. But sometimes a balance had to be struck between art and commerce, and since Enoch was careful how he rationed the inheritance he primarily lived on, his art by necessity supplied an irregular source of additional income.

He hadn't really expected any of his pieces at the *Gallery of the Grotesque* to sell, the way he had priced them—though he would be damned if he underpriced them—but one had. And this was the reason for his return to Salem today. The buyer wanted to take possession of the artwork now, rather than wait for the exhibit to end next week, on Halloween. Furthermore, the man wanted to pay Enoch in person, so that he might meet face-to-face the artist who had so impressed him.

The commuter rail disgorged its passengers, and Enoch climbed a series of steps to the level of Bridge Street. The sky was bright blue, the air crisp but not biting, and the city with its quaint tree-lined streets, brick sidewalks and many historic buildings seemed bent on coaxing Enoch into giving it another chance.

Still, with the city in the grip of its annual "Haunted Happenings," it wasn't long before its indigenous spooky folk and the influx of spooky pilgrims became manifest. Enoch gave an inward groan ... and yet, many of these creatures, both male and female (and often it was a challenge to differentiate), were as fetching as they were ludicrous in their dramatic black outfits, their abundance of improbable jewelry, their extreme hairstyles and makeup, their piercings and tattoos. Perhaps he would rent a room here in town and stay the night after his business had been conducted, so that he might partake a bit of the exotic fauna. Once again, Enoch Coffin was reminded that he was often drawn to that which repulsed him, and repulsed by that which attracted him. Once again, reminded that the only clear-cut black and white he knew was the relationship between ink and white paper.

II.

When Enoch arrived at the rented shop space that housed the temporary *Gallery of the Grotesque,* the purchaser of his artwork was already there waiting for him, presently in conversation with one of the artists who had organized the showing. Introductions were made, after which the artist excused herself to return to her duties at the front admission desk, leaving

Enoch and his new patron alone.

This person had been introduced to Enoch as Walter Mason, who appeared to be about thirty. "Appeared," because there was a curious ambiguity about him that allowed for the possibility that Mason was ten years younger, or ten years older. In addition, he was androgynous in appearance, even his soft voice lost between the masculine and feminine, his long black hair falling about a face so pale that Enoch wondered if the man wore whitening foundation. He had the look of a geisha who had let down her hair, and even cloaked his tall frame in a long black robe like a kimono. Ah, Salem.

"Oh, Mr. Coffin!" Mason cooed, at last slipping his hand from Enoch's own after having prolonged their handshake. The man wore long black velvet gloves that disappeared up the sleeves of his robe. "I cannot express my gratitude that you agreed to meet me in person! Your piece is so exquisite and so important to me—like a sacred thing!—that I didn't even want to touch it with my own hands until you yourself removed it from the wall for me."

"I'm flattered," Enoch said politely.

"I'm not in possession of a bank account, so I trust that cash will be acceptable?" Mason reached inside the front of his robe and drew out a bundle of money, pressing it into Enoch's hands. "Three thousand dollars. Please count it."

"No need. Thank you." Enoch stuffed the wad into the pocket of his brown suede jacket. Though unchallenged, he somehow felt the need to explain, "I charged conservatively, considering that the work itself took over thirty hours in total."

"I can believe it—such an intensity of detail! Worth every penny; there's no need to explain. But I ask, is pen and ink your preferred medium? I see you represented here with oils, as well."

"Oils are my preferred medium, though I've sought versatility in regard to my art."

"And so you have achieved it! But I myself find your pen work, in the pieces represented here at least, to be the most impressive. Shall we move on, into the presence of your masterworks themselves?"

"After you."

They walked across polished wooden floorboards into another of the rooms, Mason's feet making sharp clacking footfalls under the flowing hem of his robe. Did stiletto heels account for some of his height?

They came to the white-painted wall where hung five of Enoch's artworks: two oils, an acrylic painting, and a duo of pen and ink drawings.

Both pen and inks were similarly dense in detail, though one relied more on pointillism while the other utilized a crosshatching technique.

"Escher has nothing on you, sir!" Mason gushed, sweeping his arm toward the two drawings—the smallest of the five pieces—framed under glass. "I daresay, not even Piranesi with his *Carceri* etchings captures such a hellish sense of vast and otherworldly architecture ... such mind-bending geometries. Are you a trained architect, as he was?"

"I learned some drafting in school, but I never studied as an architect. You're very insightful; I will admit that Piranesi was one of my inspirations for these." Enoch didn't go on to reveal what other inspirations he might have had—such as his dreams.

"But they're very much your own, certainly! How did you envision such scenes? Did you sketch them out first, or just let your pen take you where it would?"

"The latter. I suppose I worked mostly from the subconscious." Again, Enoch felt disinclined to discuss the dreams he had experienced during the period in which he had worked on these two recent drawings, and several more in the same vein that he had opted not to include in the showing.

As if through fresh eyes, Enoch turned to face his drawings again, particularly focusing on the one with the obsessively intricate crosshatching that Mason had just acquired.

As Mason had indicated, both portrayed strange environments. The one done in pointillism illustrated an exterior view of a complex, gigantic city—seemingly abandoned and falling into ruin—while the one Mason had purchased revealed the interior, perhaps, of one of those cyclopean structures. Its ceiling soared impossibly high, while an overabundance of staircases and ramps crossed the scene, leading everywhere and nowhere. Shadows and light cut in from every direction, in angled planes and curved arches, creating an eye-straining interplay of black and white, line and absence of line—a maddening web of geometries.

No figures populated the exterior cityscape, but Enoch had placed a single person in the interior drawing, at its center, like a fly caught in that mad web. The figure was distant, barely a silhouette, apparently regarding the viewer as the viewer regarded it. Enoch couldn't even remember consciously deciding to include the lone inhabitant. As he had said, much of his approach to this series of drawings had been to trust his subconscious to take the reins.

But there had also been a recurring solitary figure in the dreams he had experienced, some weeks back, that had first inspired this pen and ink series. He remembered little more about the figure, though, than what he had captured here.

Mason cut into this thoughts with further praise. "Normally the guidelines of perspective anchor two-dimensional art in the laws of reality, but here you've used the mathematical laws of perspective subversively, against their own purpose. On a flat page, you've managed to convey dimensions beyond what can be plumbed!"

"You're very kind. You've articulated my intentions."

"My compliments are well deserved. But Mr. Coffin, may I impose upon you for one more favor? Could you, with the hands that gave life to this masterpiece, remove it from this wall and carry it to my home, and once there hang it again for me? My house is only a short, pleasant walk from here, I promise you. I feel that my own crude aura would only sully the magic of your creation. Call it superstition."

Once more Enoch gave his patron a polite smile. Was this the opening overture of a seduction? He was not yet desirous of Mason in that way, but he wouldn't rule out the possibility. Anyway, it wasn't a bad feeling to be appreciated for his work, nor a bad feeling to have three thousand dollars in his pocket, and so he replied, "Yes, certainly. Lead on."

Enoch took down his picture from the wall, and thus carrying it under one arm accompanied Mason outside, where they traversed the brick-paved sidewalks of Salem, upon which Mason's feet clacked sharply.

III.

"How fortunate you are," Enoch observed, "to own such a lovely home, in such a location."

"Yes, yes," Mason agreed, "I am."

The house they arrived at was situated just down the street from the museum called the Witch House, formerly the abode of Judge Jonathan Corwin, who had been involved in the Salem witch trials.

Mason's house itself was narrow but long, with one of its ends facing onto Essex Street. Its roof was in the gambrel style, with two sloping surfaces to each side. There were three floors, including the attic. As they passed through a white picket fence to reach a door at the side of the house, a voice cried out behind them and they paused to look around.

"Mr. Mason," called an elderly woman from the thin strip of yard at the side of the house next door, separated by another length of white fence, a rake in her hands with which she had been gathering autumn leaves. "How has your uncle been? Still unwell?"

"Yes, yes, afraid so," Mason replied, smiling. "I'm still seeing to his needs. Hopefully he'll be up and around again soon."

"Please tell him I asked about him, will you?"

"Of course, of course, I will. Good day, Mrs. Howe."

The old woman waved, and Mason turned away. Enoch followed suit, and waited while his host unlocked the side door.

As Enoch started to follow Mason inside, he saw that the mailbox affixed beside the door was overflowing. He reached in, pulled out a thick handful of material, and glanced at a mailing label stuck to a coupon brochure, printed with the name *SAMUEL CORWIN*. When he was inside he held the bundle toward his patron. "You've been neglecting your uncle's mail, I'm afraid."

"Oh yes, yes, how forgetful I am," Mason said, accepting it and depositing it immediately onto a side table. "I'll go through it later."

"So it's not your house, then."

"Ah, no, I don't actually own it. My uncle has lived here in Salem for many years, and when he fell into ill health he summoned me to come and look after him, in return for which he takes care of my needs as well."

"Such as purchasing art?"

Mason's lips, too red in his pallid visage, pulled into a tight smile. "He doesn't care what interests I pursue with the money he so graciously grants me."

"Do you have a sizable collection?"

"I've only collected one item previously, but surely today marks a more valuable acquisition."

"Again, I'm flattered." Enoch held up the framed drawing. "So where did you intend to hang it?"

"My uncle provides me a room in the attic; I'd like to hang it there."

"The attic? Such a large house, and your uncle lives alone, but you stay in the attic?"

"Oh, it's a lovely large room in fine condition—you'll see. It's my own choice; my uncle gave me free rein. I happen to love attic rooms ... so artistic."

"Well," Enoch conceded, "my studio is in the attic of my home in Boston, and of course it's my favorite room in the house, so I can understand your sentiments."

"But let me show you," Mason said, leading Enoch toward a staircase.

"So your uncle must have been related to Judge Jonathan Corwin, then," Enoch said as he followed Mason, who clumped loudly up the stairs.

At the second floor, Mason turned toward his guest and smiled curiously.

"I saw your uncle's name on his mail," Enoch explained. "Corwin, not Mason."

"Yes … he's my uncle on my mother's side. And yes, my uncle is a descendant of the judge. But we can't ourselves judge Corwin too harshly, since we're unsure today of the extent of his role in the witchcraft investigation, and what his feelings were on spectral evidence."

Enoch was familiar with the term. Spectral evidence was evidence not based upon hard fact, but upon visions and dreams. Spectral evidence at the Salem witch trials had consisted of such testimony as the alleged victims of the accused witches claiming that so-and-so had harassed them in a vision, in the form of an animal for instance. The Reverend Cotton Mather, who happened to be buried in the graveyard opposite Enoch's home in the North End of Boston, had recommended that spectral evidence be heard in the trials, but had advised that it could be the Devil himself in such dreams, merely pretending to be the accused witch.

Discussing this matter further, Mason said, "The Devil—ha. Humans always try to put their tiny anthropomorphic face upon the mysteries of the universe, eh, Mr. Coffin? I'm sure a sensitive soul like yourself, so obviously more finely attuned to the cosmos, understands how foolish such notions as the Devil are. The common ape confuses his own evil with the forces of the universe, in an attempt to place that evil outside himself, but the cosmos is not malign; the cosmos is indifferent. Cosmic entities would be no more evil than is a spider who traps a fly."

"You speak of humans as if to distance yourself from them."

"Ah, if only we could, eh, Mr. Coffin?" Mason smiled more broadly than he had as yet done, and Enoch could understand now why his smiles had been more subtle before. The man's small teeth appeared quite black, more so than decay would account for. Perhaps it was another intentional aspect of his dramatic appearance. Geishas covered their teeth with black wax, so that their teeth would not appear yellow in contrast with their white faces, so perhaps Mason was going for something of a geisha effect, after all.

They continued up the next flight of stairs, and when they arrived at the attic level Mason again turned to face Enoch and said, "As it happens, on my father's side we're related to another person involved in the Salem witch trials, though her name is much more obscure. I believe a concentrated effort was made to eradicate mention of her from the record books."

"And who would that person be?"

"Her name was Keziah Mason, and though she hailed from Arkham she was one of those accused of witchcraft in Salem. She was no doubt the only authentic witch among those poor folk."

"Why do you say she was an authentic witch?"

"Well, in her testimony at the trial she made mention of curious practices that might be dubbed, for lack of a better word, magical. Such as utilizing, in her words, 'lines and curves that could be made to point out directions leading through the walls of space to other spaces beyond.' But she was not hung with the rest, because she mysteriously escaped from the jail. The Reverend Cotton Mather was quite perplexed, I understand, by what she left behind in her cell."

"Which was?"

"According to the only remaining document, which seems to have been suppressed, what Mather observed was, 'curves and angles smeared on the grey stone walls with some red, sticky fluid.'" Mason chuckled in that soft voice of his. "Perhaps in her own way, Keziah Mason was something of an artist, herself."

IV.

"This is where I dream," Mason said oddly.

The attic had not been finished into an apartment as Enoch might have expected from Mason's words; its beams and rafters were open and bare, motes of dust swimming in rays of sunlight slanting in through its few windows. It did show signs that Mason inhabited it, but his bed was no more than a mattress without a box spring or frame, pushed against one wall. Candles had been burned in abundance upon an old steamer truck, melted pools of wax standing in a profusion of saucers and other containers. Books were stacked about the room, many of them almost crumbling into dust. Such features as the candles and books, however, did in fact put Enoch very much in mind of his own house's attic.

Because of the house's gambrel roof, the angles of the long, single attic room were interesting. But most interesting was one corner in particular, not far from the mattress. Here, it was plain that newer pieces of wood had been nailed, spanning the space from one corner wall to the other, and from the floor to the sloping ceiling, in overlapping layers … but surely not for a practical purpose such as lending the roof further support. There were two-by-fours, wider planks, even lengths of thin doweling, crisscrossing in a kind of intricate wooden web. Further, lines had been painted upon these wooden pieces in a red pigment. The planks allowed a broader surface for some of these markings to form curves. Depending upon where one stood to regard the composition, these red lines intersected in different ways.

"So, you're an artist yourself," Enoch observed, "rather in the manner of your ancestor, Keziah. I have to admit, now, that I have heard of her history before."

Behind him, Mason said, "Really? But I shouldn't be surprised. You obviously have much arcane knowledge. You couldn't create such artwork, otherwise. It cannot be accident or mere intuition, your ability."

Where Enoch stood there was a concentrated icy draft, like a cold steel knife blade pressed flat against his leg even through the material of his trousers. Looking down at the ancient steamer trunk beside him, he noted a red light glowing from within, showing through cracks and peeking out here and there under the lid.

With a cocked eyebrow, he turned from the trunk to face Mason, and found that his host had shut the attic door. Painted upon its inner surface in the same red pigment was a large odd symbol of overlapping circles, lines, and tiny lettering in an alien script.

"If you would be so kind as to remove your drawing from its glass and frame," Mason said, as he pulled the long velvet glove from his right hand. In so doing, he revealed odd tattoos on both the upper surface and his palm. Red lines ran down each finger, top and bottom, and the natural grooves in his palm had been traced in red as well, though overlapping circles and more alien lettering had also been added. When he removed his other glove, Enoch saw that his left hand had been identically tattooed.

"Do you have a better frame to showcase it in?" Enoch asked, feigning innocence.

"Yes. There." Mason pointed beyond Enoch, at the wooden web in the corner. "I'd like you to nail the drawing in the center of the widest plank, there. I'll help direct you. You'll find a hammer and nails on the floor directly below."

"You can't do it yourself, because of your tattoos. Why, Mr. Mason?"

"I told you—I don't want to disturb your magic with my own."

"A magician like your ancestor, are you? A witch?"

Mason winced. "Such an ignorant term, Mr. Coffin, please. 'Witch.' It's no better than 'Devil.'" He then turned to confront the closed attic door, and spread the fingers of both hands in such a way that the lines on his digits matched the angles of certain lines on the symbol painted on the wood. When he pressed his hands to the surface, the red pigment there took on a fiery glow. It was a seal. A seam of weird red light now shone under the door, accompanied by another cold draft that speared into the room.

When Mason bared his black teeth in a smug grin, as if waiting for

Enoch to show fear, the artist merely asked instead, "Where is your uncle?"

"Not far."

"Indeed." Enoch then whirled and with his arm swept most of the candles from the top of the steamer trunk. When he threw the lid open, the rest of the candles clattered to the floor. Red light burst up into Enoch's face, but it wasn't that which caused him to stumble back and shield his eyes with his arm. It was the frigid blast of arctic air that had been released. Still narrowing his eyes lest the icy air freeze them into balls of glass, he peered over his arm into the maw of the trunk.

Through plumes of churning vapor, which caught the ruby glow emanating from the impossibly deep throat of the trunk, Enoch made out a weirdly bent figure that appeared to be floating in a vividly red sea. Throughout this sea were strung a countless multitude of black cables, but the thickest cables appeared to pulse as if they were something organic. The pathetic figure snared in this black web and thus suspended in the crimson void was a nude elderly man, his mouth wide in a silent shriek and his eyes bulging in terror. Enoch knew that Samuel Corwin was still alive, trapped in that web like a fly, and staring back at him in helpless horror.

Mason came toward him and kicked the lid of the trunk shut. In doing so, the hem of his black silk robe rode up and his foot was revealed. It was a cloven hoof, tufts of black fur about his ankle.

"That will be quite enough of that," Mason said mildly. "Let's not be rude."

"You're being rather rude to your uncle, don't you think?"

"He's not my uncle. He's the descendant of one of those who persecuted my true ancestor, Keziah."

"I thought you said we mustn't judge old Jonathan Corwin too harshly because we aren't sure how much he had to do with the fates of the accused."

"Well," Mason chuckled, "just in case. Anyway, I had to have somewhere to stay; rents are expensive in this part of town."

"And why did you need to find a place in this particular town?"

"I had no choice; this is where I found myself. Thanks to you. It was your dreams that summoned me at first, Mr. Coffin—beckoned me to the window, if you will. Then you cinched it when you drew that." He pointed to the artwork in Enoch's hands. "You pulled me through the weave, along the lines and curves. You, playing with magic you only half understood, hooked me like an unwary fish and drew me into your wretched, limited mortal plane."

Enoch turned the drawing around in his hands to squint at it. Particularly, at the vague ant of a figure in its center. "So that's you."

50

"Yes. An unintentional portrait. Here." Mason moved to a crude shelf and took down a magnifying glance. As he returned to Enoch he continued, "It took me a number of days to follow the scent of your drawing, once I manifested in this realm from which my ancestor was spawned. When I tracked the energies to their source and viewed your creation, I understood how I had been brought here." He passed Enoch the magnifying glass.

Enoch accepted the implement and studied his own handiwork through its lens, but the figure was not that much more distinct: just a few strokes of his nib, a splotch of India ink, with a tiny open area suggesting where a white face would be. And yet, even as Enoch watched, he saw the rudimentary figure's long hair streaming as if blown in an arctic wind, its long black robe visibly stirring as well.

"What is it you want from me now," he asked, looking up, "that you feel compelled to seal me in this room with you?"

"I need you to reverse your artistic spell. I only want to return to my own realm and those who are like me—such as Keziah, who still lives and dwells in those other spaces. Unlike her, I was never part of this world, never fully human, nor would I want to be."

"You need only have asked. You didn't have to try to trap me here like you did your poor faux uncle. Just tell me what to do."

"As I say, you must nail your drawing at the nexus of my formula. I'll help direct its placement."

Enoch removed his pen and ink drawing from its glass-fronted frame, and then brought it to the corner where Mason had nailed his many crisscrossing lengths of wood, marked with their red lines and curves. Enoch knelt down to position the drawing against a broad central plank, and found he didn't really need Mason's direction. Painted tracks upon the wood aligned perfectly with certain angles in the drawing, formed by staircases and other architectural details that cut into the image from the edges of the paper. Several curved lines on the wood perfectly continued curves begun in the drawing by an arched doorway or a partially seen circular "rose window," such as one might find in a cathedral. Enoch could feel in his nerves an inaudible click as the lines of his drawing fell into place and the proper links were connected like electrical currents.

Holding the drawing against the wood with one hand, he picked up a nail and the hammer his host had indicated.

"A nail in each corner!" Mason instructed behind him. "Yes! Each corner must be bound!"

Enoch nailed the upper corners of his drawing to the central plank, and the bottom corners to another, narrower plank running parallel beneath it. He then rose, still holding the hammer causally, though now he had a crude weapon.

"A pleasure to see an artist such as you at work," Mason told him. "Despite the inconveniences you've caused me, my admiration for your ability is sincere. Now, if you'd kindly move aside."

"Don't you want me to remove you from the drawing? Maybe with a brush and some white correction fluid …"

"Now that the final puzzle piece is secure, your work is done. At last, I can touch it myself."

As Enoch watched, the creature that had taken the name Walter Mason knelt before his strange construction in the corner and carefully positioned both hands over the pen and ink drawing, spreading his ten fingers just so. When he seemed satisfied with their alignment, he pressed his palms forward, making physical contact with the drawing. The red lines tattooed along every digit continued various angles that Enoch had inked in.

And then, every red line Mason had painted along the wooden pieces began to glow, creating a net of fiery strands so bright that Mason's form became merely a silhouette. From out of the attic corner came such an intense, blasting cold wind that Enoch involuntarily stepped back and again covered his face with his arm. The wide-brimmed slouch hat he favored was blown off his head and his hair was ruffled by the roaring gust.

But the arctic wind quickly died away, and the luminous scarlet web dimmed to its natural state. When Enoch lowered his arm, Walter Mason was no longer in the attic room.

He moved closer to his drawing and crouched down to examine it, having again taken up the magnifying glass. Peering through the lens, he saw that the vague dark figure standing in the center of his drawing of an immense, otherworldly chamber had vanished.

Enoch turned toward the steamer trunk, approached it and once again opened the lid. There was no longer any red-glowing void, nor icy vapors. The uncanny portal had reverted to a mere musty and empty old steamer trunk. Poor innocent Samuel Corwin was irretrievable now, and Enoch Coffin preferred not to speculate on his fate. It wouldn't be the first time a miscarriage of justice had taken place in the Witch City.

He used the claw end of the hammer to pry the nails from the four corners of his drawing, and then replaced it in its frame. He'd bring it home with him, instead of returning it to the gallery, lest questions were asked.

Enoch was not rattled by the experience he had just undergone. In fact, he was pleased that today's excursion to Salem had been rather more interesting than he had anticipated. He was quite gratified that one of his drawings had proved so potent. Though to be honest, he was also a bit relieved that this drawing was the only one in the series of pen and inks in which he had incorporated a figure.

The three thousand dollars in his pocket wasn't detrimental to his mood, either, even if it did come from an old man perhaps forever ensnared in the spider web of a vengeful part-human entity.

Enoch moved to the door upon which the seal had been painted, but the symbol no longer glowed crimson. Red light and a freezing draft no longer seeped in beneath the door. Enoch turned the knob and stepped from the room without any unsavory consequences.

Once again in the street, and hurrying away lest the neighbor woman notice him again and mention him should there ever be an investigation into the disappearance of Samuel Corwin, Enoch took note of the goth-types he saw walking along Essex Street here and there. Yes, Salem was full of their ilk.

Yet how many of them, he wondered, had not come here as tourists from other cities or states, but as visitors from someplace much, much farther away than that?

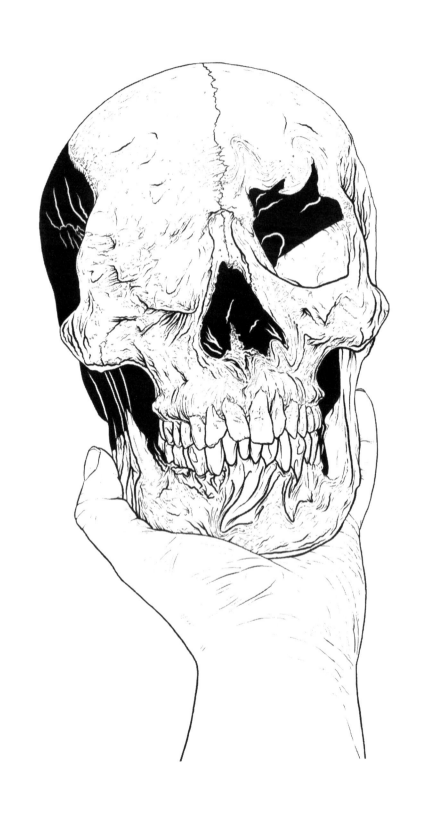

W. H. PUGMIRE

They Smell of Thunder

In memory of Karl Edward Wagner

I.

Enoch Coffin drove his truck along the rutted road, past the stone wall of what might once have been a habitation, although no house stood within sight. There was just a wide dry field that reached to where the lush forest took over on the rising slopes, with here and there growths of high weeds mingled with the tall yellow grass. The sky was overcast and the weather cool, but Enoch liked the window down when he drove and didn't mind the chill. "Lonesome country," he mumbled as his pickup bumped over the road's furrows, and he cast a backward glance to make certain the artistic gear in the rear cargo bed had remained secure. Further on, the road inclined and he could see the mountains above the dense woodland, and something in the primeval aura of the sight excited him—he felt very far from Boston. As his truck crossed over the bridges that spanned ravines and narrow rocky vales, he studied the curious manner in which some of those ancient bridges had been constructed, how various combined portions of timber seemed emblematic in the signs and sigils they suggested. The domed hills were close now, and he stopped the truck in order to step out and piss; and as he relieved himself he marveled at the stillness all around as his eyes scanned the shimmering line of the Miskatonic River that passed below the wooded hills. As he stood there a ratty jalopy passed him on the road, and he smiled at the way the suspicious eyes of its driver studied him. Whistling, Enoch raised a hand and made the Elder Sign, which the other driver hesitantly returned.

He drove onward and came to a bumpy riverside road and then drove slowly across an ancient bridge that crossed the Miskatonic, experiencing a sense of nervous expectancy concerning the soundness of the bridge. The structure's hoary age affected Enoch's senses and filled him with foreboding—such things should not be, should not exist in this modern age. The artist was delighted that it did exist so as to spin its macabre spell. But the tenebrous bridge was merely prelude. As the pickup truck slowly crossed it, Enoch sensed a change in the air that wafted through his vehicle's window. The shadowed atmosphere felt, somehow, heavier, and it carried an extremely unpleasant smell such as he had never experienced. Reaching, finally, the other end of the bridge, his truck drove again across a rough road and Enoch laughed out loud at the sight of Dunwich Village before him, huddled beneath what he knew from his yellowed map was Round Mountain. His fingers itched for pen and pad so that he could capture the uncanny sight with his craft. How could such squalid, disintegrating buildings still be standing? In what era had they been raised? Enoch then began to notice some few lethargic citizens who shuffled in and out of one ridiculously old broken-steepled church that now served as general store, and the artist was amazed at how the inhabitants of the village were so in tune with its aura of strange decay. He had entered an alien realm. The fetid stench of the air breathed in was almost intolerable, even to one such as Enoch who relished decayed necromancy.

He drove for another three miles, checking with the 1920s map that his correspondent had sent him, and stopped at the pile of ruins that had once been a farmhouse just below the slope of Sentinel Hill. He sat for a while in his stilled vehicle and watched the three persons who worked at a curious construction of wood, a kind of symbolic design that reminded Enoch of the patterns he had seen on the bridges he had crossed on his way to Dunwich. Finally, he pushed open his door and stepped onto the dusty road, holding out his hand to the frantic beast that rushed to him and licked his palm.

"Spider," a man called to the dog, which moved from Enoch and trotted to his master. The artist approached the stranger and they exchanged smiles. "Mr. Coffin, I recognize you from the newspaper photos. I'm Xavier Aboth." Enoch reached for and clasped the young man's extended hand. "You found your way easily?"

"Oh yeah, your grandpappy's map served me well. I took very good care of it, it's so delicate." He looked to the top of the high hill and could just see some of the standing stones with which it was crowned. "The infamous Sentinel Hill. And this must once have been the Whateley farmstead."

"Aye, that it is. We're just sturdyin' up the sign here. Hey—Alma, Joseph." The lad motioned for his friends to join them. "This is the artist who was hired to illustrate my book of prose-poems. Enoch Coffin, Alma

Bishop and Joseph Hulver, Jr."

Enoch shook their hands as the woman studied him. "Clever of our Xavier, writin' his own book. Course, he's been to Harvard and Miskatonic. Mostly them as gone to university never return. We're glad this one did." She smiled slyly at the poet.

"I'll let you two finish up. The powder is in that plastic bag there. It needs to be sprinkled exactly as ye're sayin' the Words." He turned to Enoch. "My place is up a mile and a half yonder. No, Spider can chase after us on the road, he loves that. Yeah, I walked over, it's a nice stroll. I like to stop and bury things in Devil's Hop Yard, over there. You know, things that help enhance the alchemy of the bleak soil." The two men entered the pickup, and Xavier whistled to his canine, which barked joyously and ran beside the truck as Enoch drove. As he drove, Enoch glanced nonchalantly at his companion's dirty clothes and soiled hands. Xavier was extremely unkempt, living up to the image of Dunwich folk that had been related to Enoch by some who learned that he was journeying there. The word about Dunwich and its denizens was that they were little more than ignorant hill-folk who rejected modernity and lived primitive and solitary lives. Rumors of inbreeding were prevalent, and Enoch's one friend who had visited Dunwich Village complained of the hostility he encountered there from people who mistrusted those who were not kindred.

Enoch drove for a while and then the road turned and passed near another high hill, below which stretched an infertile hillside that was naught but rocks and corroding soil. The young man leaned out his window and called to the dog. "It's okay, Spider, jest run." Then he turned and smiled at Enoch, shrugging. "He gets nervous near the Hop Yard." The truck continued to follow the road until coming to a small plot of land on which a cottage that was little more than a shack leaned beneath the dark sky. "Go ahead and park next to my old jalopy there." The artist did so and climbed out of the vehicle, offering his hand once more to the friendly canine. He joined Xavier in taking out some of the gear from the cargo bed.

"Smells like a storm is brewing," Enoch said, looking up at the sky.

"Aye, we'd best get this lot inside."

The young man's language gave Enoch pause: was this the poet who had crafted such beautiful and compelling prose-poems? The lad's spoken language was simple and at times uncouth. Perhaps returning to this forsaken homeland after spending years away at University had killed any elegance of tongue and returned him to the local patois. He followed Xavier to the door of the house and inside, and was relieved that the place was bigger on the inside than it looked on the outside.

"I'm givin' you the upstairs with the bed. I often just sleep down here on the sofa. The light's real good up there cos I put in a winder in the roof above the library, to help with readin'. I like lots of light when I read. Come on up. Oh, them steps are firm, don't worry, you just need to balance yourself cos there's no handrails."

They walked up what was a combination of ladder and steps, through a rectangle in the living room ceiling and into a cozy bedroom. Xavier tossed the equipment he was holding onto the bed and stretched as he sauntered into the next room, which proved to be a spacious study filled with books, two tables and three sturdy chairs. The ceiling was very low, just an inch from Enoch's crown when he stood at full height. He set his gear on the bed next to Xavier's pile and nodded with approval.

"This is nice. You're certain you want to surrender your bed?"

"Rarely use it. And I suspect you'll want to work up here. It's real quiet, not another neighbor for half a mile."

As if on cue, a faint sound of rumbling came from someplace outside. Xavier nodded.

"What was that?" Enoch asked.

"Oh, that's just the hills. They get talkative just before a storm." He raised his face and shut his eyes; he inhaled deeply. "Can you smell the thunder?"

Enoch's nostrils gulped the air, as from above the ceiling window electricity flashed. The sky boomed as the deluge broke.

II.

Once alone, Enoch sat on the bed for a little while and listened to the storm. He found his host an enigma. Xavier was much younger than expected, and when Enoch reached into his knapsack for his own copy of the boy's privately printed chapbook of macabre prose poems and vignettes he saw that there was no personal information concerning the lad except that he resided on a family homestead in the town of Dunwich—no age or other biographical tidbits were offered. How could such a simple-minded fellow write such strange and mature work? The artist rose and walked into the other room, the "library," and sat at the larger of the two tables, the surface of which was littered with piles of books and holograph manuscripts. Nearest him was a tea tin filled with pens and pencils, and next to it were old hardcover editions of the prose-poems of Charles Baudelaire and Clark Ashton Smith. Atop one pile of manuscripts was a chapbook edition of the prose poems of Oscar Wilde, the cover of which was smudged with dirty fingerprints. Moving that, he reached for the topmost sheet of paper and squinted his eyes in an attempt to read its minute handwriting. The sheet was covered with crossed out words and eliminated lines, but with effort Enoch could make out a cohesive text, which he recited in his soft low voice.

"I am the voice of wind and rain through leaves that move beneath one black abyss. The limbs of trees bend to my song and shape themselves with new design, forming sigils to the haunted sky in which I originate. I taste the husks of mutant trees that are rooted in the tainted soil, and I whisper within the sigils that have been etched into that shell of wood, the Logos that awakened me as mortal pleas. I am the voice of tempest spilled from depths of black abyss. Awakened, I sing so as to arouse that which is Elder than my immortal self."

Outside the small house, the rain stopped and all was still except for an occasional chattering of night birds. Enoch stepped down the ladder stairs so as to bid his host goodnight, but the lower regions of the abode were vacant of inhabitant. Shrugging to himself, the artist climbed back up the steps and undressed. The bed was comfortable and its blankets kept him warm in the cool room. He was almost asleep when he thought he heard movement within the room and imagined warm breath on his handsome face. Strangely, Enoch did not dream as was his wont, and it seemed that very little time had passed before he awakened to the smells of breakfast food from below. Slipping into shirt and trousers, he stepped barefoot to the lower room and saw movement in the small kitchenette at back. Xavier smiled as Enoch entered the place and skillfully placed eggs, sunny side up, onto two slices of soda bread that sat on a plate next to sausage and bacon.

"Mother got used to soda bread during her months in Ireland, when she went back to attend some family burial. I've changed the recipe a wee bit by usin' buttermilk instead of stout. Help yourself to fresh coffee and we'll eat in the front there."

Enoch poured himself a cup of coffee, which he drank black with heaps of sugar, and accepted the plate of food offered him. Walking into the main room, he fell into a comfortable chair and placed his plate on the small stand beside it, then cursed when he saw that he had forgotten eating utensils. Xavier joined him in the room and set a fork onto the artist's plate, and then he sat at a small table, moving away a bunch of books to make room for his dish. The dog lay before the hearth, its paws next to a food bowl.

"It's kind of incredible."

Enoch looked at the poet. "What's that?"

"That Rick would send you here to—what?—get a handle on me and have me collaborate with your illustrations for the book. You don't find it insultin'?"

"Not at all."

The boy shrugged. "Art is personal, right? Individual. My things come from these weird places inside me. But your stuff will be your interpretation of my stuff, you know, triggered by the pictures it puts inside your noggin. I don't want to explain my stuff to you—I want you to find the parts of it that I don't see so clearly. When I write, it's like I go into a trance and become somethin' ... someone else. Sometimes I'll read over a thing and say, 'Where the hell did *that* come from?' It's like seein' a photo of yourself for the first time, when before all you knew was your reflection in the mirror. You're all different and you don't even recognize yourself."

Enoch laughed. "Well, Richard wants your first hardcover edition to be rather special, limited though the edition will be. He produces beautiful books. I have those weird places inside me, too, and thus I know their feeling and can reproduce them with my art. The outré is my forte, Mr. Aboth."

The poet cringed. "I hate being called that. Xavier, please. Well, I don't really know what you and Rick are expectin' of me, cos I don't know fuck-all about art technique and all of that. How is this gonna work?"

"All right, here's what's expected. We have been brought together because we are alchemists, as is our publisher. Our art is predicated ..." The poet frowned. "It's established on a foundation of love for arcane things and our knack for evoking mysteries beyond corporeal time and space."

"I'm gonna let you down if that's what you think. I'm not ashamed of my witch-blood and all, but it doesn't guide the way I live."

Enoch finished the food and set his plate down roughly. "How can you say that when you've written the prose you have? Your language is skilled and gorgeous, and it sings of alchemy."

"But that ain't me—or, it's a part of me and a part of somethin' else, my Muse. It's the thing I conjure when I put my mind to workin'."

"And where does it come from, this something else, if not from a place inside you?"

"Nah, it's the part of me that leaves and joins the others in that secret place, and they dance with me and make me dream, and then I'm still kinda dreamin' when I sit up there and scratch my words out. It's ritual, sure."

"And where do you go, when you 'leave' and mingle with these others?"

Xavier turned to gaze out the window. "To the hills, and under them, to the secret places that we know in Dunwich." Enoch watched as the boy's eyes began to darken. "And they sing to us, as our mammies sang when we were babes. We hear them there, beneath the hills and in the clouds. We smell them atop the rounded summits among the standing stones and skulls. The storm is their kiss, with which they claim us." The poet sat dead still for some few moments, and then he blinked and smiled. "I can show you, if you like. You'll need to draw the hills for the book, they're important. Bishop Mountain is real close."

Without finishing his breakfast, the boy stood up and snatched a shoulder bag from a peg on the wall by the front door, and then he opened the door and vacated the house as Spider trotted behind him. Cursing, Enoch rushed up the stepway and got into socks and shoes, and then he joined the poet outside. The boy led Enoch toward a hill that rose behind the house, and as they walked toward the back area Enoch noticed three low mounds in the ground, two of which were topped by boulders on which curious symbols had been etched.

"That's Mother, and that's Grandpa," Xavier said as he pointed to the two graves.

"And the other?"

The lad shrugged. "Just some body we found atop Sentinel Hill. Didn't feel right to leave him up there, with his hide all melted onto his bones and all, so I brought him down here and gave him ceremony. Felt right. People go up there to open the Gate without really knowin' what the hell they're aimin' at. Usually they just get scared and scat, but this un had a bit of success. That was a noisy night," he concluded, laughing. He pointed to the hill. "It's a bit of a trek, but it feels good climbin' up there, and the view is mighty nice. Let's go. You comin', Spider? He doesn't always like to join. Dogs are super sensitive."

Enoch watched the beast tilt its head at them and watch as they moved toward the hill, and then it walked in a circle and settled on the ground, its head on its paws.

They walked toward the hill and began to ascend it, wandering into its growth of woodland. Xavier's stride was steady and rather jaunty, and this walk was obviously a favorite activity. Enoch glanced at his wristwatch now and then, and after a forty-minute hike they were out of the woods and approaching the apex of the hill. They followed a footpath that led them to the place where standing stones formed a circle.

"Come on to the other side, you can see better there. Watch your step, there's a bunch of stones that's easy to stumble over, and some of their edges are kinda sharp. There, that's the Devil's Hop Yard that we passed, and there's my place. It used to be where the Seth Bishop house stood, that was destroyed during the Horror, and Grandpa was able to buy the land and build our stead. Farm never was much, and I hated that kind of work anyway, so I've found work in the Village. Won't never make much livelihood writin' my stuff, but that's more a hobby anyways. Nice clear mornin' after last night. Did the storm keep you awake?"

"No."

"I can't never sleep during a storm. I like to listen to it talk, all soothin' like. We get plenty of storms in Dunwich. That's Sentinel Hill to our right."

"Where you found the stranger's corpse."

"Yeah. He was probably some kid from Miskatonic who got in good with the librarian and read the old books and had ideas. Tried to open the Gate, most like, not understandin' it needs to be done durin' the Festivals and all. I can't be bothered with none of that. Grandpa knew a lot about it and tried to get me interested. Dunwich heritage and all of that. You were wrong, Mr. Coffin—okay, Enoch; I'm not really an alchemist, not the sort you probably think me to be. I know enough about the signs and callin' to the hills, and I tend the Hop Yard and a few other sites cos I'm part of the land and its people. But I use my weird skill for my writin'. I conjure words, language. Whoa, words are powerful little devils. Poetry is just as potent as some passage outta the *Necronomicon*. And not so lethal to them as don't know what the hell they're doin'. Bad poetry just makes you look like a damn fool. Bad raisin' up can leave you a dead fool." He turned to stare at Enoch. "Is your art your alchemy, Enoch?"

"Not really—it is my *art*, and therein lies its potency. But I paint the esoteric things without explicating them."

"There you go again—big words. But I think I know what you mean. You peel back the shroud without explainin' the rotten mess beneath it. Do you always understand your vision?"

The artist laughed. "Almost never. I allow the secret things to keep their mysteries, few of which I fully comprehend. I don't want to kill mystique—I want to suggest the secret things that may be found within fabulous darkness and let them have their aesthetic effect. I want to conjure art as it seduces my brain and enhances vision. Do you understand that?"

"Hell yeah. That's what I do. I hear the others in my head and let them fuck my brain, and then I write the visions they leave beneath my eyes. That's what it is—*vision*, seeing somethin' old and secret, and tryin' to explain how it feels inside your soul, where it plants all kind of roots. Hell yeah."

Enoch walked away from his new friend and went to touch a hand to one of the standing stones. "Were these erected by aborigines of the land?"

"What, by Indians? Nope, they wouldn't never climb up the hills of Dunwich. These stones were probably here afore any of them squeezed outta their mammies. Too bad there ain't no wind, it sounds awesome when it dances around these stones."

"Wind is easily conjured." Enoch smiled slyly at the lad.

"I know. Grandpa used to call it when he was feeling lonely for his kindred." Xavier's face grew slightly sad. "Mama used to call the wind now and then, when she couldn't sleep. I think that's what she was doing, singin' real low and weird, and then outside you'd hear the wind arisin'."

"Something like this?" Enoch placed his other hand onto the pillar and began to whisper to it, and then he rested his ear against the surface of stone and shut his eyes. When he heard the song beneath the stone, he pressed his mouth against the pillar and repeated the ancient cry. Xavier shuddered as an element entered into the air around them, and then the tears began to blur his vision as Enoch sang the ancient song that the boy remembered from childhood when it was murmured by his dam. He tried to speak the arcane words but found that his voice choked with sudden sobbing.

Reaching for him, Enoch brought the young man into his embrace and pressed their moist lips together with what was almost a kiss. He raised his mouth to Xavier's eyes and warbled the primordial melody onto them, and he smiled as the boy panted onto his own face, a sensation that he remembered from the previous night, when someone watched him closely as he sank toward slumber. Enoch moved his face away and peered into the boy's eyes, and then he smiled and kissed the fellow's streaming tears as, around them, an alien wind began to hum between the spaces of the standing stones. Enoch raised his eyes skyward and watched the shapes that formed as sigils of shadow far above them. He then took Xavier fully into his arms and sang the song of tempest at the youth's ear, clasping the lad's quivering form in his strong unyielding arms.

III.

The men sat in silence and lamp light in the main room of the small house. Enoch had just read aloud some few pieces from the manuscript of Xavier's forthcoming collection, and the young man was curiously moved by the sound of his work read by another. The artist sipped at his cup of coffee and gazed at the fellow near him. How old was the poet? Was he even twenty? He looked, in the soft light, like a little lost boy as he scanned the sheets that Enoch had read out loud.

"Your prose is beautiful, Xavier. The prose poem is, I think, the perfect form for the macabre. One can express anything and everything, concisely yet with force. These are finer than those in your chapbook, your language is more mature."

The boy laughed. "The instructors at school were always tryin' to correct my speech. 'Stop talkin' like a Dunwich farmer,' they'd yell. Like I was supposed to be ashamed of where I come from. They've had a thing against Dunwich at Miskatonic for ages, and I was glad to leave early cos of Mother's illness. Didn't want to go to damn University anyway, but she wanted it and it made her happy. She thought they could learn me how to write 'with more distinction' was how she'd phrase it. But I didn't want to be molded by their ways. My talent is mine own, a gift from them outside. Don't need no mollycoddlin' old fool in spectacles fussin' over me and tellin' me how to write and pretendin' to care so much about my 'gift,' their eyes all shinin' and stupid." His laughter had a bitter ring. "Anyway, had to come home and tend Mother as she was dyin'. She went a little witless near the end and used to sing with the whippoorwills. But she'd get all quiet when I conjured the others and spoke to her all elegant-like; and she'd put her soft hands on my face and call me her lovely boy."

Not knowing what to say, Enoch glanced around the room and let his eyes settle on a round wall hanging that was composed of connected sticks. "I saw those totemic sigils on some of the bridges that I crossed. You were attending one when I first saw you."

"Oh, the river signs are different from the Whateley charm."

"No one has cleared the Whateley wreckage and claimed their land."

"Nope. The memory of the Horror runs deep with some. Grandpa was thought crazy for buildin' on this spot, but ain't nothin' wrong with it."

"And the Whateley land?"

"Best left undisturbed. There's just a few of us visit it and tend the charm and the lair and all. Ah, I see that look in your eye. Ain't too late yet. We'll take my jalopy. Nah, Spider don't venture out after dark. Good boy, Spider," he said, patting the beast's head. "No, you won't need a jacket, it's a warm night." Exiting the house, they boarded the lad's old car and drove through darkness. "You remind me of Grandpa, the way your eyes shine when there's magick brewin'. I've never felt the thrill, and Mother was kind

64

of blasé about it all. I think the Horror scared most folk more than they'd ever admit, cos it weren't never figured out what the Whateleys were up to. We just know it was somethin' awesome, somethin' for a special season. But the season has passed, and now there's just what was left behind."

"An aftermath of Horror?"

The boy chuckled. "You're kinda a poet yourself, when you speak sometimes."

The rough road took them to the Whateley ruins, and Xavier turned to reach down behind the driver seat and pulled out what looked like an antique oil lantern. Stepping out of the car, the boy motioned for Enoch to follow him as he pulled a lighter from his pocket and lit the lantern's wick. Silently, they walked to the ruins, and the artist was aware of an alteration in atmosphere, and of an aged old smell that permeated the place. Something untoward had had its origin here, of that there was no doubt. He stopped to gaze to the flat apex of Sentinel Hill and felt a thrill of horror course through his flesh. What else had trod this unholy ground, on what grotesque gargantuan hoofs? It had left its aftermath absolutely, an eidolon that tried to spill its shapelessness into one's skull and teach one's lips to shriek its name. Finally, Xavier stopped and bent to move some planks away that covered double doors built into the ground. The lad pulled open one door and descended, his shadow playing weirdly on the stone steps and walls of dirt as he stopped to flick his lighter to a torch that protruded from one surface. The underground chamber was revealed. Enoch noticed that the hideous stench was not so strong in this lair beneath the house. He breathed quietly as his anxious eyes scanned the entered realm, and when he passed a small antique chest filled with ancient gold coins he let his hand bury itself therein.

"Wizard's booty," Xavier whispered. "Best left alone."

The artist raised his hand out of the pile and surreptitiously pocketed one gold coin, and then he moseyed toward the unearthly lattice structures that hung on one wall. What they were he could not fathom. They seemed composed of bleached sticks from trees and thin lengths of board that had been fastened together in weird display, although he couldn't tell in the poor light with what they had been conjoined. He couldn't bring himself to touch them, for something in their outré nature confused him. He backed away and was amazed at how bizarre the sticks seemed, more phantom-like than physical, like the fossils of spectral things.

"I've never seen their like," he whispered.

"Nope, Wizard Whateley was unique. Some old journals of folk that had visited this place before his death said that these things were fastened on some sealed doors in the house and on the old clapboarded tool-house. If you look at them too steadily they find you in dreamin'. Had a shared dream with those folks you met t'other day, and from it we built the one afore the house. Keeping somethin' out, or somethin' in, I guess. The hill noises get loud here on the Sabaoths. It's Roodmas on Tuesday. If you're interested we can light a fire on Sentinel Hill and such." The young man looked around and frowned. "Kinda grim in here, ain't it? Let's get."

Without waiting the lad walked to the wall torch and snuffed it out on the dirt floor, and then held his lantern before him as he ascended the stone steps. Enoch waited for a moment in rich darkness, the one illumination in which came from the lattice designs on the wall. Enoch studied them in fascination, and it came to him that they resembled doors on a fence. He wondered what he would find, should he push one open and peer into the other side. Then the artist cautiously found his way to the steps and climbed toward outer aether.

IV.

Enoch, alone in his rooms, sat at the smaller table and sketched onto a pad, trying to recreate the lattice designs that he had seen in the Whateley underground lair. He found it curious how his vision blurred as his mind tried to recall the exact shapes of the designs he had beheld, and how cold his brain felt when he concentrated too fully on remembering. Finally, he gave up and, rising, stretched his arms until his palms touched the low ceiling. Glancing through the ceiling window, he saw many points of light in the black sky. He was restless and a little bored, and so he slipped into his jacket and quietly walked down the steps to the lower room, where Xavier was sleeping soundly on the sofa with one lowered hand resting on his dog's head. The animal did not move as it watched Enoch go to the door and step outside. His truck sounded loud when he switched on the ignition and drove slowly down the rutted road to Devil's Hop Yard. The artist stopped his vehicle and stepped onto the road, sneering at the odorous Dunwich air as it crept into his nostrils and tainted the taste in his mouth. The desolate field was acres long and absolutely barren, and he hesitated for some few moments before finding the nerve to step onto its precinct. Bishop Mountain loomed above him, beneath moving clouds that were lit up by soft moonlight. Yes, this was cursed sod, and Enoch muttered protective spells as he trod its wasted demesne. Finally, he knelt and placed his hands on the surface, flatly, trying to sense what, if anything, was held beneath the ground.

"Perhaps a drop of witch blood will awaken you," he whispered as he took his switchblade out of his pocket and opened it. Holding the steel blade to moonlight, he made signals to the sphere's dead light, and then he quickly sliced the blade through an index finger and watched the dark liquid spill onto the dirt. A sound arose from beneath him, a faint rumbling that grew into a kind of cracking or quaking; and then a current of chilly air poured down the great round hill, to him, air that babbled senselessly at his ears. The earth below him trembled as from other distant hills came a response of other rumblings. "Gawd, what visions would you plant if I slumbered on your sod?" He then reached into another pocket and brought forth the ancient golden coin that he had pilfered from the Whateley warren, the metal of which felt weirdly hot in his hand. He raised the coin to his mouth and kissed it, and then he used one side of it to etch a diagram into the dirt. Chanting, he dug into the earth with the hand that held the coin, burying it as deep as he could burrow. All around him, the noises silenced. Enoch spat into the small dark area of his bloodstain and then staggered to his feet. How heavy were his limbs, as if some force below were trying to coax him underground. Like a clumsy drunk, he lurched from the Hop Yard to the road and his truck. He frowned at the blurriness of his vision and drove extremely slowly to the Aboth homestead. Entering the house, he found the living room vacant of man and beast. Heavily, he climbed up the steps and sat on his bed.

Dunwich was dead silent, and he was sleepy. He reached down so as to remove his shoes, and as he held the heel of one his hand was littered with the debris that clung to it—the particles of soil from Devil's Hop Yard that he had carried with him. Mumbling incoherently, he removed the other shoe with his other hand, onto which other particles of dirt adhered. Enoch clapped his hands but the soil would not fall from them, and so he cursed and ran his fingers through his hair and over his face. Granular fragments fell onto his eyes, which he rubbed wearily, thus pushing the substance into the choroid. Something beneath his face tickled him, and the artist laughed as he pulled off his shirt and reclined on the bed.

The artist raised his face to eerie amber moonlight as he danced upon a gravesite. Below him, the rumbling from some deep place underground kept rhythm to his movement, and when he bent his head so as to watch his happy feet, he saw that he was frolicking upon the grave of the stranger whose dissolved corpse had been found atop Sentinel Hill. *What a lonely little grave*, the artist thought, *and how wretched must be the solitude within the pit of death.* He knelt and moved his hands into soft earth, and when his hands found the flimsy object he pulled it up and out of earth. The skeletal mouth was open, and some dried fleshy substance still covered one eye socket. The artist reached into his pocket for the golden coin, with which he would cover the other socket, and he was mystified to find the coin missing. No matter, he could still entertain his captive; and so he lifted the thing in moonlight and wondered at the way some of the bones had been deformed with melting, as if kissed by acidic lips. He brought the creature's skull close to his face and tried to imagine the countenance that had once covered it.

They pirouetted among the other gravesites until he heard the baying of a winged thing that sallied to him through the mist of moonlight. The hound-like thing was familiar, for he has seen its likeness in the *Necronomicon*. He did not like the way the beast leered at his partner's skull as heavy liquid slipped from bestial tongue, and so the artist placed his hand protectively over the cranium. Yet the beast was not to be deprived, and it bayed again as it stretched its liquid tongue to the artist's hand and licked it; and as the rough member lapped at his flesh, the artist saw that skin slip from his appendage and cover the skull, which took on fleshy form in which boiling black liquid, churning inside sockets, formed new orbs that blinked and laughed, and new mouth that breathed upon him.

Enoch groaned in slumber and pushed away the canine head that nuzzled his hand as the young human mouth so near to his breathed language onto his eyelids.

V.

He awakened to find Spider reclined on the floor next to the bed and studying him with poignant eyes. Smiling, Enoch called to the dog and clapped his hands, to which the dog responded by leaping onto the bed and licking one hand happily. "Your tongue is smooth, not rough like the feline variety," the artist said, to which the beast tilted its head as if attempting to contemplate the spoken sound. Now fully awake, Enoch pushed out of bed and slipped into clothes, and then he was preceded by Spider down the steps, to the living room where Xavier and the girl Alma Bishop smiled at him. Enoch thought he could detect the tang of new-shed orgasm in the air, but it may have been mere fancy. Smiling at the couple, he sat at a small table at which Xavier had been working and on which sat two piles of paper. In the shorter pile, the paper was filled with the poet's minute handwriting, and in the other pile the paper was blank. Unable to resist, Enoch slipped a blank sheet near him and picked up a pen, and then he began to sketch. The youngsters did not move as they watched the artist work, aware that they were posing. After twenty minutes, Enoch smiled and stood, handing the sheet to Alma, who murmured appreciatively as she saw the drawing in which she and Xavier were expertly portrayed.

Outside, Enoch raised his face to the sun and felt its welcomed warmth as he ran his hands through his hair, in which he still felt particles of Hop Yard grime. He moseyed to the small well and, yanking its rope, raised a sunken wooden bucket out of semi-clear water; and then he set the bucket on the well's stone ridge, cupped his hands into the liquid and then raised those expressive hands so that the water spilled over his hair. He dipped his hands into the bucket again and lowered his face into the cupped water. Wiping his eyes, he caught sight of his battered pickup truck, which he had seldom seen in daylight. The pickup had belonged to an artist chum who had committed suicide, and it was usually kept hidden in a rented garage—Enoch preferred the keen pleasure of riding on trains to that of driving the vehicle. Yet he confessed to himself that he had enjoyed driving it around Dunwich, had enjoyed a sense of freedom of movement that it had given him.

The young couple came outside and the girl kissed Xavier goodbye, then turned to smile at Enoch. She held the sketch in her hand as she wandered from them down the road. Xavier strolled to where Enoch stood, dipped one hand into the bucket and brought water to his mouth.

"You did a strange thing last night."

"No I didn't. Your work is about the land, the land I need to become intimate with. I need to eat it with my eyes and taste it with my hands, get the feel of it underneath my skin and in my blood. Such a rich mythic land, darkly fertile." He stepped nearer to the boy. "I appreciate it. I like its inhabitants. I'm going to start working on your portrait tonight, per your request that an illustration portray you rather than a photograph." His hands lifted so as to explore the young man's visage. "I like your face, with its length of nose and compressed lips. You keep your mouth so tightly clamped, as if afraid of spilling secrets."

"We'll have to do that project before nightfall. It's Roodmas. I've got somethin' to do atop Sentinel Hill."

"I can sketch ye up thar."

The boy laughed. "Nah, I don't think so. Your hands will be occupied with—other things."

They parted, and Enoch, feeling restless, took his sketchpad as he walked for hours so as to investigate some bridges. He enjoyed drawing the ancient structures, which were becoming rarer in New England as they were replaced with modern structures. On one bridge he found a particularly enticing lattice diagram that had been worked into the structure with newer wood than that with which the bridge had been constructed, yet as the artist tried to draw the graph he experienced an aching behind the eyes. He rubbed his eyes with his fingers, and then worked those fingers in an attempt to ape the diagram on the bridge; but as he did this his hands became sharply chilled, kissed with occult frigidity, and his witch-blood advised him to desist.

The sun was sinking behind the hills by the time he returned to the house, and he was surprised to find Alma there again, sitting at the hearth with her arms around Spider's neck.

"Ah, good," the poet told him. "I thought you'd miss it. Do you want to drive? Okay, hang on a tick." Xavier went into the kitchen and opened a cupboard, from which he took a small jar that was filled with pale powder. He signaled with his eyes that he was ready, and together the men walked out and into the pickup. They drove through the decadent Massachusetts countryside as sunset deepened into dusk, and the silent boy scanned heaven in search of birth of starlight. Enoch parked his truck just in front of the large lattice diagram that had been erected before the ruins of the Whateley farmhouse, and getting out of the truck the artist went to handle the joined sticks.

"This is a bit different from the others on the bridges, a bit simpler in motif. Is this your work?"

"Hell no. We learned it from that worn by Wizard Whateley. The others are inspired by dreams and all, and they're true as far as they go; but they're mostly for water and what it calls with flowin'. This one is more—cosmic." The lad smiled at the use of what he considered a sophisticated word.

"And where is Wizard Whateley, Xavier?"

Coyly, the lad smiled and nudged his head toward Sentinel Hill. "Up thar." Holding tightly to the jar of powder, he moved toward the incline, and Enoch followed silently. Strangely, as they walked over stones and high grass that led into woodland, the boy began to sing.

> "*An' un day soon ye day'll come*
> *When heav'n an' airth'll drone as un,*
> *An' chillen o' Dunnich hear ye cry*
> *O' eld Father Whateley from all sky.*"

They tramped through the woodland, and out of it, toward a twilit sky, toward the round apex of Sentinel Hill and its rough-hewn stone columns, its large table-like altar, its tumuli of human bone. Enoch knelt beside one pile of reeking remains and noted how some of them were oddly deformed, seemingly melted at places—and this reminded him of something he could not quite recall, a dream perhaps. As he was hunkered by the bones, Xavier stepped to a brazier and took a box of wooden matches from an inner coat pocket. One struck match was tossed into the brazier, which exploded into soaring flame. Enoch arose.

"Over here," the boy called as he moved over the coarse ground to a place when a length of oblong stone lay flatly on the earth. Had it been composed of wood the object might have served as lid for a small coffin. Enoch studied the symbols that had been etched into it, most of which he recognized from having studied them in tomes of antique lore. "Help me shove it a bit," the boy instructed. "I could do it alone, but it's best to have an assembly. Just this top part here, yeah, there ya go. Phew, you never get used to the stink. Funny that he should smell still, havin' been gone so long; although, of course, it ain't all him that's reekin'."

The huddled skeletal remains were of a small lean fellow, and although most of the flesh had long erased, one patch of dry hide clung to the skull and formed a kind of face to which a growth of beard still clung. The thing was naked of clothing except for a thick robe of purple thread. What really captured Enoch's attention was the design of latticed wood attached to a cord that wound the throat. This small item was far more identical to the designs in the underground Whateley lair than any of the others Enoch had seen. He stared at it as the boy next to him sprinkled a little of the powder from the jar over the dead thing's face and uttered whispered words. Below them, sounds issued from beneath the hill, and the flames in the brazier soared as if they had found new fuel. Enoch stood and sniffed the dark air.

"Storm's brewing," he informed the lad.

Xavier rose to a standing position and stared at stars. "Nah, it's them."

"Them?"

"The others—them old ones. They smell o' thunder. They loom among the stars, and between them." His eyes grew odd and shadowed. "They sing of deceased glory and show the silhouette of what has gone before, as they bubble between dimensions and weep the antique cry. Let us sing with them now, my brother, as they split the veil and show the thing that was, the thing that is, the thing that will be. They walk supernal among the smoldering sparks above us, craving the scent of mortal blood, which nourishes them weirdly. They form themselves with blood and debris of starlight so as to gibber in the mortal plane. Cthulhu is their kindred, yet Cthulhu sees them dimly. They pulse between the planets and kiss the palms of the Strange Dark One, Avatar of Chaos. We sing for them to unlatch the Gate, so as to usher forth the time of Yog-Sothoth. We see it there, the Gate and Threshold, between dimensions. We call it with our tongues, our hands."

The poet raised his hands and latched his fingers together, his digits impossibly aping the design of the dead wizard's icon. The hill noises escalated, and with each new pulse of sound the brazier flames expanded. Enoch watched what looked like smoke coil among the stars, which extinguished one by one. Xavier stood upright, an elect messenger who held his fleshy signal to the flowing obscurity of the sky. He bleated arcane language to the dark cosmic abyss, and in answer to his cry a pale form began to reveal itself. It was the esoteric lattice design, perfectly formed, fluid and sentient. It was the awesome Gate of Yog-Sothoth, a thing that trembled as it sensually divided itself so as to reveal the eidolons beyond it, the ghosts of they who lived brief mortal lives. There was the frail white-haired woman of fearsome and foolish countenance, and there was one offspring of her loins, a dark and goatish beast. And there—there was the awesome one, the one of such abbreviated promise, with its gigantic face that stretched across the sky, that face of which one half replicated the suggested visage of the interred wizard.

Enoch watched this display of lost glory and future promise, and knew that he was naught. Shaking uncontrollably, he flung himself before the Messenger with pleading in his liquid eyes. But the Messenger merely glanced for one moment at the frail and puny freak before him; and then in contempt he struck the artist's head.

W. H. PUGMIRE

Mystic Articulation

I.

He took the train from Boston to Salem, and from there he traveled eastward in a taxi, to Kingsport. He had been to the ancient seaport before, at Yuletide, but this was the first time he had journeyed there in early summer. After his weeks in hospital and then bed-bound at home, recovering from injuries secured during a job-related trip to Dunwich, Enoch Coffin wanted to be somewhere peaceful, lovely, where he could feel far away from mundane modernity. He knew that he had chosen well when the taxi followed the descending road that took him into the well-preserved colonial town and to the agency at which Enoch's Kingsport chum had left a key to the cottage where the artist would be camping. He paid the cabbie, tipping generously, and then struggled out of the vehicle as he held firmly to the cane he required for walking with one hand and his suitcase with another. His ongoing dizzy spells were mostly a thing of the past, but the cane gave him a sense of security that was more mental than physical. Having got his cottage key, Enoch returned to the street and felt a faint regret that he had sent his taxi away. It would be a half-hour trek to the small house in the Central Hill district where he would be staying, and his earlier certainty that he could make the trek without incident was now not so confident.

He began to walk down the quiet lane, past the shops, some few of which were still open. Passing a dark men's shop reminded him of his plan to buy some new clothes in the city, one reason he did not need to bring more than one medium-size suitcase with him now. He stopped for some moments and looked at the clothes dummies displaying tasteful fashion, and then he walked further along until he spotted a bookshop across the way, its door wide open and lights burning inside. It was a temptation he could not resist, and so he hobbled across the street and stepped into a spacious room where the walls were lined with bookshelves. Enoch observed the large sofa and the low table before it, some few chairs and two additional small tables. He thought he was alone in the room when he espied a cowled, cloaked figure bent unmoving over an antique spinning wheel. Enoch thought that the figure was napping when it slowly shifted and lifted its hooded head, and he wondered why the woman wore a mask. The mask smiled wanly.

"I shall soon be shutting up. Were you looking for anything in particular?"

"Poetry?" He spoke in a hushed voice, matching the quiet tone of the creature at the wheel.

"That wall. Do set down your suitcase, you look positively weary. Will you have a cup of tea?"

"That would be delightful, thanks." He looked over the poetry shelves and through the glass door of one locked case, in which he was startled to see a copy of the 1927 privately printed first edition of Yeats's *The Trembling of the Veil,* limited to 1,000 signed copies. It had been some time since he had read the poet, and so he turned to the shelves and found a volume of the Irishman's verse as the bookseller returned carrying a tray laden with tea things. He began to hobble toward her.

"Do not entertain the idea of assisting me, you are quite incapable. Sit here on the sofa." She set her heavy tray on the low coffee table before the sofa and poured Enoch a cup of tea, and the artist sighed gratefully as he sat. "You've been ravaged, young man."

"I was raped indeed," he mumbled. "I've come to Kingsport for a three-week rest. My friend rented a cottage for me up on Central Hill." The tea, as he sipped it from a delicate china cup, was steaming hot and delicious. He poured a bit of cream into his cup and reached for a sugar cookie. He turned to smile at his hostess and tried to nonchalantly study the peculiar face beneath the cowl, which she had kept in place. Although she was obviously past middle age, her face was strangely smooth, and Enoch wondered if it was indeed her face or some tight-fitting synthetic mask; and as he studied it he saw the way the soft light of the room was reflected upon the surface of her countenance, and also how an essence of that light was caught within the creature's shimmering incandescent eyes.

"Are you a poet?" the woman asked as she glanced at the book he had chosen.

"No, I paint." He finished his tea and struggled to his feet. "That was great, thanks. And I'll get this. I don't want to keep you, you said you were shutting up."

"Yes," she answered, rising slowly. "The day's earnings are already locked away, so you can come back another day and pay for the Yeats. That's the Oxford 1940 first edition printed in London. Twenty dollars—some other day. No, we'll leave the tea things there—the mice will enjoy the biscuits. I see my taxi has drawn up outside. You were planning on walking to Central Hill, I suppose, an absurd idea. Come, we'll deliver you to your cottage."

"You're very kind," Enoch answered as he limped to where his suitcase sat and then followed the woman out the door and into the waiting taxi. "I'm Enoch Coffin," he informed her as they rode to the Central Hill district.

She nodded to him but offered no hand. "Patricia Olney. The weather has been cool this week. The tourists aren't flocking quite as steadily as is usual, so you've chosen a good time to stay. Being that you are interested in poetry, you may want to know of a little—gathering—tonight at the Old Town Pub. A local (I suppose we must now consider him so) poet has had a new collection published by a resident patron. Should be rather a good show. Ah, here's your address. Charming," she said as she observed the small house. "Enjoy your Yeats, and we shall meet again anon."

Enoch stood on the pavement and watched the vehicle drive away, and then he shambled to the cottage door and let himself in. Charming was exactly the word with which to describe the place. The rooms were clean and well-furnished, and he found the refrigerator well-stocked with groceries and beer. Although he had no appetite, Enoch clutched a beer and glass and moved into the small living room, where he turned on a tall lamp and fell into a cozy armchair with his Yeats on his lap. He drank half of the bottled beer and shut his eyes; just for a moment, he told himself. When he awoke, an hour later, he saw that night had fallen outside the cottage window. What had awakened him was someone unlocking the front door and boldly walking in. A young mulatto woman stood before him, shaking her head and smiling ruefully.

"Honey, you're a mess. Look at those circles under your eyes."

"Denise—how charming, your invasion. No, I've not been sleeping well. What time is it? I want to attend this poetry thing tonight. I need people. Lots and lots of people."

"Well, you're not going out looking like that. I know you said not to get you any clothes because you wanted to shop in town, but I got you a nice casual suit that's quite sharp. Take a shower and shave. I guess you're talking about the Scot poetry reading. He's a freak, so you may enjoy it. Go, get your ass in the shower and make yourself presentable."

The artist did as he was commanded, and had to acknowledge that it felt wonderful to shower his damaged body and brush his teeth and hair. He didn't bother shaving but went to slip into underwear, and then went to the bedroom closet and found the beige summer suit that Denise had chosen for him, and hanging above it was a matching summer hat. A cool cotton shirt went well with the suit and completed the ensemble. Re-entering the living, he found his friend sitting in the armchair and reading Yeats.

"This is nice," he said, indicating the cottage. "Who owns it?"

"I do. I rent it out to various chums who need to get away from their lives for a while." She rose and stood very near to him. "Well, you certainly look a lot better. How are the limbs and all?"

"I'm just glad to be out of the hospital. I'm okay."

"I don't know what weird shit you got yourself mixed up with, Enoch, but I hope you'll settle down for a while. You're not the lad you used to be. Your wild ways are gonna catch up with you before you know it."

"My 'wild ways' aid my art, my dear. How do I look?"

She got a little closer. "Baby, I could eat you alive."

"That will have to wait until I'm feeling more myself. Let's go."

"I'll drop you off, but that's not my scene and no thank you."

They walked into the night and Enoch whistled as he saw her car, which was a testament to the lady's wealth. The plush lining of the seats was like nothing he had experienced, and he moaned in pleasure as he leaned back, shut his eyes and ignored her reckless driving. Too soon the car came to a halt and the lady kissed his cheek. He stepped out of the vehicle and leaned on his walking stick as he watched his friend speed away. A couple passed him and entered the pub, from which a raucous racket issued. He was in the mood to party, certainly, despite the soreness of his limbs, and he clutched his cane securely and limped into the establishment. Ah—the loud obnoxious city life, how he loved it. And yet how queerly alien he found it, here in Kingsport, where such sport didn't quite belong. The crowd was mostly young, reminding Enoch that the city was a place that attracted many young artists who created a hip and youthful 'scene' drenched in bohemian ways; and yet he thought that he detected a newer element of riot than he had previously noted in his few visits to the city, although perhaps it was merely this one occasion that had triggered this present zeal. He recognized no one, and his attire and extreme handsomeness caught everyone's attention. He passed the tables to the few rows of chairs that had been set up before a small platform, on which an intoxicated fellow addressed the crowd and inspired bursts of caterwauling.

"You all know that I had promised ne'er to set pen to pad again, but to follow the sage example of exiled Wilde and merely dream and talk. But our exceptional proprietor," and here the speaker held a glass of booze toward the bar, "a blessing on his head, has promised me a year's imbuement of his cheap whiskey if I composed a new volume of my sardonic verses." The crowd cheered, over which the fellow yelled. "How could I refuse? And now our generous Mrs. Prampton, of Kingsport Press, has issued my genius in chapbook form. So get out your pennies, my hearts, and spill them onto the lady's table yonder, and scan my rhymes and sigh with me for this sad sick sphere, this mortal dust into which we all will fall. Nay, don't be sad! There is drink and debauchery enough for all!"

It was obvious that the fellow was playing up to the crowd, and it was doubtful that the poet was as inebriated as he pretended to be. Enoch went to the bar, ordered a drink, and was flirted with by a woman who invited him to join her group at their table. He accepted and entered that sexual atmosphere that was his forte, suavely playing with the smoldering lusts he nonchalantly ignited. He answered the usual questions about the artistic scene in Boston and explained his own work in simple terms, and then he asked his own questions.

"Who is this fellow being celebrated tonight?"

"Oh, that's Winfield Scot. He's been around ever since I've been coming to Kingsport. Kind of a weird dude, hangs out at some abandoned hovel up on Water Street."

"It's not a hovel," corrected the young woman whom Enoch had met at the bar. "It's the home of a former sea captain known as the Terrible Old Man. Supposedly the guy was way over one hundred years old by the time he finally died. It's said he left behind some treasure chest full of Spanish gold, but that's never been confirmed."

"Why not?" Enoch asked, intrigued.

"Bad juju," piped up an older woman who wore a superior air. "If you stay in Kingsport for any length of time you'll discover a rather infantile and superstitious fear among the locals. It's never given concrete expression, but it's palpable nonetheless. And some of it is centered on that two-story cottage where Scot has made his street-urchin nest. The place does have an undeniable aura of menace ..."

"It's those fucking stones," a young man interrupted, "painted all weird and grouped together like something out of Easter Island. They give me the willies every time I pass the place when I want to paint at the piers."

"And this Scot fellow lives there?"

"Camps out would be the proper term," said the superior lady. "On the front porch, huddled in blankets and reading by lantern light. We think he subsists on government money."

"Psycho money," someone said, and everyone laughed. "Scot's always said he was a poet but for all the years I've been coming here no one has ever known him to write a line—until now. They say his little book is okay," the fellow concluded, unable to resist a condescending smirk.

Enoch had had enough of the little clique. "Well," he said as he stood, "you make him sound intriguing. Think I'll mosey on over and check out his scribbling." The others raised their glasses and bleary eyes to him, and he returned their sloppy smiles with a wink and foxy grin. As he walked to the table he saw that the poet had joined the woman seated behind it, smiling disdainfully at the crowd that ignored them. Enoch picked up a chapbook and skimmed through it.

"I'll take three copies," he said as he plucked his wallet from his pocket and set a fifty-dollar bill before the astonished woman. "I have a couple friends who have a fondness for the esoteric thing."

Winfield Scot laughed. "You're right there, mister."

"I seem to see a Clark Ashton Smith influence in some of these lines," Enoch continued as he perused the pages of the copy he held. "It's a shame America isn't more acquainted with one of her finest poets. Do you know his prose poems?"

"Exquisite," the lady rejoined as she handed Enoch a twenty-dollar bill and two additional copies of the chapbook. "I'm Sally Pont," she said, offering Enoch a genuine smile. The artist took her hand.

"Enoch Coffin, of Boston."

Miss Pont smiled with recognition. "I have your illustrated edition of Naomi Neptune's scandalous short stories. Your work is amazing."

"Thank you, that was a fascinating project." He waved a hand to indicate the crowd. "Lots of fans here?"

Winfield Scot smirked. "No, this is just a party crowd, here for the booze. Some of them will buy the book on their way home, maybe, as an afterthought. I told Sally that her 500-print run was far too optimistic."

"Not so," she countered. "Most of my customers are online, and this will please them enormously. But thank you so much. I think you'll like it."

"I like it already," Enoch replied. "I can tell an authentic poet when I read one, and this seems excellent."

The woman observed his cane and reached below for a small plastic bag. "This has handles, it'll make it easier for you to hang on to your copies."

"Thank you. I think I'll find some silent place in which to read. Good night." He smiled and moved away, worked his way through the packed crowd to the door and sighed at the taste of fresh air. His initial zeal for the party life had indeed departed. Stopping to lean against an antique lamp post that showered him with golden ambiance, Enoch opened the book that he had been scanning and read the opening poem. Its title was "Andromeda," and it skillfully played with both the spiral galaxy and the figure of Greek mythology, creating an intoxicating evocation of mortal age and cosmic grandeur. Caught within the spell of the words he began to speak out loud, Enoch was not aware of the fellow who silently watched and listened until he paused and turned a page. The artist slid his head around and saw the poet watching him. "Making your escape?"

"Gawd, at last!" He looked at the specter of the moon behind its miasmic curtain. "Ah, the night mist is coming in from the sea. The *real* Kingsport beckons. Been here long?"

"Got in today, but I've visited before. I've never really explored the local nightlife."

Scot spat. "There's a new constituent, crasser than what we've known before. But I don't think the coarser kind stay for long—I hope not. Of course, I don't commingle with the crowd, I did this tonight for Sally, who now realizes it was a mistake. The place for this kind of event is a bookshop. Let's walk into the mist and get away from this electric fire."

Together, the gentlemen traversed down a crooked street that led toward the waterfront, from which a dull horn sounded. "I found a charming bookshop earlier this evening. Couldn't believe it, they had a copy of Yeats's *The Trembling of the Veil* behind glass."

"Wants a pretty penny for it too, so she does. I like Yeats. In that work he wrote something about finding his style too ornamental as a young man, and so he decided to sleep upon a board. He didn't, and he wouldn't have found it much help to poetic style. I spend most of my nights on a porch, so I know what I'm talking about."

"Are you homeless?"

"Not at all. So, you've met Miss Olney."

"Hmm?"

"The old broad who owns the bookshop. How did she strike you?"

Enoch sucked in air. "I was dumbfounded by her face. Couldn't decide if it was some kind of covering or reconstruction."

"Yes," the poet answered, nodding slowly. "She's looked like that since returning from the High House, where she went to gather whatever elements she could find of her grandfather's soul." He laughed at the expression on Enoch's face. "Or so the story goes. The face is strange enough, but it's no match for her luminous eyes. I passed her once, in mist much thicker than this we're walking into, and her eyes were absolutely glowing, scared the piss out of me. She arrived shortly after I did, almost thirty years ago now. I barely remember the way she looked when she first arrived, but whatever happened up there it did indeed transform her."

"Up where?"

"The inaccessible pinnacle and its sinister northward crag—Kingsport Head and its house o' dreams. No one ever mentioned it to you on your other stays?"

"No."

"Well, very few would mention it, that's right enough. And the mist often hides it at night, when one might chance to look up and see the lights glowing in the small windows."

"And Miss Olney journeyed up this 'inaccessible' peak and—?"

"Legend, dear fellow. What was your name? Ah, Enoch. A Hebrew name, the man who walks in the clouds with god or some such thing— just like old lady Olney's grandpappy did, according to whispered legend. Wasn't Enoch supposed to have invented writing? I think I read that somewhere. A blessing to his memory, if so." He noticed that the artist was looking tired and studied Enoch's cane. "I know where you can get a better one."

"Excuse me?"

"Your walking stick. Come on, you'll be impressed. It's a twenty-minute stroll to my place. Let's go." Scot began to whistle a jaunty tune, the sound of which echoed in the vapor through which they journeyed. Enoch walked slowly, clutching his cane and limping through the mist after the other fellow's lead, until they came to a raised plot of land encased by a tall black fence of wrought iron. Scot led Enoch up three stone steps and past the gate, into a yard where gnarled trees twisted over a curious display of large stones, oddly grouped and painted and slightly reminding Enoch of photos he had seen of the relics of Easter Island, although the way these present stones were grouped disturbed him queerly and alerted his arcane senses.

They passed beneath the trees on the cracked stone pathway, and Enoch studied the aged and neglected house that leaned in darkness and billowing mist as he detected a bad smell that was a mixture of sea and death. Raising his eyes so as to peer above the antique abode, he detected three small objects with round owl-like faces and incandescent eyes that watched them high in the thickening vapor, until finally the beings were swallowed by the mist, taking the polluted reek with them. Enoch became aware of the fellow beside him looking at him inquiringly. "You attract things, don't you?" And then the poet laughed and led the way up warped wooden steps to a long length of porch whereon were piled many blankets, books, and what looked like a gas-operated single-burner stove.

"I think some freaks at the pub were talking about this place, something about a Terrible Old Man."

"Yep," Scot answered as he hesitated before the front door of the dwelling.

"So what made him Terrible?"

"His age—and his secrets. He was an old sea captain. Hand me that ship's lantern, will you? Thanks." Scot hesitated a few more seconds, and then he opened the door.

Enoch followed him into what looked like a large bare room. The poet then struck a wooden match and lit the lantern's wick, and Enoch gasped as he saw the gallery of queer booty that gathered dust along the walls. The room seemed strangely warm and Enoch began to unbutton his jacket. "Yeah, it holds warmth in some peculiar way. So does the porch, in all weathers, making it a handy place to camp. It's weird, isn't it? There is some unfathomable air of danger in the place, but also a subtle sense of security. One can be safe from the outside world of mortal men—but the Outside world breathes this air assuredly."

"It's potent, indeed. I don't like it. Let's leave."

Scot placed a hand on Enoch's arm. "Wait. The old feller kind of made me guardian of the place before he—left. We're going to make an exchange. I owe you for the pleasure you gave me in buying my verses and actually reading them. Give me your cane. It's a sorry thing."

"Got it cheap in a second-hand shop. Didn't think I'd be needing to use it for such a length of time. My limbs aren't healing as quickly as I expected they would." He let Scot take the cane from him and watched as the fellow went to one corner of the room and then returned to him holding another walking stick. He could feel the extraordinary quality of the gnarled thing. The lantern light shimmered on the highly polished surface of reddish wood. Reaching out, Enoch took hold of the walking stick and was startled as the lantern's flame momentarily burst as brighter ignition.

"Holy hell," the artist muttered.

"You're a bit of a wizard, aren't you?"

"I'm au fait with the arts. I know what I need to know. Look at the designs etched beneath the thin shellac—I seem to remember them from when I was allowed to scan the *Necronomicon* in the British Museum. This is an implement of power."

"He used it as such. It gave him his strength, and other assets. But I think you need to be a wizard to be able to evoke its properties. I have no knack for that kind of thing, never thought about mumbo-jumbo stuff until I settled in Kingsport and got to know the old codger. I'm not really comfortable with the occult or whatever you want to call it. Anyway, I have the authority to bequeath it to you, and I think it may help with your recovery. Just be careful with its potency. He told me once that magick can intoxicate."

"Where is he now, this centuried fellow?"

"Oh, he went away—into the mist." The poet smiled, happy to have a mystery of his own. Enoch found the fellow more and more fascinating. He sensed that Scot knew many esoteric things, despite his protestations. He watched as the poet began to tug at his shirt collar. "Ugh, it's hot in here. Let's scat." Without waiting, Winfield Scot trotted out of the habitation, down the stairs and near to the grouping of large stones. Enoch laughed at the fellow's sudden nervousness and followed him, and then bent among the stones so as to fondle the sigils that had been painted onto them.

"Shine your lantern over here a bit, I think—yes, look. Some of the symbols painted on these stones match some few of the sigils etched into this staff. I seem to recall…" He stood and thought hard, trying to remember what he had read so long ago in a forbidden text, which he had tricked a librarian into showing him. The lines of script filtered to his brain, hazy at first, then more clearly. Enoch raised his curious walking stick to the mist as he stood among strange stones, and he began to call to things that slumbered beyond the rim. Scot screamed as the lantern's flames shot out and licked his hand. Enoch paid no heed, for he sensed the black shape that boiled above them in the air, the bubbling void that spilled its essence into Enoch Coffin's eyes.

II.

When he awakened, he was reclining on a bed of blankets that had been spread on a wooden surface, his head sunk into a soft pillow. Winfield Scot, attending a teakettle that was screeching on the portable gas burner, smiled down on him. A bit of gauze was wrapped around one of the poet's hands. "Did she wake you up? I've only got instant." He opened a container of coffee and poured two teaspoons worth into a large chipped cup, and then he picked up the kettle and added water. "Sugar?"

"Uh, yeah, three spoonfuls. I like it sweet. How's your hand?"

"Slightly cindered is all. It'll be okay."

"What the hell happened last night? My mind's a blur."

"You called some kind of ichor out of the mist—well, it might have been a shadow, or a portal. I don't really understand all of this mumbo-jumbo. Hey, don't look at me like that; it's the truth."

"You know more than you let on. You're a sphinx of untold secrets."

"You're babbling. How are your eyes?"

"They're okay. Why?" Still a bit groggy, Enoch wasn't aware of the curious way in which the poet was studying his face.

"Oh, nothing. Three spoonfuls of sugar—ugh! Too sweet by half. Here you go, Coffin. Is that your real name?"

The artist reached for the cup. "Yeah," he replied, grateful for the brew. As he drank, Enoch scanned the day and saw that the weather was clear. Above the low gnarled trees he saw the mammoth towering outcrop of rock that rose one thousand feet above the harbor. Atop the highest crag, beyond a scattering of trees, he could just make out the peaked roof of what looked like a very small house. He let his eyes scan the rest of the impressive titan of rock. "What's that other building lower down?"

"Oh, that used to be a wireless station for the *Arkham Advertiser*. They built it sometime in the 1920s. Something strange happened there and it's been abandoned for decades. Arkham's on the opposite side about two miles yonder. Just below the other side is where the Miskatonic flows into the sea."

"Huh. You ever been up there?"

Scot laughed lightly. "No one ever goes up there. It's not safe."

The artist bit his lip and nodded slowly, and then he pushed himself to a standing position. "Well, thanks for tending to me during last night's incident. You're not telling me things, but I'll find them out. Take care of that hand."

"Don't forget your bag." He picked up the plastic bag that contained the copies of his chapbook. "I went ahead and signed them for you." Smiling, he winked. Returning the poet's smile, Enoch took his bag, reached for the cane that was leaning against one portion of the porch and hobbled down the steps. He fancied that the air grew colder as he moved farther from the ancient house, but maybe it was just an effect of the weirdness he felt as he walked past the curious stones that stood in the yard.

As he continued his walk, he found it remarkable that he was neither stiff nor in pain, and he moved with more and more confidence as he held on to the top of the old cane, which in daylight revealed itself to be a beautiful bit of craftsmanship. The daylight brought out the beauty of the reddish wood, and Enoch marveled at how "right" the cane felt in his grasp. Happily, he began to whistle, and the day was so lovely that he decided to walk all the way to Central Hill.

The cottage looked very comfortable as he entered it and hung his crumpled hat onto a peg. Leaning the antique walking stick against one wall and tossing the plastic bag onto the armchair, he went into the kitchen and made himself a plate of breakfast grub and a pot of fresh coffee. He wolfed down the food as he stood inside the kitchen and gulped one cup of coffee, and then he filled his cup again and entered the small living room, where he looked around for the edition of Yeats before espying the plastic bag he had thrown on the cozy chair. Setting the bag on the side table, he pulled out one of the chapbooks and began to read. The longest piece was a narrative poem in free-verse form entitled "Ancestral Tugging."

Enoch began to read and soon forgot about his coffee. The poem was obviously about Kingsport and had many points of reference to local spots, such as The Hollow district and the artist's colony in what was known as Hilltown. The poem's strangest portions concerned a ritual of danse beneath an autumn moon in what was meant to be the antique burying ground on Central Hill, the city's primogenial cemetery where the oldest graves (dating to the 1640s) leaned beneath growths of pale willows. The narrative followed the dancers to a church, and beneath that church, to a hidden grotto wherein eldritch ritual was conducted by masked things.

He stopped to rest his eyes, which ached oddly, and knew that he was more tired than he realized. Shutting his eyelids, Enoch let his fanciful mind move through dreaming. When his body startled into wakefulness he had no idea how long he had slept. Glancing around, he espied the Yeats, which reminded him of the money he owed Miss Olney of the bookshop. Rising, he was suddenly aware that he still wore the light summer suit from the previous evening. Contrary to his usual custom, he felt too weary to wash up and groom himself. He moved into the bedroom, where his suitcase lay open on the bed, took off the light jacket and put on a hefty sweater of green cotton. Not bothering to study himself in any mirror, Enoch ran his fingers through his wavy hair and headed out, snatching up the walking stick to which he had become rather partial. The reading of Winfield Scot's poem had made him want to investigate the old cemetery on Central Hill, but first he would venture to the bookstore and frolic with its curious curator.

He stepped into thick fog and clasped the end of his walking stick as he found his way to the trolley stop. He waited, alone, until the old behemoth rolled to him and allowed him passage, and he sat and studied the fog as the vehicle took him to the downtown area. The miasma had added atmosphere to ancient Kingsport, and he felt indeed that he had stepped out of time and journeyed into another era. Tapping his walking stick before him, Enoch found his way to the bookshop, stopping just once to observe the obscure winged shape that watched him from the sky. He approached the shop, the door to which was open. The large main room was vacant of occupant, and Enoch moved smoothly to the locked bookcase of rare items so as to ogle the first edition of *The Trembling of the Veil.* He had heard of someone purchasing a copy for $2,000, and found it incredible that Miss Olney would leave such a thing unguarded in the unoccupied room.

And then he felt her shadow press against him. "Have you read it?"

"Long ago, in a library. It served to whet my interest in Oscar Wilde, which blossomed into an obsession. It's odd, how some bygone authors seem so—present. Yeats's poems have never lost their immediacy for me. I love that he was a mystic, an occultist, became a member of the Ghost Club—all those fascinating things that have now become my common reality. Richard Ellmann, in his biography, quotes Yeats as saying something about the mystical life being the very center of his existence. Yes, yes—he peered beyond the veil and past dimensions."

Enoch suddenly realized that he was prattling on, and turned to the woman with a rueful smile. She was dressed smartly in black slacks and sweater, and although she was not young Miss Olney still wore traces of beauty. Yet there was an aspect of her face, in the expression in her bizarre milky eyes, that confounded him. She nodded her head slightly, as if to herself. "You, too, have peered beyond dimension. What has happened to your eyes?"

"What?" The woman took his arm and guided Enoch to where an antique mirror hung on one wall. He gazed at his reflection and touched one hand to his face. "I called something last night, under the influence of this sorcerer's cane, I think. It used to belong to the Terrible Old Man, and was perhaps a source of his unholy strength and longevity. I don't really remember much of last night. I blacked out."

"Your eyes have partaken of the void, as mine have eaten of the One."

"The One?" He turned to take in her gaze and saw the subtle way in which her eyes changed shade, as if they contained elements of moving cloud and mist. Tilting to her, he touched his fingers to the smooth unearthly mask that was her countenance. Lifting her hand to his, she kissed his fingers with icy lips, and he could not help but shudder.

"Do you know what exists Outside, Mr. Coffin? Darkness and light and language, that is all. Fire and shadow and articulation. But they who mutter in the cosmos are chaotic, idiots divine. Their language has no import, for they exist in meaninglessness. It fills me with such an ecstasy of liberation, to know that our mortal essence, such as it is, will spill into that stupid void and coil without form or place among the dead and dying stars. My grandfather, I had been taught by my mother, had been a teacher of philosophy, and when I was a girl that sounded so grand. I wanted to follow in his footsteps. It was only much later that I was told how he had altered after he was called to this city in the mists and its High House on Kingsport Head, of how when he arrived here his eyes had grown weary with looking too long a time on dull reality. He was summoned, by something, to this magical city, and here he looked upon the past and future shadow. He recognized the sea for the first time as the great body of mystery that it is. He did the insane thing and climbed to the strange High House that had so captivated his imagination when he beheld how its lights shone at evening. When he returned to the harbor a sense of wonder had been siphoned from his eyes, and some of the very old folk whispered that a portion of his restless soul had been lost among the swathes of clouds that often conceal the topmost crag of Kingsport Head. Listening to the story of my grandfather was like a summons. I journeyed to mist-enshrouded Kingsport, and I climbed to the High House as he had before my time. I was determined to win back whatever portion of my grandsire's soul had been forfeited to the dweller on the crag. Boldly, I pushed through one window of the peak-roofed house, and I confronted the One who dwells amongst memory and mist. And I *commanded* him to return the aspect of his soul that my grandfather had neglected to bring back with him. And the dweller in the strange High House smiled his ageless smile, and he *commanded* that I should partake of his eyes. And so I feasted. My mask is the result."

"Why are our eyes so affected?"

"The Outside is jealous of the living light of mortal eyes, just as the scent of corporeal blood arouses weird appetite within them. Ah, the power of our penetrating gaze, our purple fluid! Some Outside thing has sapped a little of your light, but you may find that in darkness you will sense secret things that will leave you awestruck. You are an adept in the occult, I could tell that when I first saw you. You may find this transformation amusing, for a little while."

"How can I reverse it?"

"That will happen when the time is right."

Enoch shook his head, bewildered, and then he reached into his pocket for his wallet. Miss Olney waved the twenty-dollar bill away and touched his face again. "Light and darkness," the artist mumbled, "the potency of blood."

She smiled at him then and took his hand, and he remained silent as she led him to her spinning wheel. "Touch your finger to the spindle, sir, while I whisper secrets to your soul." Her cool mouth touched his ear, into which she heaved esoteric sound; and as she whispered to him her hand guided his to the wheel's spindle, upon which he pricked one finger that soon dripped blood into the woman's other hand. Miss Olney raised her blood drenched hand to her eyes, the murky surface of which seemed to soak in Enoch's liquid stain. She spoke again, to enchanted air in which her words formed spirals of spray that washed the artist's haunted eyes. Turning from her, he walked through fog, not knowing where his feet were taking him until he saw the black fence form itself in the mist. He quietly walked along the stone path, past the painted stones, to one golden window at the side of the house, through which he peered. Winfield Scot, utterly inebriated, sat at a long table before a row of olden bottles in which dark pendulums hung from wire that was fastened to the stoppers. Enoch listened as the poet cooed to the pendulums, which answered him with faint vibrating buzzing. He then moved away and walked out of the neglected yard to where he caught a trolley that returned him to Central Hill, at a stop near the old forsaken burying ground. He moved through mist onto the cemetery sod and heard the whisper of wind through willows. The fog began to lift so that he could see Kingsport below him, where one by one the small-paned windows of the colonial houses filled with enchanted light. Falling to his knees, the artist brought the walking stick to his mouth and kissed an arcane signal to which he then whispered, and he marveled at how the occult language spilled from his mouth as coils of sentient gloom. He raised his eyes heavenward, to where the three winged things watched him from lingering patches of mist; and then he laughed and chanted unfathomable articulation to those beasts as they sallied to him and feasted on the shadow that vomited from his mouth.

III.

"Do you ever sleep at home in bed?"

Enoch opened his eyes to the friendly voice and found himself beneath a willow tree with Winfield Scot looking down at him. The poet was leaning on Enoch's old cane. "What time is it?"

"Almost noon. You have a very strange way of finding rehabilitation. Or perhaps you were seeking artistic inspiration in such dreams as may be nourished by this committal sod? You seem to have scratched yourself while dreaming."

Frowning as he sat up, Enoch rubbed one hand against his face and felt the scars near his eyes. "I did have dreams—of your poem and its tunnels." He knocked upon the ground. "But this place is free of ghouls, unlike Arkham and Copp's Hill." He sniffed at the air. "There is something in this elemental aether that ghouls find fearsome, far-fetched as that may seem."

"Did your dreams tell you this? Yes, there are tunnels under this hill—they connect with the ones in the old churchyard. You read that poem? I recited portions of it at a little public reading before Sally published my little book, and the reaction from some of the old-timers was fascinating. I stirred ancestral memories and dreams with that one. The legend is well-known locally, but no one likes to mention it. I found an account of it in an old diary at Olney's shop. There used to be a kind of Festival held here in ancient times. I showed the passage to Patricia Olney and she found it captivating. She's a bit of a wanker, really. After I showed her that passage she designed a kind of hooded robe exactly as it was described as being worn by the queer old folk of Festival. Caused *quite* a panic when she first strolled through town wearing it, ha ha! The old-timers won't step inside that bookshop when she's there. She shares ownership with an old gent who is always away on book-buying trips. She likes to thumb her nose at local legend, but her boldest act was to climb up Kingsport Head and mingle with the occupant in the house up there. *That* really got local tongues wagging." He laughed again.

"So what are you doing up here?"

"Walking off a gnarly hangover. I'm using your cane, it's nice." He glanced at the walking stick that he had given to Enoch. "You been conjuring more madness out of time?"

"I think so. Winged things in the sky with queer faces,"

"Ah, the psychopomps. I've known others who have encountered them. Not a good sign, buddy. To see them means that you've encountered the darker mists of Kingsport, with their shadows of dead and dreaming things."

"For someone who ain't 'into' the weird shit, you sure know a lot. Where is this haunted churchyard and its tunnels? Take me there."

"The one from my poem? I don't know, the way you've been calling to the darkness I don't think it would be wise to take you there."

90

The artist grabbed his walking stick and struggled to his feet. "Fine, I'll find it myself. I know it's here on Central Hill. Shouldn't be too difficult to find, there won't be many antediluvian houses of worship still standing."

"Oh, they tore it down over a decade ago. I don't know what the city was planning on doing with the land. There was the problem of the churchyard and its tombs, so eventually whatever they had planned was abandoned. It's a forlorn old site. Well, if you're so insistent on seeing it, I'd better go with you and be your voice of reason. The way you've been behaving you'll decide to take a nap in the pool. Come on."

Enoch stood for a moment on the hill and gazed down to the city below, with its colonial roofs, its twisting lanes, and its sleepy harbor. It was a beautiful old town, exquisitely charming in a quaint way, and Enoch loved how it evoked a very real sense of the past, which he so loved. The sea was free of mist, but Kingsport Head was enshrouded in thick clouds. He nodded to Scot and they walked to the bending path that led to the street below. What a comical sight they made, two unsteady gentlemen of middle-age tapping their walking sticks on the ground and creeping to their destination. Scot observed his companion and witnessed Enoch's strength grow more assured the longer he grasped the Terrible Old Man's staff, and after a while he had to increase his pace to keep up with the artist, who seemed to sense the way they were to wander. He smiled, amused, as the visitor strode exactly to the site they sought.

"Man, this looks desolate," the artist sighed. "It must have been a magnificent old edifice, the white church."

"Yes, it was white ..."

"And betimes the great orange star in the zodiac constellation of Taurus would seem to balance itself on the building's spectral spire. And they would trail over the crest on moonless nights so as to partake of Festival each hundred years, their lanthorns in their grasp."

"Um, that is the legend. Wow, your eyes have really darkened. Can you see?"

"I have never seen more clearly."

"Great. I don't have my 'lanthorn' with me, but I've got this powerful LED flashlight." He reached into his jacket pocket and produced the small aluminum instrument. "Now, this is where the pews were, probably, and just beyond them—here we go, the trapdoor to the vaults."

"You've been down there?"

"Once, with Captain Holt—probably twenty years ago."

Enoch tapped on the trapdoor with his walking stick, and then he bent down and took hold of the rusted iron ring and lifted. "Pah!" The stench was indeed foul as it crept into clean Kingsport air. "The pulpit was just there," he said as he pointed to an area just beyond the hatch that had covered the floor; and then he held up his staff to some absent effigy and muttered a phrase in Latin. Scot hoped it had a Biblical source and was not an evocation from some nameless tome. The artist waited for the poet to lead the way, following close behind as Scot turned on his flashlight and climbed down the worn stone steps that led into an underground crypt. They came upon a second aperture, entered it and descended a narrow spiral staircase that oozed its fetid stench into their nostrils. The rough-hewn stone on which they walked was moist and slippery, yet they were cautious and did not hurry, anxious as Enoch was to see the pool of which the poet had spoken. And then they were there, in a place where pungent seepage dragged downward from the walls of an underworld and kissed the large squalid pool of greenish water.

"It's worse than I remembered," Scot whispered as he shuddered. "We won't linger, Coffin. This place is diseased."

Enoch knelt before the edge of the pool and dipped the tip of his walking stick into the water, moving the staff as if it were a writing tool with which he could etch sigils onto the liquid facade. The two men watched the sea green mist that began to form above the pool's surface. Enoch sucked in the noxious coils of film that floated to him from the mammoth pond, and he did not shut his eyes as the coils clothed them so as to blend with his transmuted orbs. "Let's go for a dip," he told his companion playfully; but Scot did not reply, and so Enoch slipped out of his clothing alone and oozed into the liquid body, swimming some feet away from the rocky earth whereon the poet stayed. And he was confused, when he turned to wave to his cohort, to see that Scot was bending over a sprawling figure whose trunk reclined in the poet's embrace, a figure that grasped the enchanted walking stick with one hand.

Then the sound of whining summoned, and the artist revolved in the water to look at another portion of land where stood an eidolon; and beside the figure, squatted at her feet, was an enigmatic shape that pressed a feeble flute to malformed mouth. And as the artist listened to the sound the place in which he found himself began to alter, and his expanse of pool became a sluggish river in which oily things swam by him as the walls of fungoid stone melted and rose again as blackest gulf. He watched the woman, whose only attire was a hooded robe, walk onto the water, to him; and when she reached down to him the artist clasped her proffered hand and rose above the slothful tributary. He scanned the creature's cowled area that was absent of visage and contained but two smooth and luminous spheres that mocked his mortality. The phantom led him from the water, onto stone, as three winged beasts drifted through green mist and bleakest gloom. Portions of the black gulf beyond him began to shimmer, as did his midnight eyes, those mutated eyes that watched a darker form stalk toward them, a haughty figure that reached into the woman's cowl and brought forth the smooth and shining mask with glowing eyes. The strange dark one turned to the artist and pressed the waxen veil against the artist's face, and then the daemon pressed one talon into the artist's forehead and engraved a secret sign such as had been etched onto the Terrible Old Man's walking stick. Forcefully, the fiend slapped his ebony hand against the mortal's face and shrieked his name.

Enoch Coffin awakened in a darksome place, in Winfield Scot's embrace, as the poet's hand struck him once again. "Wake up, damn you!" The artist scrambled free from the other's arms. "This is one place where you're *not* napping! Come on, I can't fucking breathe. Don't forget your wizard's cane."

Something in the poet's alarm caught on, and the two men moved swiftly through the nitrous atmosphere and up the moist stone stairs, not stopping until they stood within the gathering gloom of new dusk, while from the Kingsport Harbor came the solemn tolling of buoys that were moved by the waves that pushed toward rotting wharves.

Scot steadied his friend with one strong arm as Enoch caught his breath. "You've scratched yourself again." Enoch did not move as Scot raised a hand to his face and smoothed an area on the artist's forehead. "Come on, this time I'm making certain you sleep in your own bed." They moved through gathering mist and violet shadow, watched secretively from above by the winged beasts that floated in the ghostly sky.

IV.

(From the personal journal of Enoch Donovon Coffin)

I woke up to the smell of bacon and coffee, pushed myself up so that I sat in bed, and tried to remember the night before. Winfield Scot poked his plain-faced mug into the bedroom and asked how I liked my eggs. "Sunny side up, with well-done hash browns and buttered toast, no jelly. I like my bacon chewy."

"You got it," he replied and disappeared. I pushed off the bedclothes and saw that I was still wearing my boxers. How many days had I worn them? I pulled them off and sat there naked when Scot returned with a tray of what turned out to be excellent breakfast cuisine. He set the tray on the bed and gave me a look that seemed to dare me not to move so that the juice would spill, and then he picked up my boxers from where I had tossed them on the floor. "Where do you keep your clean underwear?"

"I'll attend to that later. My balls need to breathe. Where'd you sleep?"

"That chair in the living room is extremely comfortable."

"Hell, you could have slept here, the bed's big enough."

He kind of smirked. "I don't swing that way, pardner." Then he bent to examine my face and frowned. "You look worse than ever. Alchemy doesn't seem to suit you. Maybe I shouldn't have given you the old man's staff."

"Bullshit. It's just this—place, Kingsport. It's awakened elements inside me that are new, unique. Or maybe it's you, inexpertly channeling some forces despite your conviction that you're not into the weird stuff."

He bent to my suitcase, which he had moved from the bed to a small chair, and took out a clean pair of briefs. The bloke would have made someone a nice little wifey. He sat on the end of the bed and tossed the briefs at me. "I came here from New York almost thirty years ago, in desperate need of a change. I'd always had this ... fantasy ... about belonging to an artistic community, but the scene in New York was getting so cliquish and I hated it. The scene here was different then than it is now, not so touristy. I loved it, and I relished the atmosphere of this city with its mists and its memories. Kingsport is like no other place I have known— not that I've traveled all that much. I joined a little group that had formed a kind of artistic co-op in one of the old hotels, and it was great for a while, rent was cheap and friendship was easy. I decided to stay, and over time I got to know the city fairly well. I discovered the curious undercurrent of restless fear that one finds among the older fisher-folk. They don't often express it, but drink sometimes loosens their tongues when you talk to them one-on-one. Then they whisper tales about the mists and about the sea, about things found and things imagined. They tell of enigmas pulled from the depths of water or vaguely viewed in the clouds that gather over Kingsport Head. They warned me against the Terrible Old Man and cautioned me to stay away from his yard and its painted stones. He rarely left his home, usually paid boys to get his groceries and all. He paid well, so that offset the fear the lads usually experienced when in that yard and the old captain's company. But now and then I'd see him wandering the older sections of town visiting certain reclusive folk, or he'd take the trolley up here to Central Hill and amble through the old cemetery. That's where I met him, and as we stood side by side and looked down over the roofs and at the harbor, he told me outlandish things as one by one the small-paned windows of the houses lit up all dreamy-like. I was pretty poor, and I had heard about his hoard of Spanish gold with which he bought his supplies; so I offered to assist him with the errands of life and such, and he agreed—said he liked my dreamy face and suspected I was a poet. I took to visiting him at night and reading poetry to him, and the more I was in his company the more I was—seduced, something in his nature was so intriguing and compelling. I didn't have many belongings, just a few books and things, and so I moved out of the co-op and took to sleeping on the old guy's porch. He was growing older and feebler, although he seemed to find a fund of strength whenever he went out trekking around town, grasping his old walking stick. He'd make us a weird brew of tea at times, and it'd make me so sleepy drinking a couple cups of the stuff that I'd fall asleep on his floor, where I always sat. I'd wake up and see him at that table, talking to the pendulums in those antique bottles and watching them stir and purr in reply. He'd sometimes tell me that he was depending on me to 'take care o' things' when he was gone, and I thought it was his old age talking. And then he was gone. Some folk said they had seen someone creeping up Kingsport Head toward the crag where the ancient house is usually covered by the clouds. But no one knows for sure. So, yes, I have become attuned to the 'weird stuff'—you can't sleep in that yard, on that porch, and not be. But I don't put into practice the arcane arts as you enjoy doing. Or, rather, you seem unable to resist their lure."

I finished eating and sank back into my pillows. "I love it, true, as an aid to my art. I live for artistic experience and expression—it's the very air I breathe. But I am a realist in my craft. I capture a dark actuality and express it with authenticity."

"You've been seduced, Coffin, however grand you want to paint it. I've seen it time and time again: the allure of what is called, around here, the Outside. It's got you by your balls."

I scratched my scrotum and then slipped into my briefs. "I'll return the old codger's cane if you want me to, but I've grown rather fond of it. I want to study its symbols some more."

Scot laughed. "That's exactly what I'm talking about—you're fixated on the occult. Yeah, sure, keep the staff. I've done my Florence Nightingale duties, I'm outta here. Take my advice and get some real rest, you look like crap."

I chuckled as he picked up the tray and took it to the kitchen, and then I closed my eyes as I heard him exit the house. I did feel ragged, but I had no intention of spending the day in bed. What I really needed was a shower, so I pushed out of bed and staggered to the bathroom, where I stopped at the sink and let cold water fall into my hands and then threw it on my face.

The face that looked back at me in the mirror was shocking. I used to scratch myself during sleep when I was a kid, but it hadn't happened for decades, and it was not cool to see the marks around my eyes and on my forehead. I vaguely remembered one weird dream about birds or weird winged things that feasted with sharp mouth on elements of my eyes, and I figured the dream had been inspired by the sensation of my nails on my face as I slept. The mark that had been engraved on my forehead was another matter. It resembled one of the marks that had been etched onto the old man's walking stick, and I recalled having seen it in the *Necronomicon,* although I couldn't remember its significance—something about dreams, perhaps, and the things that can be evoked from them. I washed cold water over my face again and then slipped out of my newly-donned briefs and ran a shower. Man, it felt good, the rush of hot water and the soapy wash cloth rubbing all over. I decided not to shave because I didn't want to look at my face again. There were clean jeans in my suitcase and I slipped on the warm sweater that I had worn the previous evening. I felt good. Maybe at this time of day the pub would be free of the pretentious imps I had encountered at Scot's reading, and the idea of simple bar food and cold beer was especially appetizing, even though I had just devoured a large breakfast. Maybe I'd take my time walking into town and work up further appetite. Yeah. And stop at Olney's book shop and scout for another volume of verse. Hell yeah, that was the plan. I grabbed my wallet and walking stick and beat it, and it felt good to move along the lanes and descend the hill toward downtown. Kingsport charmed me as never before, and I took curious turns and walked past venerable residences and over quaint wooden bridges that crossed streams. The harbor spread below, filled with crafts of all kind and with just a faint blanket of mist rising over it. It was like a charming picture-postcard come to life, haunted by the far-off cry of gulls and toll of buoys. Perhaps I would investigate the wharves after I spent some time in the bookshop.

I really did feel great, clean and invigorated, clutching the cool old stick of polished wood and strange inscription. Got to the main street and was surprised to see that the bookshop door was shut, but the knob turned easily in my grasp and I entered in to find the lady at her spinning wheel, dressed in a long black gown and modest black sweater that showed off her still-youthful figure. Her gray hair had been brushed back away from her face, and the soft light of the room seem reflected in her weird shimmering eyes.

"Mr. Coffin," she said in her low-toned voice, and that was kind of strange because I didn't remember ever telling her my name. Guess I was getting forgetful in old age.

"Hey," I saluted, and then I walked to the shelves of poetry and scanned the titles, stopping to pull out a volume of Swinburne.

"I'm just about to lock up. I shall be leaving for a brief holiday, as my partner returns tomorrow to tend the shop. I have a present for you, to repay you for your company. I don't have many who dwell with me as consistently as you have. I've enjoyed your company."

"Shucks, the pleasure has been all mine." I watched as she went to a desk and took a woven shoulder bag from it, which she presented to me. The workmanship was exquisite, and the mauve material soft to the touch. The bag was weighty with whatever had been slipped inside, and I peeped into it and nearly fainted. "You can't be fucking serious." The first edition of Yeats's *The Trembling of the Veil* was inside the bag.

The crazy lady shrugged. "I purchased it, I shall do with it as I like. Ah, the wonder of your wounded eyes—how priceless."

I was shaking, trembling like a pup in love. This was too rich a gift. As I stood there, she went to a place on the wall where her hooded robe hung. Removing it from its peg, she donned her mad apparel, and then she motioned to the door and escorted me outside.

"Let me walk with you a while, or better yet let me treat you to a little feast. What's the best place for fine dining?"

Miss Olney shook her head. "I have no appetite—of that kind." Her eyes moved upward. "Look, the mists begin to assemble near the strange High House. Ah—the air up there is sweet and outré—how the lungs tingle as they breathe it in. Delicious, delicious." She was very near to me and peered at the scratched area of my forehead; and then she kissed her hand and pressed it to the emblem that had been etched into my flesh, as if I were some weird mezuzah. Lowering her lips, she kissed my mouth—the sweetest kiss that I have ever tasted. As she moved from me I could not help but follow.

I can't quite remember where we walked or what we passed. We were near the wharves for a while, and the mist over the water was beginning to thicken and spill toward land. We followed a road along the harbor and then traversed a bend that took us to an incline, which we ascended. The way grew steep and stony, and I grasped my staff more securely and let its properties strengthen my limbs exponentially. Time ceased to exist as we trod over tall grass and beneath giant trees; and then the trees disappeared, replaced with steep naked rock. I chanced to turn my head at one point and glimpsed Kingsport far below us, cloaked in whorls of mist and shadow. Had it grown so late? Where was the sun? Indeed, where was the sky? All I could see above us were banks of gathered cloud and the dark shapes concealed within them. We climbed out of a kind of chasm, through vapor and up steep stone, in a realm between earth and sky; and then, suddenly, the venerable dwelling came into view. Gawd! Who could have built such a strange house? How had they managed to bring the needed supplies to this fantastic height? It seemed insane and esoteric. I clutched tightly at my staff and muttered verses beneath my breath, patting the shoulder bag that swung beside me and feeling the treasure inside it. The clouds crawled chaotically around us and the house, humming in accompaniment to my whispered poetry. Patricia Olney pulled the cowl over her head as she passed by the silent house, with its peaked roof of worm-eaten shingles that met the rocky ground. I heard what might have been a north wind's howl as my companion reached the edge of the crag that stretched out to the macabre mist.

She turned to me, and my heart shrank at the sight of her burnished eyes, those glowing orbs. She held out her naked hands to me and bade me join her, but I couldn't move my feet, and so she floated to me and touched my face with her hand's tapered nails. "Come," she commanded, "feast upon my eyes. Thus will your own be healed and rectified." Tilting to me, she kissed my eyes and then offered me her own. I was filled with sudden craving. My tongue stretched to her smooth waxen visage and licked the liquid of her iridescent eyes, and then my ravenous teeth chewed into their jelly. Oh, the ecstasy of her moan. When I moved away, I saw that her eyes had altered and appeared more human; but the sheath of semi-flesh that was her face had slipped a little. Smiling apologetically, Miss Olney lifted her delicate hands to her countenance and straightened it. Without turning away from me, she pulled the cowl over her head so that it completely covered her face, and then she held up her arms as if in anticipation of some happy crucifixion and began to walk backward, toward the edge of the mist-drenched crag. Without hesitation, Patricia Olney moved off the earth, into the roiling clouds. I watched those billowing bodies welcome her, as the monstrous phizogs within those clouds leered at me and laughed.

Protectively, I held my staff before me and uttered articulation to the mist, that film in which I saw the churning faces of myth and madness, bearded faces that taunted me with wild laughter, sprites that sang of ancient arcane things. They conjoined into each other and melted into other forms, until all were subsumed by an outline of utter blackness that

I remembered from some subterranean vision that I had witnessed in an unearthly spot. I grew afraid, but the only weapon that I had was the staff of the Terrible Old Man. Howling curses in unfathomable language, I hurled that walking stick through the air, into the outline that crawled like chaos toward me. A portion of the outline lifted out of itself, shaped as a head of some fantastic beast, into one eye-socket of which my staff had been implanted. Heaven groaned, as in the mist three beasts took form, winged and with pale faces that watched me disdainfully. And then the mist folded within itself and was gone, and I stood beside the strange High House and looked down at sleepy Kingsport and its harbor washed in gorgeous sunset flame. Standing near one window of the dwelling, I pressed my hand onto its diamond-shaped panes where I found my bright reflection. My eyes, no longer wounded, watched me with queer emotion. My mug was unmarred, its flesh smooth and whole. I stared at myself for a little while, until suddenly someone, someone inside the strange High House, unlatched the window from inside. I hurried from the site.

JEFFREY THOMAS

Every Exquisite Thing

I.

For painting in oils, which was his favorite artistic medium, Enoch Coffin preferred not to buy paint in tubes but to create his own. To achieve this, he purchased little jars of dry pigment that he mixed with walnut oil (which cut down on the yellowing engendered over time by linseed oil). But he would also add his own unique ingredients to the recipe, which he felt imparted additional power to his work. Sometimes quite considerable power. Some of the ingredients he required, according to obscure grimoires in his library—such as a facsimile of the Voynich manuscript—were for him best found in Boston's Chinatown district.

Enoch always made a full day of his Chinatown excursions, riding in early from his home in the North End on the subway system's Orange Line. He would visit a Vietnamese restaurant for a bowl of *pho*—beef noodle soup—and a cup of strong *ca phe sua nong* thick with sweetened condensed milk. Or maybe some Chinese *dim sum* instead. Before the ride home, he'd stop at the corner Hing Shing Pastry bakery for some pastries filled with lotus-seed or red-bean paste. Life was as much for the sensual pleasures of the moment as it was for learning what lay before and after life, and Enoch didn't believe one needed to starve for one's art, in any sense of the word.

Ah, but he loved this little tease of Asia, which reminded him of travels he had taken when his finances, or the generosity of patrons, had allowed. Strolling here past arrays of exotic fruit on the sidewalk, or spying live chickens pacing about in a building's vestibule, put him in mind of exploring the back streets of Seoul, where someone had once spat blood at him from a balcony, and upon looking up he had glimpsed a furtive figure with the obsidian face of a demon. Up sprang memories of Vietnam—of riding a ferry across a wide black river in the wee hours of the morning on his way to visit the Phuoc Dien temple complex by the Cambodian

101

border. He had been intrigued to find that young transvestite prostitutes plied their trade on either shore and upon the ferry itself, and in flirting with one of these beguiling creatures he had peeked into its bra to find it stuffed with toilet paper.

And so it was that Enoch raised an eyebrow in appreciation, albeit tinged with a bit of confusion, when he entered his favorite Chinatown apothecary and found a beautiful woman tending the back room, instead of the wizened old man who owned the tiny establishment. The stranger stood behind the counter where he had only seen elderly Shun situated in the past. Behind the woman, the small room's back wall was lined ceiling to floor with wooden drawers labeled in both Chinese calligraphy and Vietnamese lettering.

The woman's eyes were already locked on Enoch's when he entered, as if his arrival had been anticipated, though he never called ahead prior to a visit here. "Hello," she said in accented but accomplished English, "may I help you?"

"Ah, I was looking for my friend, Shun," Enoch explained.

"Oh, I'm sorry, but my father passed away about a month ago."

"What? Oh no … I had no idea. I'm terribly sorry." Enoch had liked Shun, but he fretted more about obtaining the materials he needed to enhance his paints. "Your father, you say? I never knew Shun had any children. So did he train you in his special craft?"

"Yes, he did; very thoroughly. I'm sure he sensed the end was coming."

Enoch judged the woman to be in her mid to late thirties. She was tall, with wavy black hair framing a pale handsome face. Her long nose, strong jaw, and composed mouth gave her an aristocratic bearing, but her eyes struck him as deeply sad. It was the sadness of her eyes that most accounted for her beauty. Enoch recalled that Oscar Wilde had said, "Behind every exquisite thing that exists there is something tragic."

He wondered how long she had studied with her father, because he'd never seen her in any of his previous visits to the herbalist. He believed he would have remembered her.

Enoch said, "Well, what is your name, my dear?"

"Jiao."

He explained in as little detail as possible, feeling a bit self-conscious, how he added special ingredients to his paints to "empower" his art. The woman nodded as she listened, as if this were the most normal of concepts. When he had finished, Enoch said, "So I have a bit of a shopping list today, Jiao."

"Please begin." She smiled politely. Her smile was as sad as her eyes.

He leaned forward on the counter between them, and one by one related the materials he needed, having by now memorized them. He watched as the woman named Jiao went from drawer to drawer, filling small brown paper lunch bags with dried leaves, seeds, or what looked like twigs and bark. Into one bag she dropped a number of tiny mummified seahorses. She stapled the bags shut when finished, and soon ten of these stood in a row on the counter. She gathered them all into a plastic shopping bag for him.

"Very good," Enoch said, watching the woman's face carefully. "Now, what I need are some of the more obscure ingredients Shun kept upstairs. Such as his 'Essential Saltes.'"

Jiao held his stare for several beats. "He brought you upstairs? He gave you Essential Saltes?"

"Yes. He never told you?"

"No."

"I assure you he did, or else I wouldn't know any of this."

Jiao nodded slowly. "That's true. What is your name?"

"Enoch Coffin."

"Very well, Mr. Coffin. I'll take you upstairs."

Jiao came out from around the counter, and Enoch followed her into the main part of the shop. She spoke to a young worker in Chinese, and apparently he wasn't expecting to see her beside him, for he looked around with a startled gasp. Enoch had the impression the lad was afraid of his new boss. Apparently she told him to keep an eye on the back room, and that she was taking a customer upstairs. The boy, whom Enoch recalled having seen on earlier visits, nodded quickly with understanding.

Then, Enoch was following Jiao outside the shop to the street and another entrance to the building. Within, they found a shadowy staircase and Jiao led him to the familiar third floor, where she unlocked the door Shun had always unlocked for him, no doubt with the very same key.

II.

The apartment was murky, its shades pulled and drapes drawn, its air a mix of exotic scents. Incense, yes, but other odors unidentifiable, and not all of them pleasant. As he trailed Jiao into a central room perhaps intended as a dining room, Enoch said, "I need to paint you."

The woman stopped, and turned to meet his avid gaze. She was restraining a smile, but was it one of pleasure or derision? She said, "Why do you say that?"

"Well, aside from the obvious reason, that you're strikingly lovely, it's an intuition of mine—and I've come to trust my artistic intuitions more than I trust the rising and setting of the sun."

"I see. And I suppose you would want to paint me in the nude."

"You mean you nude, or me nude?"

"Very funny."

"I wouldn't protest if you were willing, but I wouldn't insist upon it."

"Hm. You're very handsome yourself, Mr. Coffin. Has anyone ever painted your portrait?"

"Me? Oh no, I'd never permit that. I'm like those savages who are afraid a photograph will steal their soul."

Neither consenting to nor declining Enoch's request, and still holding that enigmatic little smile, Jiao moved across the room to an antique Chinese kitchen cabinet. Normally this would have housed dishes and utensils in the upper section and food in the lower, but instead Shun had stocked the hundred-year-old cabinet with cures, potions and concoctions not available to his common customers.

While Jiao opened its cupboards, Enoch turned toward an altar he didn't recall having seen in the apartment before. It seemed to represent the practice of ancestor worship, featuring as it did a framed old black-and-white photo portrait of a handsome young Asian man, before which were arranged flowers, offerings of fruit, and joss sticks burnt down to their yellow stems. "Who is this dashing young fellow?" Enoch asked his host.

"My husband," Jiao replied.

"Oh—and here I thought the photo was quite old. I'm sorry to learn you're a widow. What losses you've suffered."

"Yes," Jiao said, facing him now and holding a glass container close to her chest. She had removed it from the cabinet. "You said you needed the Essential Saltes of the *con rit?*"

"Yes." As they had ascended the stairs, he had told her that much. *Con rit* was the name the Vietnamese had given to a legendary sea creature with a fifty-foot-long segmented body like that of a centipede. A rotting specimen was said to have washed ashore in 1883, and Shun possessed a bottle containing some of that carcass's distilled Saltes. Enoch told his host, "When painting a seascape, I like to add a touch of the *con rit's* essence to the mix. In the same way that, when painting a forest, I mix vegetable matter with my paints, or add cemetery soil to my hues when I render a graveyard scene."

Jiao held out the container she carried, and now Enoch could see that it was empty but for a dusty residue. "And my father sold you the Saltes of human beings as well, did he not? Such as these?"

"I can't read the label," Enoch said, gesturing toward the bottle she held, "but yes … yes, he did. Sometimes I add them to the flesh tones with which I portray the living or the dead—whatever that painting calls for. But also, there are times when I use them throughout the entire painting, whatever its subject, if these Saltes represent the crystallized remains of some great artist or poet, so that their psychometric force might be imparted to my own work. Your father managed to collect quite an array of specimens in his travels. He was a singularly gifted alchemist. As an artist, I am an alchemist myself. He understood my motivations, and my needs."

"But did he sell you any of the contents of *this* jar?" Jiao asked in an insistent tone, further extending the labeled empty container.

"As I told you, I don't know. One jar looks the same as the others to my eye. Why do you ask? Whose remains did that contain?"

Jiao took in a long breath in preparation to speak, but she was cut off by a loud thud above their heads and looked up sharply. Enoch glanced at the ceiling. It sounded to him as if someone in the apartment above had dropped something heavy on the floor.

Enoch returned his gaze to his host, and looking strangely stricken, she resumed, "My father did indeed gather quite a collection of human remains, sometimes already rendered by other alchemists into their Essential Saltes. But most of these remains he himself distilled."

"So he boasted to me. As I say, I'm aware he accumulated arcane knowledge."

"You are familiar with the Cultural Revolution, that swept my country from the sixties into the seventies?"

"Yes. It was a terrible time."

Jiao snorted a bitter laugh at his understatement. "Theories vary on how many people lost their lives in that time of savagery. I have heard anywhere between one to twenty million lives lost. In Guangxi there were public ceremonies, banquets, in which people were cannibalized. Of course during this dark time, artists were persecuted. Some managed to hide their art under the floorboards of their homes, and return many years later to retrieve it."

"It's all very horrid."

"This jar, here, once held the remains of an artist named Song Yi. Yi's art was not shocking or challenging. He painted simple rustic scenes of people at work, people laughing and living. Lovely portraits. But forty-three years ago, he was handed over to the authorities by a traitor he believed was a friend. This friend told them that Yi was subversive and dangerous, and so at the age of thirty-eight, Song Yi was publicly beaten until he died from his injuries."

Enoch said, "Yes … yes, I know. I do know this one's history."

"You do."

"Your father sold me some of this artist's Saltes on several occasions, so that I might use them in my own art. In so doing, I believed some of his essence—"

The bottle slipped through Jiao's hands then, struck the floor and shattered into several large pieces.

"What is it?" Enoch asked. The woman was visibly trembling now.

"It is evil, what Shun did. Evil, what you did, too."

"Look, Jiao, I'm sorry you don't approve of what I've done for my art, or what your father did for his own purposes. Not that I ever understood all his purposes. I thought you might carry on in his footsteps. If I was mistaken, and you'd rather not sell me any of the materials from this cabinet, then I'll go."

"Now I understand everything," Jiao said as if she hadn't heard him, sounding close to tears. "Now I know what went wrong."

"What are you talking about?"

"I should show you. Come with me."

"Where are we going?"

Jiao pointed above her. "Upstairs."

III.

The apartment upstairs, when Jiao had unlocked it and let him inside, proved even gloomier than the one below, but as if to compensate for this there were other stimuli to assail Enoch's senses. A profound heightening of the odd, unpleasant odors he had detected downstairs, and a distant, pitiful moaning. He supposed it *might* be a human being making that sound.

Jiao led him through the apartment, and he shuffled along carefully lest he bump his shins or trip in the dark. The moaning, increasing in volume though still muffled, seemed to guide them. Were there garbled words? Why was the voice so horribly, inhumanly *wet*-sounding?

They came to a short hallway, and Jiao positioned herself to one side of a closed door, into the wood of which a narrow horizontal gap had been sawed out, at face level. Enoch noted another modification to the door: a hasp screwed into the wood, so that the door could be padlocked from the outside.

In the murk, he couldn't make out Jiao's face as much more than a ghostly smear, but Enoch felt the weight of her stare. "Look inside," she told him in a flat voice.

As if reluctant to turn his back to her, Enoch hesitated, but then moved to the slit cut into the door. Warily, he leaned his face close to it. He held his breath against the stench.

The small chamber was no doubt intended as a bedroom, though it was empty of furnishings aside from a bare mattress on the floor. Boards had been nailed over the single window, so that only a few chinks of light penetrated the gloom. But as Enoch peered at a pale, indistinct shape sprawled on the mattress, his eyes became a bit more acclimated. And as if the shape on the mattress had just awoken and seen his eyes at the slit in the door, it suddenly stirred with weird, agitated movements.

"Good Lord," Enoch muttered.

The thing that rose up, as best it could, from the foul mattress was without clothing, and Enoch wasn't sure if he was grateful for the darkness that obscured the thing's form, or more unnerved by the fact that he couldn't quite make sense of what he was seeing.

It should have been a human, that much was certain, but it had either been altered from that state or had never been able to achieve it. Half the chest was missing, and one arm with it, the creature so shockingly compromised that it should not even be alive. Its pelvis was askew, its legs disproportionate, one skeletal and the other a bloated knobby mass, apparently with no foot at its end. And the head … if that translucent, gelatinous blob could be called a head …

The monstrosity hobbled toward the door with a awkward limp, rushing at Enoch as if it meant to burst straight through the wood to get at him. He backed away, and a moment later it thudded into the door and rattled it in its frame. Fingers curled in the slit, but the pulpy hands were too swollen to squeeze through.

Just before backing away, Enoch had caught a glimpse of the thing's visage. Only a glimpse, and yet he had the keen eyes of an artist. That face, though it seemed to have lost one eye under a bulge of its lumpen head, was the same face from the black and white portrait on the altar downstairs.

"That photo I asked you about," Enoch said. "You said it was your husband. Is this creature your husband, then?"

"I lied," Jiao replied. "My husband was Shun."

Enoch switched his gaze from the fingers scrabbling in the peephole, to the woman standing opposite him. "Shun wasn't your father?"

"My husband, Mr. Coffin. Over forty years ago, during the Cultural Revolution, I met a handsome young artist named Song Yi. He was a beautiful soul—nothing like my cruel husband. We fell in love. He painted me, as you have asked to do. You briefly charmed me with your request. You reminded me of him. And yes, he painted me in the nude. One day, my husband discovered this painting hidden amongst my things."

Enoch glanced toward the door. It was all coming together now. "The man in the altar photo. That was Song Yi, not Shun."

"Yes."

"So this creature, in this room …"

"Shun turned Yi over to the authorities, and after Yi was beaten to death Shun managed to steal his body. He had perfected his evil magic even then. Perhaps it was sheer spite, some malicious gratification, that inspired him to practice his arts on Yi. He reduced my lover's body down to its Essential Saltes."

"And yours, too … am I right, Jiao?"

"After he strangled me in a fit of rage, Shun told everyone I'd run off and left him. Yes, Mr. Coffin, my husband practiced his alchemy on my dead body as well. Maybe he gloated over the two bottles that contained Yi and myself, in the decades that followed."

"So how then did you become reconstituted?"

"Shun grew old, and perhaps sentimental. As he confronted his own mortality, maybe he felt guilt for what he had done to me. And so, the lonely necromancer raised his wife from the dead."

The wet, bestial voice behind its door blurted out an inarticulate cry, as if reacting to her words.

"So Shun resurrected Song Yi, as well?"

"No. He sold Song Yi, bit by bit … to *you*. I had no idea, until this day. Enough of Yi's Saltes remained that I suspected nothing when I set about resurrecting him myself. Because you see, Mr. Coffin, my husband had trained me to be his assistant herbalist. And his assistant in his demonic experiments, as well."

Enoch looked to the peephole in the door and saw one eye there peering out at him. One eye with an Asian epicanthic fold … one eye that hinted at a living, human mind somewhere behind it. An artist's eye. He could understand why the woman hadn't destroyed the abomination.

"I'm sure Shun was secretly amused selling you pinches of my lover's essence," Jiao said. "Sadistically amused. But what of you, Mr. Coffin? Didn't you ever pause to consider your own actions?"

"My dear, I never thought that anyone would ever want to restore this man."

"Perhaps you should have entertained that possibility."

"Perhaps I should have," he allowed.

Jiao reached toward the peephole in the door, and squeezed her slim hand inside to run her fingertips along the creature's cheek. It let out a soft, pained groan. It was the first sound this being had uttered ... because the moaning Enoch had heard, and which hadn't ceased, originated behind another closed and padlocked door in the hallway. It too had a slot sawed into it.

Enoch gestured toward this second door. "And your other tenant?"

"Who do you think?"

Enoch stepped to the door and drew close to its peephole. This room too benefitted from a few slivers of light through the boards covering its solitary window. Here too was only a soiled bare mattress on the floorboards. Here too an uncanny pallid occupant. But this creature couldn't rise to its legs, for it had none. It dragged its abbreviated lower half after it, flopping crazily about the room on its misshapen forelimbs as if searching endlessly for a means of escape. Perhaps sensing Enoch at the slot, it whipped its head around and its noises became more plaintive. The artist recognized its wizened face, however distorted.

"*Enoch!*" the tortured figure gurgled in its awful voice. He could only just understand it. "*Enoch ... help me ...*"

The ruined thing crawled to the door and thumped its rudimentary, flipper-like forelimbs against the wood, but couldn't rise to the level of the peephole.

"I'm sorry, Shun," Enoch spoke through the door, "but this isn't my story. I'm afraid I'm only a customer."

"*Enoch! Enoch ... help me! Help meee!*"

Enoch turned back to face Jiao. "I suppose I should be going."

IV.

The young man whom Jiao had left in charge of the shop in her absence rang up Enoch's purchases at the front counter. Jiao had disappeared, but just as Enoch was prepared to leave she returned to the shop from outside. In both hands she carried an object inside a plastic shopping bag. It was obviously a container of some kind. A jar.

She extended it to Enoch, and he accepted it. The beautiful woman with her mysterious, sad eyes explained, "I'm afraid I won't be able to provide you with any more Essential Saltes in the future, Mr. Coffin, but I'll give you some just this last time."

"I understand."

"Consider them a gift," she said, smiling. "With them, I think you could paint a very dark and demonic vision indeed, if that's what suits you."

"Whose are they?" he asked, though he knew he didn't need to.

"Unused bits of my beloved husband, of course."

Returning to the North End of Boston on the Orange Line that evening, munching some flaky pastries filled with lotus-seed paste from the Hing Shing Pastry bakery—and with the jar of Saltes in his knapsack with his other prizes—Enoch Coffin felt regret indeed that his favorite apothecary would no longer make available to him the rarest of the ingredients he favored for his customized paints. But even more, perhaps, he regretted that he had not been able to bring himself to make a request of the apothecary's new proprietor.

He had little doubt she would have denied him, yet still he wished he had asked her if he could come back to her home in the future, in order to paint two portraits.

As striking as Jiao was herself, Enoch's interest had shifted to two other models even more unique, more remarkable, more in agreement with his taste in subject matter.

But then, Shun's establishment had always been a source of terrible wonders—and one person's tragic horrors are another person's exquisite things.

JEFFREY THOMAS

Impossible Color

I.

Enoch Coffin accepted that he must suffer for his art. He also accepted that sometimes other people must suffer for his art, as well.

Though Trent was an exceedingly handsome young man, with a thick mop of dirty-blond hair spilling across his eyes, Enoch had him posed nude in the most grotesque of positions, looking like a gargoyle struggling against its stony nature in the hopes of flight. Enoch had kept Trent in this pose for over an hour, as he sat in the youth's favorite armchair sketching him in charcoal. He could have finished long ago, but he was punishing the boy for his insolence. Not that he minded gazing at his uncomfortable model, either.

"I thought the idea of a sketch is that it's fast," Trent complained, without turning his head when he addressed Enoch. The last time he had moved significantly, Enoch had jumped up from the armchair and kicked him in the hindquarters.

"How would you know anything about sketching?" Enoch replied. "You, whose hand has only ever known the feel of a computer mouse?"

They were in Trent's apartment in Brookline, Massachusetts, home of the New England Institute of Art, where Trent was a student. Enoch liked downtown Brookline, with its diversity of restaurants, nice little shops and bookstores, its civilized and artistic atmosphere, but it was in Boston's Museum of Fine Arts that they had first met and struck up a conversation several months earlier. Trent's father was a successful Boston optometrist, and paid not only for his son's schooling but this comfortable apartment as well.

"I think this one's complete," Enoch sighed casually, perusing his handiwork.

"Thank God!" Trent began to rise from his twisted crouch.

"Wait! I'm starting a new one with a sanguine crayon."

"I don't think so!" Trent said, straightening up with a pained expression as if gargoyle-like his limbs had indeed begun to ossify. "What's a sanguine crayon, anyway?"

"It's the end of the world," Enoch muttered.

"Well, do you know what vector graphics are?"

"If Goya made do without your vector graphics, I'm sure I can as well."

"I tell you, someday digital art will make paintbrushes and your sanguine crayons as obsolete as e-book readers are making physical books obsolete. Really, Enoch, I wish you'd let me show you the art program I use. I think once you got past your inhibitions, you'd be intoxicated by the possibilities."

"Inhibitions? You nasty pup—I should boot your little white ass again." Enoch set his pad and charcoal stick aside. "I don't want a computer to cross my doorway, but I've seen enough digital art and it isn't that I haven't been impressed. As in any medium, some artists are more gifted with these tools than others. But it's simply not my religion. I need paint on my hands—I want to smell it. I want to feel clay shaped between my palms. Next you'll be telling me that internet porn will make sex between two human beings obsolete."

Standing naked before the the older man, thrusting his pelvis forward as he massaged his cramped lower back, Trent smiled seductively and said, "Now that's one thing I *don't* want to become obsolete."

Enoch rose from the chair to stretch his own body. "So what are you patching together now from the ether?"

"Patching together," Trent snorted. "What I'm into now is 'forbidden colors.'"

"*Forbidden Colors*—the novel by Mishima?"

The younger artist laughed. "No. They're also called 'impossible colors.' They're colors that supposedly can't be seen under normal light conditions, because of the way our brains process information from our rods and cones, which is called the opponent process. But under certain experimental conditions that challenge this process, test subjects have been able to see colors they couldn't name—like yellow-blue. Not yellow and blue blending into green, but a color that looks both yellow and blue *at the same time*. And the same with red and green, which are two other opponent colors. Imagine a color that appears both red and green."

"Are you sure you're talking about real colors, and not just tricking the eye with illusion?"

"Aren't all colors illusion? Just frequencies of light … immaterial things?"

"So you're trying to create such an impossible color on your computer?"

"Yes! It's my obsession now. Imagine being the first artist to render a work of art in colors no one has ever seen before! Maybe you can't achieve this with your old smelly oil paints, Enoch, or else it would have been done centuries ago, but with new technology why shouldn't we be able to figure out how to teach the eye to see new colors without test conditions?"

"Teach the eye? The eye is a machine. Can you teach your hand to feel scent?"

"Oh Enoch, and here I thought you were a true adventurer of the arts!"

"It's one thing to talk, brat, and another to achieve. Anyway, to me you're still talking about earthly colors. Red. Green. Red *and* green. How about a color that has nothing analogous, nothing to compare it with at all?"

"Sure, why not?" Trent agreed enthusiastically. "That too. Maybe that can be achieved. That's what I'm after."

Enoch shrugged. "Well ... it is an exciting concept, certainly."

"Here, let me show you my latest test." Without bothering to don his clothing again, Trent moved to a desk upon which his computer system was set up, and leaned over it to tap at his keyboard. Enoch came to stand beside him.

On the computer's monitor, against a black background standing shoulder-to-shoulder, were two identical human silhouettes, one red and one green. Trent explained, "The red and green have to be the same brightness, and just the right opposing hues. I've been trying this with a white background, too, to see if it makes any difference. Anyway, you see that white X on their chests? Now, if you cross your eyes and combine those two Xs ..."

Enoch barked a laugh. "Cross my eyes? My dear, do you really expect people to come into a gallery and cross their eyes to view a piece of art? Maybe if they stand on their head it would work even better."

Trent turned to glare at his guest. "Fuck you, Enoch. I would never laugh at any artistic project of yours. This is just a test! Maybe you're intimidated by my ambition. Or too proud to open that dusty old mind of yours."

"Pah." Enoch strode across the room, retrieved his sketch pad and his slouch hat, and fitted the latter on his head. "Cross your eyes now, my boy, and you'll see two of me leaving. But I'm afraid we're both composed of the same hues."

II.

It was three months before Enoch Coffin heard from the art student again. By that time he'd put Trent out of his mind altogether, engrossed as he was in his own art projects. But then one night, while he was working on a painting in the attic studio of his narrow little house on Boston's Charter Street, Trent called. Enoch hated being disturbed while working, and always screened his calls, but when he heard Trent's excited tone he couldn't help himself. And it was the words even more than the tone that made him pick up, for what Trent had said was: "Enoch—I think I've found my impossible color!"

❧

"I've always got my antennae up," Trent said. "Always trawling the net."

"Of course. You and your precious internet."

Trent ignored the older man's disparagement; they'd been over such things before, tiresomely. "I found out about this estate sale … an eccentric old character in Swampscott named Charles Gardner. A real hoarder, but instead of hoarding piles of newspapers and worthless shit like that, this guy collected all kinds of weird antiques, rare books, artwork from obscure artists all over the world. They said his house was floor to ceiling with his treasures; there were just barely paths through it all. And what first caught my eye was that this guy's family originally came from nearby Arkham. And you know all those stories out of Arkham …"

"Some intimately," Enoch replied. He sipped the coffee Trent had served him. He liked his coffee the way he liked his lovers: varied. Today he had asked for it black.

Trent was pacing the floor of his Brookline apartment excitedly, jabbering a mile a minute as if stimulated by some drug more potent than coffee. Enoch knew the drug well. It was the muse.

Trent went on, "Well, I saw a very interesting object listed for sale so I decided to contact the agent about it, and this agent is also a local historian so she knows her stuff. It seems an ancestor of Gardner's had a pretty strange thing happen on his farm, back in 1882. A meteor—*apparently* a meteor—crashed on this farmer's land. At the core of the meteor people found a smooth sphere of a color that was, according to a contemporary newspaper account, 'almost impossible to describe.' *Hm?*" Trent smiled provocatively. "The sphere had some funny properties, such as 'attacking silicon compounds.' But the fallen object's worst property seems to have been radiation, which took its toll not only on the farmer's livestock, but on his own wife and sons as well … and eventually poisoned the poor guy himself. When locals came to investigate the deaths, they witnessed a beam of light radiate from the property's well—a beam of light of a color that was said to be of an 'unfamiliar hue.'"

"Interesting," Enoch admitted.

"I guess this was one very freaky light show, and really rattled these guys. Anyway, supposedly the meteor and the strange sphere inside eventually disintegrated without a trace, and the old farmhouse is long gone. The agent told me the area where the farm stood is even today a dead plot of land where nothing will grow, and no one has ever built anything there again. Maybe that in itself isn't enough to corroborate such a story, huh? Ahh … but then there's *this*."

Trent turned toward a side table and lifted a riveted metal box, tarnished dark with age. He raised its hinged lid, and turned back toward Enoch as if offering a cigar from a humidor. Instead, what Enoch saw inside the box was a pile of glass squares.

"What are these?" he inquired.

"The farmhouse had casement windows composed of multiple small panes, as was the style back in the day. It was from this window that the witnesses watched that weird light show erupt from the dead farmer's well. Someone had the presence of mind to rescue these panes, and they got passed down into the hands of old man Gardner. Someone with an eye for the unique. Someone who understood they were a treasure worth preserving, whereas another person might have thrown them away. Even the estate sale agent, who recognized them as a historical curiosity, doesn't suspect their potential value both scientifically and, more importantly to me, artistically."

"May I?" Enoch poised a hand over the proffered box.

Trent grinned, his eyes seeming illuminated from within. "Yes, Enoch … hold one to the light. Look *through* it."

Enoch picked up the topmost square of glass, and as his host had suggested raised it to a nearby window through which glowed bright, prosaic sunlight. Trent watched his friend's handsome face, upon which the brows soon gathered and sensuous mouth turned down in a contemplative scowl. Enoch angled the glass slightly, this way then that, and next pivoted in his chair to hold the little pane up to the artificial light of a wall lamp. Again, he shifted the glass slightly to observe its subtle effects.

Trent said, "There's a kind of iridescence, isn't there? Like the oily colors in a soap bubble. It's faint, but it's there, isn't it? Imprinted on the glass somehow, the way they say lightning can etch a photograph onto glass. And glass is silica, is it not? Didn't they say that the funny globe had an odd effect on silicon? But you tell me now, Enoch. *What color is that?*"

It was as the young artist had said: the effect was delicate, but undeniable. Enoch set aside the pane to select another one, then a third. The anomalous quality was present in all of them—a subtle iridescence. But what color or colors indeed? Enoch opened his mouth as if to suggest a hue, but quickly closed it. Once again he started to speak, once again stopped himself. "I don't know," he conceded at last. "My God ... there's a ghost of color trapped in this glass, but I'll be damned if I can put a name to it. It's not related to any known color, and that's just not something you can envision with your imagination, the way you can imagine how another planet might look, and the life upon it. This is something that we've been denied, even with all the countless sights our world has to show us. It shouldn't be possible, but—"

"Yes," Trent cut him off. "*Yes.* Impossible color."

Enoch rose from his chair, and now it was his turn to pace the living room, as he again and again gazed upon the glass square he held before windows, then artificial light sources, back and forth. Having set down the metal box again, Trent watched him, and at last Enoch faced the student and said, "So what are you attempting to do with this find?"

"In regard to my art? I'm not sure yet. Just because we can see it doesn't mean we can copy this effect with paint. I've been trying to think of a way to record it somehow. Get it into my computer. Maybe find a means of scanning the glass ... or if not that, then photograph the glass and—if that captures the quality—then scanning the photograph. If I can't replicate the color with physical pigment, maybe I can move it onto a virtual palette."

"You have enough of these panes—you could still pursue the scientific possibilities as you pursue you art."

"Enoch, you disappoint me more and more! You, the pure old-fashioned artist, the man of personal integrity, thinking of money that could be made from this?"

"Artists do have to eat, young man; pappy can't carry you forever. Never mind that for now. You have enough of these that you can let *me* have one of them." Enoch slipped the pane into the pocket of his brown suede jacket.

"Hey!"

"Don't worry, I am indeed a man of integrity; I won't try selling your miraculous discovery myself."

"But you may find a way to incorporate it into your art before I do!"

"Me? With my primitive smelly paints? Oh I doubt it. But still, it's captured my imagination. I want to study it further. You won't deny me, will you? Perhaps I'll discover something that might even aid you in your own pursuits."

Trent sighed, then shrugged. He knew the older man was right. But also, he was just afraid enough of the odd artist Enoch Coffin that he didn't care to oppose him.

III.

Before he began, Enoch propped the pane on the sill of an attic window so that sunlight might stream through it. Misty suggestions of color spread upon the worn floorboards. Dust motes swam in the beam like alien microorganisms. He stepped into this beam himself, reverently, as if into the glow through a cathedral's window. This caused him to wonder what his late father Donovon Coffin—a stained-glass artisan—might have composed from pieces of this glass.

Enoch held out his artist's hands like receptive instruments that might somehow, intuitively, detect and *grasp* the proper frequency of light. He watched the pastel illumination play across the skin of his hungry appendages.

He realized it would most likely prove a fruitless—the word was *impossible*—endeavor, but with this appropriated prize as his inspiration he set out to duplicate the pane's strange tint in a conventional painting. On that first day he tried watercolors, for their translucence and delicacy, but the next afternoon he switched to oils, which he preferred. Yet both approaches resulted in the same: a compounded muddiness that was nothing like the effect trapped in the glass.

For both paintings Enoch had used the same subject matter: a stone well in a rural setting, created solely from his imagination, and in both paintings he portrayed this well in the deep of night. Uncanny light in a bright, vaporous column churned straight upward into the sky, where it bored through a ceiling of clouds and reflected upon their underbellies. The result in each rendering was not unlike the erupting mushroom cloud of a nuclear explosion, and was all the more ominous for that. They were not at all a bad pair of paintings … they just didn't reveal anything like the color he was attempting to replicate.

That hue was so elusive in the glass's faint tint—what he wouldn't give to see it in greater, purer intensity! The thought drove him on in his frustrating attempts, and it was this that leant more power to the scene in the oil painting, which he kept working at stubbornly. For dramatic effect Enoch ended up adding sinister trees with their leaves all burnt to ash and the ends of their denuded branches sheathed in glowing luminescence. Branches that appeared to have become sentient, reaching futilely toward the sky as if to hold onto that nameless force, as it returned to the cosmos from which it had plummeted like the essence of Lucifer.

Eerie green phosphorescence like luminous rot, glowing on the grass around the well and the underbellies of those clouds …

No!

A blue phosphorescence, then …

No!

An orange kind of glow … a purple and orange kind of glow …

No and no. Failure and failure. In the end he could only concentrate on the setting itself. His uncanny pillar of light was a cheat … green blending into blue into purple into orange. All terrestrial colors. Never had the limits of his art shackled and chafed him so. Illusion and lies, that was all he was good at, and not so good after all. In the end he flung his mess of a palette away from him in self-loathing.

IV.

On the third day following their last encounter, Trent phoned Enoch and they compared notes. Enoch reluctantly described his frustrations with his twin paintings, expecting Trent to use this as fuel to criticize Enoch's outdated artistic methods, but the younger man actually expressed keen interest in having a look at the art when he had a chance. "It sounds like your intuitions are attuned to the scene," Trent remarked, "if not the color. Myself, I've tried photographing the glass with my digital camera, then moving the pictures into my art software and stealing the color with cloning, adding it to a custom palette, other techniques…but they all seem to lose something in translation. The color either disappears altogether or get changed into other colors, from the common spectrum."

"Maybe what we're seeing is a head trick … a mirage …"

"Oh, Enoch, that we're failing to capture this phenomenon doesn't mean it doesn't exist! We have to be more humble than that."

"If we were humble we'd never be trying to reproduce this color in the first place."

"Well, if lightning can make pictures, then we can do it. What are we if not bundles of lightning in bags of skin?"

Enoch smiled at the phone. "Sometimes I remember why I decided to be friends with you."

"I'm flattered. Well, anyway, my father is working on something for me that might broaden my artistic vision."

"Your father?"

"You shall see, when it's ready … you shall see."

The next day, Enoch mounted the steps to the attic with uncertainty as to what he might do next to approach the matter of the otherworldly color. He was reluctant to concede defeat, though, as long as he knew the younger artist was still pursuing his own methods. The pane beckoned yet taunted him, like a glass microscope slide containing a species of life that had yet to be identified. As he reached for the door to his studio, he wondered if there were some type of photoreactive paper that he might spread on the floor in the projected beam from the pane, which might accept a transfer of the color. Not a way to work freely with the color, perhaps, but a start along the path of directing and controlling it.

As it turned out, he found his daunting challenge had already been dismissed for him. He was certain he had left the small square pane leaning on the window sill. Now it was gone. When he approached the window, all he discovered was a fine sprinkling of glittering dust on the sill and partly spilled onto the floorboards.

Within minutes, Enoch was calling Trent in Brookline. But the student didn't pick up. Was he attending class? Enoch left a message for him.

"My boy, I suspect there was good reason your eccentric old man Gardner kept the panes in that metal box, which I further suspect might be made of lead. I just found my sample of glass reduced to dust. I'm not lying, if you find that hard to swallow. I don't know if it was exposure to light, or the air, or what else that might account for this, but I remind you of the story of the meteor you related, and the sphere within it. You told me after a time both of them dissolved, leaving nothing behind."

A beep, as the allotted message time ran out. Enoch set down the phone and turned to contemplate the sparkling dust. Each grain seemed to trap a particle of weird light as its nucleus. Though he had handled the pane by its edges quite a bit, he was now reluctant to make contact with its possibly irradiated remains. He swept up the dust carefully, poured it into an empty pill bottle of light-resistant brown plastic, sealed that in an airtight sandwich bag, and stored the package away in a dark drawer.

Later that afternoon he called Trent again. When there was no answer, he chose not to leave a second message. But Trent still didn't pick up his phone when Enoch tried two more times that evening.

Several days passed silently and Enoch didn't attempt phoning Trent again. Either the young artist was making no progress and didn't want to talk about it, or making progress and hoarding his discoveries jealously. Enoch wasn't one for collaboration—his vision was too personal, his ego too great—so he didn't care much one way or the other. He wasn't going to beg for attention like the pathetic needy creatures that often haunted his own privacy, so he engrossed himself in his various ongoing projects.

Then, one night in the wee hours, a call came. Enoch was still awake, not at all unusually, in his attic, bent over his scarred old worktable. With a palette knife he had scooped some gel medium, used in conjunction with acrylic paints, from a container and spread it on a small canvas panel. The gel was thick but would dry clear. He made a little concavity with the knife in the center of the goop, then into this hollow he poured the fine grit of a drinking glass that he had smashed with a hammer after he'd wrapped it in an old towel. He then mixed the granules throughout the gel evenly and spread it across the panel to gauge its texture, and so that he might gauge the effect when it dried.

The call interrupted him in the midst of this experiment, but when he heard Trent's voice he picked up. He almost didn't recognize that voice at first, however, and he couldn't make out the words. The student sounded drunk perhaps, his voice slurred, weak and hoarse.

"So," Enoch sneered into the phone, "it deigns to call me at last, talking in its sleep."

"Yes, sleep," croaked the distant, strained voice. "We are all asleep. Our eyes are closed. We do not see."

"And I do not see what you're babbling about."

"Even as you sit there in your loft listening to me now, you don't see the aura your body emanates, Enoch. Not the way I am seeing my own aura at this moment. Like me, fire laps from your skin, flutters and coruscates, twines around your limbs like spectral eels, in ever-changing colors that have no words to label them in any human tongue. Everywhere in your loft, every object organic or inorganic gives off a different aura of different hue. Those old dead floorboards are awash in a glow that even were they gilded would not compare! An ant on your floor is an iridescent scarab to bring tears to one's eyes! But you of course are the source of most of this glorious light, this terrible color. I know, as even now I wave my hand in the air before my face, and watch the swaths and ribbons it weaves in its wake. To think that you and I sought to paint these impossible colors upon canvas! We are painting these colors upon the air with every step we take!

Flames billow from your mouth with every word and breath! Beams flare from those gorgeous eyes of yours! And around your head, in a corona, in a halo: rippling colors to put an aurora borealis to shame!"

At first Enoch thought his friend was merely ranting, but the more he listened the more his instincts told him Trent was speaking the truth, if only the truth of madness. "What have you discovered?" he demanded.

"Too much," that whispery voice rasped. "Isn't that the way? When Icarus touched the blaze of the sun?"

"Tell me what you've learned and stop waxing poetic."

"When you and I cease waxing poetic we will both cease to be. Our flame will have extinguished."

"I'll come see you in the morning."

"You left a message that your piece of glass disintegrated?"

"More or less."

"That's good, Enoch. It's better that way, my friend."

"And yours?" No answer. "And yours, Trent? Hello?"

"No. I keep them in their Pandora's box."

"I'm tired of your vague and suggestive talk. I want to come see you right now."

"The trains aren't running now, Enoch."

"I have my crappy old pickup truck."

"Are you concerned for me or just curious about what I've seen?"

"Both. I'm coming."

"If you must. When you get here, let yourself in. The door is unlocked."

V.

It was an hour like purgatory, the streets of Brookline all but deserted, and Enoch parked the beat-up pickup truck he drove when he had to in a free spot a little distant from Trent's apartment building, walking the rest of the way. His clomping footsteps had a lonely resonance.

He found the apartment unlocked as promised, but inside it was unlit as well. He made his way into the living room carefully, reaching out his receptive hands in front of him and trying not to trip or bump into anything, eventually following a feeble glow of flickering light. He found Trent sunk back in his favorite armchair, with several candles burning on surfaces around him. One candle stood beside the familiar riveted metal box.

"Oh, look at you!" exclaimed the shadowy seated figure, in a ghostly choked voice. "How you *burn!* And to think I once found your eyes beautiful when they were merely blue!"

"Can I put on a light?"

"I'd rather you didn't. I don't think I could stand it."

Enoch stood over his friend. Though the gloom was thick and cloaked the young man, candlelight was reflected in the lenses of a pair of spectacles he wore. Enoch had never known Trent to wear glasses before—and certainly not glasses with lenses that flashed with such remarkable color.

"The special aid you directed your father the optometrist to fashion for you," Enoch observed.

"Yes, and they broadened my artistic vision as I had hoped … and then some. I'm sorry I can't bequeath them to you, my friend. I can't do that to you."

"What do you mean?"

"I told my parents I was going away to visit a friend for a while, so they wouldn't come here and see me this way. I don't want them to find these glasses. I don't want my father to look through them again. I'm glad you did come tonight, Enoch. Please, you must promise me something."

"Promise you what?"

"You must swear to me, as my friend, swear as a man of integrity, that you will smash to tiny bits every pane of glass in that lead box. And when you've done that, you must promise me you'll smash these spectacles, too."

Enoch Coffin was silent for several long moments, but at last said, "If that's your wish, then I promise you."

Did he see a black crescent open in the vague, pale smudge of a face? "Thank you, dear friend."

"But what's wrong with you? What's happened?"

"What happened to old man Gardner's ancestor, and his wife, and his sons. The color demands a high price for its glory. You're familiar with many an old frightening tome, aren't you? So you must know the Bible."

"It's not my favorite frightening tome."

"I shouldn't think so," Trent hissed, his wispy voice fainter by the second. "But therein it says, 'The sun was risen upon the earth when Lot entered into Zoar. Then the Lord rained upon Sodom and upon Gomorrah brimstone and fire from the Lord out of heaven; And he overthrew those cities, and all the plain, and all the inhabitants of the cities, and that which grew upon the ground. But his wife looked back from behind him, and she became a pillar of salt.'"

Enoch nodded solemnly. "I understand."

Trent didn't add comment to that, to acknowledge that Enoch gleaned what was happening. Several more drawn-out moments ticked past, in which Enoch found himself mesmerized by the light dancing in the lenses Trent wore. At last, he stepped forward to cross the remaining distance between them, and reached out to remove the spectacles from that shadowy visage.

Briefly, when he pulled the glasses away, two hollow pits were revealed behind them, black tunnels bored far back into the student's skull. Enoch thought he heard a final sigh ... and then the top half of Trent's head collapsed and crumpled down into the hollow of the lower half. Enoch stepped back, still holding the spectacles. He heard more than saw the rest of the disintegration, rustling sounds like sifting sand. Some larger bits thumped softly onto the floor.

VI.

Enoch kept his word. When he brought the heavy lead box of little window panes to his house in the North End, he smashed every one of them, pulverized them to a fine powder. The lenses of the spectacles, too.

Then he mixed these glittering, weirdly incandescent granules into the gel medium, and began a new painting depicting the scene at the well. Normally he didn't care for acrylic paints, which he felt didn't blend as well as oils and dried too quickly for his taste, but in this instance owing to his use of the gel medium it was the right choice.

Again he portrayed a night scene, twisted trees straining to grope at the cosmos, light rushing up from the old stone well in a soundless volcanic blast. But instead of blending terrestrial colors to hint at this unearthly light, he used the gel, which would dry clear but prove a binding medium for the countless scintillating particles of glass, each like the cell of a body that could not be fully comprehended with the puny, reptilian human brain.

He would not be able to show this painting for very long at any one time, if he hoped to preserve it. Private showings, then, never a public exhibit. Any long exposure might be detrimental to the painting ... and the viewer as well.

He experienced a deep gratification that he had succeeded in besting the challenge, though a bit of guilt for feeling triumphant where Trent had failed. Well, in a sense it had been a collaborative effort, much as Enoch normally avoided such.

He had painted this scene on a much smaller canvas than usual. One that could fit inside a riveted metal box.

Ecstasy in Aberration

I.

The smooth black gentleman smoked in starlight. As he leaned against the late-eighteenth-century building that had once been a custom house he gazed beyond the harbor to the distant reef. He sucked in the Innsmouth stench of rotting wharves and decomposing time, and then he blew a cloud of scented smoke into the moist air and sighed. Behind the brick wall against which he leaned came the thump of gloomy music to which the young ones waltzed, and the sound reminded him that he was thirsty, and yet he could not get his legs to move so that he could rejoin his friends inside the nightclub; he was too spellbound by the macabre nature of the dead city and the sea. He smiled. How alike he was to the others he had encountered during his few months in the city, those lost souls who had found, in decaying Innsmouth, a portal to rich perversion and secret pleasure. Yet there was something more, something that remained hidden to most and could be ascertained by those few exotic souls who owned the capacity to taste uncanny vibration in the filthy air. Extinguishing his fag in the ashcan by the club's doorway, the black man walked to the crumbling stone breakwater that extended out into the harbor and listened to waves on sand, as behind him the music inside the club ceased and was replaced by the movement of the departing crowd. Soon he sensed the creature just behind him and her familiar perfume. He spoke her name to the waves.

"Adrianna. Come stand beside me and count the stars as they are reflected on the water. Both sea and sky are black and blend as one, an abyss of delicious pitch into which one may rise or sink, according to one's fancy. Come, old woman, stand beside me."

"Ah, Delmore Rahv—I cannot count the stars, for my eyes are too entranced by darkness." The sound of her raspy voice always startled him slightly, sounding as it did like an utterance croaked from some deep cavern. "The stars, for all their shimmer, are dead things; but darkness is alive, don't you find? Alive and rapacious." She stood taller than he, and he had to look up to study her curious head, which seemed somehow too large for its neck; and as he regarded her fantastic face he thought, as always, of alien things, for her large and lidless eyes seemed other than human, and her flat nose and wide mouth bespoke a racial heritage that confused him. He watched as her rough small hands lifted so as to pat her beautiful wig as the jeweled rings on her fingers competed with starlight. "I am enjoying your little book. But what made you abandon verse for fiction?"

"No, I won't ever ditch poetry—it is the air I breathe. But there can be poetry in prose, as I hope my book demonstrates. The short story is an intriguing form and can express so many things. I'm growing fond of finding my way into the novelette form, which despite its length demands Poe's theory of singleness in unity and effect. Did you like …"

"Your little evocation of myself? Your coy yet playful portrayal?" She laughed, a little. "You have listened to fables, but the facts escape you."

"I prefer myth to verity. And I think it conveys more truth than otherwise. The legends of Innsmouth, for example—they're rooted in dark historical fact, with which you're intimate. You were born …"

"In February of 1928—that month of fire and emancipation. No, you would not understand the freedom that came from flame and obliteration. We who survived, we of fantastic wealth, built up a portion of the city; but we left much evidence of destruction, and our ruins have served us well, for they keep outsiders from our midst. People dislike Innsmouth as much as they abhor Dunwich, and for similar reasons of a prejudice they cannot fathom. It's so amusing, to watch the ones who drive through the city as they tour New England, to see their troubled reaction swell to distaste and dread. They are perplexed and intimidated by the small packs of weird children who follow them and whistle as they whittle effigies in wood, their knives gleaming like lethal silver waves. Ha ha!" Her husky laughter erupted into strangled coughing. "Give me one of your foreign cigarettes, Delmore. I love how they savor of death deep in my lungs."

The smooth black man took the cigarettes from his pocket and placed one between his lips. He lit up, sucked briefly, and then offered it to his companion. She quaffed its fumes as the poet lit another for himself. Together, they smoked in starlight. Then the fellow leaned to Adrianna to kiss her wrinkled face, looked once more at the distant reef, and walked away. She did not watch him fade into the night, for she was captivated by the darkness of sky and sea. It moved before her with dark clouds in the air and their dim shadows on the water. She then noticed the more sinister shadows that moved about Devil Reef, those inky shapes that surfaced above the waves and then dipped beneath them, oozing away from the black reef and moving toward the harbor. The crowd from the club behind her had completely dissipated, and she stood absolutely alone, with no sound except the movement of waves on sand. She stood very still as they surged to her, the shiny bodies that caught the reflection of stars on their wet inhuman flesh. The creatures lurched forward, and she held to them her hands as they encircled her. Some few barked to night's abyss while others kissed the woman's hands with bloated mouths. She watched the approach of one final being, and sighed in ecstasy at the sight of the object that it held. The thing loped to her and lifted the tiara of white gold before her mouth, for her to kiss, for her to see her odd reflection on its façade. Then the object was set atop her wig, as the horde moved about her in honor of her majesty.

II.

The artist tried to sleep as the bus rolled along, but it was next to impossible because of the mortal din that issued from the others seated around him. He felt as if he were on the old bus that took him home from high school, especially when the pack of young people began to sing a song in French. He was slouched against the window with his knees up against the seat in front of him, which was how he knew that someone had plopped themselves before him. Trying to resist opening his eyes worked for just a little while, and then he gave up, groaned, and gazed at the skinhead girl who was staring at him with her Malaysian eyes.

She smiled timidly. "Sorry. Um, you're Enoch Coffin, the painter."

"Yeah."

"Oh, wow! I saw your show in Boston, at the Lavoria Gallery. Such potent art."

"Thanks."

"You're on your way to Innsmouth."

"Yep."

"Nice. I've been there for half a year. I work at a Wiccan shop in Arkham four days a week. We all work outside of Innsmouth." She indicated the other bohemians aboard the bus. "There's not much work in town, really, and most of it is done by the regulars there. You have your own work in town, I've read."

The artist pushed away from the window and lowered his numb legs. "Yep. I've been commissioned to do a portrait of an author—Gerhard Speare—for his forthcoming book. I refuse to work from photographs, so

129

the old codger has finally relented and is allowing me to paint him in his home. You read it where?"

The young woman smiled. "There was an article in the local rag. It's rather incredible, really. Very few of us have seen him. He's so old and sick he doesn't get around at all. I'm amazed he hasn't kicked off. How amazing that he's still writing! And you're to do his portrait for this new book?"

"Yep. What's your name, dumpling?"

"Nesa. Nesa Katt."

"So, you're a witch?"

She laughed. "No, I just work at the shop because it's way cool. I like to fuck warlocks, you know, and have hot wax spilled on me and all that cool stuff. Razor blades and bite marks."

"You're a wild one."

"Funny, that's what I heard about you. Well, here we are."

He hadn't noticed that they had entered the city, for the early nightfall was dark indeed. He arose as the bus came to a stop and watched his young acquaintance move to others and whisper to them, and then he pretended not to notice as the others gave him curious looks. "I'm a girl with a reputation," he thought. Following the others out of the vehicle, he stood waiting for one of the two porters to wheel his gear to him. He had not brought much, for Gerhard Speare had insisted on choosing the canvas for his portrait and some few shades of paint. Enoch would normally have objected, but the fee that the eccentric writer was paying for his visual rendering was so extravagant that the artist could in no way refuse the offer. He watched a young fellow with his suitcases and trunk on a long wheeled cart approach him.

"Mr. Coffin? Your cab awaits you there."

He nodded to the lad, who seemed to be slightly crippled, from the odd way that he walked, and followed him to the long black taxi. "Mr. Speare has paid your fare, sir," the boy said, actually refusing Enoch's proffered tip.

Stepping inside, he sank into the smooth leather upholstery and rolled open a window so as to breathe in the smell of wharves and sea. Seeing the Malaysian lass, he called to her.

"You need a ride?"

"No thanks," she called back. "Where are you staying?"

"The New Gilman."

"Hoo, hoity-toity. I'll see you around." She waved as a red sports car stopped near her, into which she climbed. Enoch's porter, having completed the task of loading, thumped on the back of the taxi, and the artist observed the town he passed through. Some few of his friends who had visited Innsmouth described it for him, and he always thought they had exaggerated—but he now saw, however dimly, that Innsmouth was indeed the strangest of haunts. Most of the factories he passed were obviously in ruins, as were most other buildings, the one exception being a mammoth Gothic Revival edifice that might once have been a railway station, judging by the various tracks he could just make out and a distant covered tunnel that probably spanned the Manuxet River. The journey continued, until suddenly everything changed as the taxi entered the New Merchant District. Enoch marveled at the splendor of some of the buildings, all of which seemed of recent construction. He was taken to a building composed of coral sandstone and beige marble, and a tall fellow dressed in top hat and tails opened the door to his vehicle and called him by name. How the hell did everyone know who he was?

Enoch followed the tall lean gentleman into the hotel and to a spacious elevator which lifted to the fourth floor. "Room Number 428, Mr. Coffin. Your things will be brought up momentarily. Shall I hang up your suits and such?"

"That would be excellent. I have two suits in the trunk. I'll take care of the rest of my clothes. And please don't fiddle with the art gear, I'll take care of all of that."

"Excellent, Mr. Coffin." The fellow did not refuse a tip. "Thank you, sir. I'll return as soon as your things find their way here. Enjoy your stay at New Gilman House."

"You guys still serving food?"

"Yes, the dining room serves until nine in the evening. We have an excellent halibut tonight, sir."

"Great." He nodded to the man and then was alone. Stepping into a resplendent bathroom, he checked himself in the mirror and washed his face, groomed himself a bit and made certain that he had placed one of his key cards into his wallet. He was famished, and the word "halibut" was making his mouth water. He exited his room and took the elevator to the lobby, where the main dining room was pointed out to him. Seated, he glanced at the menu and goggled at the prices.

"Your meals are gratis, sir, compliments of Mr. Speare. We have an excellent white wine to go with the halibut Provençal, which is served over rice or couscous. House salad is an excellent choice, and may I suggest the lemon tart for dessert. Very good, sir. Ah, here is your bread and garlic butter. We are famous for our butter, you know."

The guy was a trifle wearying. "Great. I'll have the salad now, and a cup of chowder."

It was a spectacular feast, such as he hadn't partaken of since the days when he was screwing Latisha Bright, who served as his patron for a season until the sex got old. He had overindulged in the wine and then accepted a glass of champagne to go with the tart. By the time he had completed his repast, the room was blurry. Pulling a ten-dollar bill from his wallet, he set it on the table and staggered to his feet. He was able to walk past two tables until he collided with a seated patron.

"Oh, fuck, excuse me."

"It's quite all right, Mr. Coffin. Will you join us for coffee? We find you rather intriguing."

"How the hell does everyone know who the fuck I am?" he slurred.

"From the small piece in yesterday's paper, of course, with its charming photograph. It's an event, your coming to paint the great and mysterious novelist. But the new book is, as we understand, a collection of novelettes."

"Did you say coffee?"

"Yes, with or without brandy. For you I suggest without, you are quite shamefully intoxicated. Sit here, beside me, so that my ancient eyes may drink your handsomeness."

He fell into the offered chair. "Coffee," he ordered in a loud voice, "with heaps of sugar, no cream. Yeah, sure, drink my beauty all you want, pumpkin. Hey missy, I'm Enoch."

"I know," said the attractive young woman. "We encountered each other earlier today, on the bus." He squinted and smiled. "Oh yeah, Miss Pussy. How ya doin'?" The girl's sudden laughter was so loud that the sound of it made the artist sink a little into his chair.

"I am Adrianna Bishop. I have your *Nesting Place* oil in my bathroom."

"Ha, that should scare the crap out of your visitors."

"Your *Father's Shadow* hangs in my library."

His smile to her was sloppy. "Let me kiss your hand, wench, I went to Prague on that sale. You must be loaded."

"Not as 'loaded' as you, my dear. Ah, here are the coffees, and here your heaps of sugar."

"Thanks. So, are you mother and daughter? Lovers?"

"Nesa assists me about the house, and I occasionally sit for her. We have just spent an exhausting evening putting my bookshelves in order. Although petite, this young woman has the strength of a tiger."

"Pussy, pussy, burning bright," the drunk man warbled. "Mmm, this coffee is good." Raising his hand, he shouted. "Hey, waiter! More nectar, yo."

"You can stop the performance, Mr. Coffin," the young girl told him. "You needn't play the bad boy for us. It's your work that impresses us, your affinity with the macabre and the inhuman. That painting of your father, for example ..."

"No, we ain't gonna talk about that. Hell, all this sober talk ..."

The elderly woman was staring at Enoch with wide unblinking eyes. "We can none of us escape our heritage, Mr. Coffin. I think you are most fortunate to have had such a sire. He has molded you in ways you don't wish to acknowledge."

"And I think you have the queerest gawd-dang face I've ever seen. Are you wearing makeup, or is your skin naturally so ashen and gray?"

"I am as you find me, young man."

"Adrianna has been here all her life, since the holocaust."

"The what?"

The older woman held the artist with her liquid eyes. "A devastation that happened long ago, a portion of my own personal heritage. A tarnish on Innsmouth, the ashes from which some few of us have risen. Something never to be forgotten." A curious quality came into her weird eyes, a kind of wistful woe.

"Something that's remembered once a year. You've come at a convenient time, Mr. Coffin. Tomorrow night is the Surge."

Enoch, woefully, was waking up. He frowned. "The Surge."

The elderly woman shrugged as she lifted a hand to smooth the silk scarf wound around her throat. "A remembrance of past pain, mostly by persons who do not understand its meaning. It's become a popular form of play for these innocent young things who visit Innsmouth so as to drink its decadence. These lovely young things, who help to bring life to a dead city."

Nesa's eyes were bright as she replied. "It begins at the railway station, where we choose our—what is it?"

How sinister, the ancient one's smile. "Where you choose your Olmstead, Mr. Coffin—one puppet in the play."

Now this was a turn-on. Enoch sensed something potent here, something unnatural and significant. "Tomorrow night, at that Gothic Revival station that we passed on the bus, right?"

"That's it," the lovely young girl responded. "Wear something old and tattered. Clothes are usually discarded just before the dash through moonlight. I heard it was wild last year."

"And will you be Surging, Miss ...?"

"Call me Adrianna. No, no—it's for the young things. I 'celebrate' in other ways, alone. You look so sleepy, Mr. Coffin."

"Call me Enoch. Yeah, I'm suddenly dog-tired. Good-night, ladies."

He arose, more steady than before, and sauntered from the room. His bed, when finally he sat upon it, was very soft. Enoch reclined, still fully dressed, and thought about the things he had been told. They soon became the things of which he dreamt.

III.

Misty morning light greeted his eyes as he lay sprawled in bed fully clothed. "World, world, let me kiss you away and dream some mo'." He then remembered that he was to meet the mysterious writer early that afternoon, and so he rose and went to the closet where his suits had been hung, chose the blue one and went to shower and shave. Dressed and groomed, he checked himself out in the bathroom mirror and nodded in approval. "Hullo Gorgeous." Going to one suitcase, he found the satchel that contained a sketchpad, some pens, and his switchblade. Taking leave of the room, he made the journey outside and wrinkled his nose at the potent smell of sea. He sauntered down the lane and stopped at a liquor store to buy a quart bottle of whiskey, which he packed inside his satchel, and then he remembered Miss Katt's suggestion that he have some old clothes to wear at the gathering tonight, the unexplained Surge. Continuing his stroll, Enoch saw a distant section of town that looked depopulated and decrepit, the sight of which aroused his aesthetic senses. "That place looks absolutely diseased," he spoke to himself, as was his constant habit. He moved toward the area as he removed his coat, the weather being muggy and inspiring perspiration.

What a contrast to the area in which he was staying! There was a stench not of the sea, or not wholly of the sea, that made him queasy. Rot was all around him, in those buildings that had not completely caved in, in the very air inhaled. Yet his finer senses detected something more, some unseen force that lurked among the debris of wreckage. Something untoward had happened here, something that had left remnants that yet breathed and waited. Enoch was suddenly aware of the ones behind him, the pack of infants clothed in shabby attire who moved the blades of their knives into the wood they whittled as they gazed at him with wide unblinking eyes. The artist smiled and knelt before the pack, reached into his satchel and took out his knife, which surprised the onlookers. Opening the knife, he clamped it between his teeth as he rolled up the sleeve of his right arm. The light of the pale sky fell onto the old scar that marred his flesh, the esoteric sigil. Removing the knife from his mouth, Enoch worked its blade into the scar that soon was wet and red. "Flesh is easier to work with than wood, I find." He smiled at the imps as he spoke, and then he lifted his arm to his mouth and sucked at blood. Moving the arm away, he blew a crimson-hued bubble of saliva that dissolved as bloodstained drool that coated his mouth and chin. Enoch reached out a hand to the nearest boy. "Come kiss me, pretty child."

The pack fled as laughter sounded behind him. Rising, he turned and smiled at the elderly woman he had sat with in the dining room. Seeing her in the light of day shocked him, for she was obviously gravely ill. Her grayish flesh clung tautly to her bones, and he had never beheld eyes so large and liquid. The silk scarf was still wound tightly around her throat, and he noticed for the first time her bracelets of white gold.

"Have you a handkerchief? Give it to me, and I shall dress your wound." She took the cloth he offered her and dabbed at his arm, revealing the wet scar. "Ah, the insignia of raising up. Rather a potent sigil to have etched into one's flesh, Mr. Coffin. Here, let me just cover it with this and tie it, thus. There, now you can put on your jacket and all is well. You don't want to spill much mortal fluid in this place, where the Outside is so near. You know, certainly, that the smell of mortal blood has a way of intoxicating They who linger between dimensions."

"You haven't been to bed," he informed her as he closed his knife and put it into a pants pocket.

Her voice, when she replied, was thick and raspy, and he thought that she was rather intoxicated. "I'm never 'to bed,' young man." She glanced around the area where they stood. "This is not a safe vicinity in which to wander."

"Yes, I can sense the delicious aura of danger. I like it. I was just scouting for a wee shop where I can get some old, easily discarded attire to wear at tonight's doing."

"Ah, you're attending the Surge. I no longer do so, my old bones protest such leaping. Come, follow me."

Her stride was a little unsteady as she led the way around one corner and down a narrow lane of what looked like unoccupied buildings, and then she approached a door and stepped into a dusky place. The reek of sea and fish, already compelling, was alarmingly potent inside the dark shop into which he had been led, and Enoch covered his nose for a moment as his eyes adjusted to the room's dim lighting. They had entered what looked like a junk shop, with innumerable items stacked on floor and tables, and Enoch finally noticed the figure that stood among the disorder. Enoch's eyes took in what he thought were Negroid features, but as his eyesight improved he saw that the fellow's skin was the same shade as Adrianna's, although of a rougher texture; and the fellow's queer features were far more pronounced than the woman's, the lidless eyes larger and the ears almost nonexistent. The hunched creature watched them and then brought the glass it held to its ungainly mouth.

"Is that local?"

"It is, Miss Bishop," answered a low, coarse voice that reminded Enoch of large stone wheels grinding against each other.

"Two glasses, Suresh." The fellow bowed to her apparent authority and exited the room as she turned and smiled at the artist. "Innsmouth brew, such a heady tonic. It will make you dream. Ah!"

The man returned, and Enoch thought he must have a slight hunchback, he seemed so malformed.

"Oh, it's the celebrated artist come to paint old Gerhard's portrait. There's some of his books over there." He pointed to a cluttered table. "Here, drink up, this'll put fur on your palms."

Or remove all hair, Enoch thought as he noticed that both these creatures seemed entirely hairless. He was certain that the woman was bald as a billiard ball beneath her stylish wig. Nodding his thanks, he took the glass as he nonchalantly studied the man's odd face, with its reptilian features and deep scar at one corner of the mouth.

"What can I do for you?"

"He needs disposable clothing for tonight."

Enoch tried to suppress his annoyance at having the woman answer for him and took a sip from the glass he held. Adrianna, laughing, caught him with one hand as he reeled slightly.

"Um, yeah—something I can discard during the orgy or whatever."

"During the ecstasy, Mr. Coffin, the delirium of the chase," the other fellow corrected him. "Come look at these, I think they are your size. And here are some old loafers, if you decide to run barefoot, as is the custom." Enoch followed the man to a table where a lamp shone its brittle light, and it was then that he noticed the fellow's large hands, which had a kind of growth between each finger.

"Um, yeah, they'll do. Don't matter if they're a bit loose, since I'll shimmy out of them eventually. Hey, I'll take that hat, too. I dig hillbilly hats."

"Put it on my account, Suresh. After all, I'm loaded." She winked at Enoch as the clothes were placed into a sturdy paper bag. Enoch took the hat and placed it on his head. "Let us go," the woman commanded, setting her glass on the table where the artist had placed his.

Enoch followed her outside and held out his hands to her as she stumbled. "You're drunk," he informed her.

"And shall be more so before the day is done. Come, here's my driver. I need to walk near water and quaff its essence. You'll join me, and then my driver can take you to your appointment with the novelist. Don't stand there looking dense, young man, get in." She indicated the long black car where a young man stood next to an open door.

"You're used to getting your own way, wench."

"I am one majesty of this realm, sirrah. In."

They drove through the section that wore its ghoulish air of death and desertion, past a grassy area that led to the sea between crumbling brick walls. The vehicle stopped and its door was opened by the normal-looking young man. Adrianna got out first and waited for her new acquaintance, and then she led the way to a place where large moss-covered stones sat on the earth near an antique wharf that reached into the sea. Enoch saw the low distant line of Devil Reef, to which he pointed as he and the woman sat on two of the bulky stones. "What's that?"

"Hmm? Ah—that's where it all began. The portal from which the leagues ascended so as to congregate with mortality. Am I a sphinx you cannot comprehend? Do you know nothing of our history? It was long ago, of course, but I would have thought that someone who is intrigued by arcane mystery would know of Innsmouth. We are more isolated from the world than ever before, that's it I suppose. A species unto itself, as we were at the time of my birth, just before the holocaust. The history of those events is like a brand burned onto my brain, although I remember none of it, of course. My family was in Europe during the epoch of bayonets and bombs. We returned to devastation. Friends and relations had been taken from Innsmouth and placed into camps or prisons or such. The government did not like our breed, you see. They did not like the webbing on our hands, see here? They were perplexed by the more inhuman manifestations of my race. Innsmouth had been a place of neglect and ruin for ages, of course, because it is such a temporary home for we Immortals—we of the Deep. You've no doubt perused our legends in the tomes that you have obviously read—yes, obvious because of your work. Your art, Enoch, reveals so much about yourself. Those little arcane touches, those titles of books that are so often displayed in background. Of course, the history of Innsmouth isn't inscribed into any tome; I suppose it's to be found in official records that have been set aside and forgotten, if it exists at all." She shrugged. "It's rather recent history as it is. The record of the discharges that were dropped from Devil Reef so as to destroy that which will eternal lie. What fools. We could have seduced them with Innsmouth gold and bought security, I suppose; but vengeance has a sweeter taste, and we have that within us that could exterminate your race if we so chose. We do not. We are rather fond of your clownish caste."

She smoothed the scarf around her throat and looked thirsty, and so Enoch reached into his satchel and brought forth the quart of whiskey. Adrianna laughed as she accepted the bottle and tipped some of its golden nectar down her throat, and then she handed the bottle back to Enoch, who gulped a bit as she continued her converse.

Her eyes, as she turned them to him, glinted mischievously. "Ever hear of a shoggoth?"

"In Alhazred."

"Ah—the 'mad' poet, whose madness was part pose, methinks, and partial authenticity. To see beyond dimension and taste the Outside dents your mortal sanity. I can see it in *your* eyes."

The artist chuckled. "What, that I'm dented?"

"More so than most. You, like Alhazred, have been tainted by the knowledge that haunts your little brain, the lines of muttered alchemy that you cannot quite stop formulating in your sleep, the tugging of foreboding things, the tools of alchemy."

"You mentioned shoggoths."

"Aye. Such sleek yet viscous tools of desolation, lethal and unstoppable. Not easy to command, but our kind have their ways. Thus was holocaust visited upon those places where our race was held captive, where fire consumed the prisons of my nation. The paltry pygmies who would hold us became our burnt, our melted offerings to the Lord of R'lyeh. Some few of us returned here to dwell in secret places, as of old; but now we mostly dwell beneath the waves, or on islands near to other portals. We swarm, on moonlit nights, to Devil Reef and sing to the splendor of many-columned Y'ha-nthlei, to which I shall soon descend. Give me that bottle."

"Keep it. I need to split and see the mysterious novelist."

"I've prattled incomprehensibly, I fear."

"No, I understood more than you may imagine. I've read the old books, after all. So much of what they record is little more than legend or drug-delirium. I recall some few hints concerning the myths of the Deep Ones, a race of aquatic immortals that sometimes mate with humans and from which legends of mer-folk supposedly materialized. But I thought they were a species whose legend is found on other continents. I didn't realize that Innsmouth was one bed of breeding. That's what you are, you of the Deep?"

But she wasn't listening to him. The whiskey was having its effect, and her bleary eyes ignored him as they peered out to sea. Quietly, Enoch rose and went to the driver and slipped into the car, in which he was driven to the home of Gerhard Speare, which was built on a high hill that overlooked the posh section where Enoch's hotel was situated. The artist stood on the gravel path as Adrianna's car sped away, and he was still examining the fantastic mansion when one of the two gigantic doors opened and a young woman stepped out to greet him.

"Mr. Enoch Coffin. Welcome. Master Speare is in his private room. Follow me, please." He followed the lithe woman into the house and up a flight of stairs, and then down a dusky hall to a huge oak door, upon which she tapped before opening it and escorting the artist inside. One thick and fragrant candle provided the dark room's only light, and Enoch could not make out anyone else in the room as the woman shut the door on exiting. Other smells came to him, of books and age and the sea—but then the smell of the sea pervaded all of Innsmouth. Still, it seemed especially pungent in this room.

"Will you have a seat, or do you prefer standing?" The whispered voice could have been a death rattle, and Enoch had to strain to understand each word. "There is a chair near you, do sit. Bring the candle closer if you must."

"That's okay, my eyes will adjust." He sank into a chair and placed his bundle of second-hand garments on the floor, then removed his hat and dropped it onto the pile of clothing.

"Excellent. I have just been for a deep swim, and my eyes dislike bright light after the darkness of the depths. The fragrance of the sea still lingers on my flesh. Do you enjoy Innsmouth?"

"I find it more captivating than I expected."

"I thought you would. Monstrous haunts give you keen aesthetic pleasure, as is revealed by your magnificent oils. I have noticed that you preserve your most suggestive works for the grand paintings and imbue them with intriguing touches in background and such. Your oil of Sentinel Hill, in Dunwich, which I have hanging there on the wall behind you—the directions in which the tall stones tilt is most indicative. And the shaping of the dark cloud—very subtle and probably missed by most."

"You paid a lot of money for that painting, and you're paying me a hell of a lot for the job I've come to perform. I've never been given such an amount for a portrait that will be used in a book to illustrate its author."

"You were chosen because you are, exceptionally, a realist, yet one who presents realism in a most fantastic manner. You imbue your work with hidden sigils, spectral forms, and occult secrets. You show humanity as the monster that it is, or may become. But more, you reveal the other races, of ghouls and burrowers beneath, of avatars of madness and they that split the veil. That is why you were elected for this especial task. You have read my books that were sent you?"

"Yes."

"And noticed the old author's photo that has been used repeatedly. The time has come for an updated image, in which I am revealed as I am. Use the candle by you to light the other two on the tables nearest me."

"I've got a lighter." He could just make out the tables and rose to step toward them as he took the lighter from his pocket and flicked it until its tiny flame ignited. Enoch didn't look toward the whisperer in the chair until both candles were lit, and then he did his best to stifle the noise that threatened to erupt from his throat. The candlewicks had held their fire dimly for some few moments, and then their flames expanded, and their light spilled onto the whisperer in darkness. The creature was small and entirely nude, although its distinct outline and features were swathed in moving shadow. It tilted forward slightly and curled its mouth, which made the face resemble a grotesque mask of mockery. Absolutely hairless, as had been the others of its race that Enoch had encountered, the being regarded the artist with bulging eyes and lips as its flat nose sniffed at the air.

"I can smell your blood, Mr. Coffin, as it rushes through your stems of veins. You have read much of the elder lore; do you understand the lure of human blood to that which lurks Outside?"

"Yeah, I've noticed the curious repetitions of improbable lore about the daemons that need human blood to take bodily form in this realm. It's crap, of course. Why would non-terrestrial freaks that predate humanity by millennia need *human* blood when humans are so recent a race compared to the ones who lurk Outside?"

"But you have just answered your own question: because they are of the Outside, creatures of appetite that lust for mortal carnage and the ecstasy it provides. To exist in this realm demands corporeal mutation in those of the Outside, a different chemistry of being. Humans as an outlet of ecstasy are a subtle yet common thread that runs through ancient arcane lore. We of the Deep are enticed by such ecstasy ourselves and use it as a vehicle for procreation."

"You of the Deep. Adrianna was going on about that earlier today."

"As you were sitting with her and contemplating Devil Reef. Yes, I saw you at the end of my carousing beneath the waves. Such a sad creature, Adrianna. She has heard the call and would resist it, but cannot. She is overfond of oxygen and would stay above one century more. But that does not concern us. You see me as I am, and will paint me thus. Because of your reputed love of the grotesque and monstrous, it will be said that your portrait is a vile exaggeration, an outlandish defamation of the author as inhuman fiend. That will be the rich jest—for your painting will be absolutely true to life. You won't mind the abuse of critics; indeed, you seem to thrive on it."

"I adore disapproval."

"Exactly." Gerhard Speare lifted his head and moved his flat nose as he regarded a curtained space. "The atmosphere is too still, I find. I like a little storm before the Surge. Will you be attending?"

"Yep," Enoch replied, indicating the bundle of old clothing that he had set on the floor near his chair.

"Excellent. Come, let us practice some alchemy and thus kill ennui. Follow me, to the balcony." Speare rose and waddled to the curtains, which he opened so as to reveal a French door that led out onto a balcony. The dull light of late afternoon greeted them. As Enoch stood, he noticed his painting of Dunwich on the wall and winced at the memory it evoked. "Come to me, Enoch Coffin, and let us call unto the clouds. You have raised storms, I take it?"

"No, I haven't, although I'm familiar with the lore."

"Ah—a new experience! The tempest I have in mind requires mortal blood."

"And your own won't do, for you are an Immortal."

"Exactly. Why do you remove your jacket?"

The artist did not answer as he tossed his jacket into the room and pulled his knife from his pants pocket. He held the knife in one hand as he used the other to unbutton and roll up his shirt sleeve, exposing the handkerchief with which Adrianna had dressed his wound. Enoch removed the dressing and heard the other fellow sigh as he beheld the symbol etched into the artist's flesh. "You know this sigil, of course."

"I do, Enoch Coffin. It will aid us well. Ah, the uproar we will evoke! Allow me, sir." Gerhard Speare took the knife from Enoch's hand and opened its blade, and then he muttered weird words as he traced the sigil with the knife's point. Enoch spoke the words as well, and marveled at the way their utterance caused his blood to bubble. "Do you smell the thunder, Enoch Coffin?"

The artist scanned the sky and saw the dark shapes that spilled from one place toward shadowed Innsmouth, the coils of blackness that conjoined as monstrous cloud from which a streak of lightning zigzagged toward the rotting wharves. Heaven thundered as together the monster and the man shouted to the sky. Sheets of rain fell to earth as gusts of growing wind tossed the storm to the alchemists who watched from the balcony. The world turned black as windstorm howled, spilling into the dark room behind them and extinguishing all candles. Enoch turned to gaze at Speare as the novelist took hold of the artist's arm and bent his flat nose to it.

"Ah—the scent of mortal blood. How it intoxicates and cajoles!" Without warning, the Deep One thrust the knife deeper into Enoch's arm and muttered esoteric language that seemed to shake the earth, and then he threw down the knife and held the spray of blood to the sky. Enoch watched, spellbound, as his scarlet liquid rushed toward the ravenous black cloud and became a part of its element. Bulbous lips pressed against the emblem on Enoch's arm and were coated with his corporeal stain as Enoch's vision finally blurred. The artist felt the monstrous mouth lift from his arm and smash against his lips as, weak and losing consciousness, he was dragged into the chamber's gloom.

IV.

He awakened in his hotel room, naked in bed, his limbs a bit stiff but otherwise in fine fettle. Propping himself up with his elbows he saw that the bundle of clothes he had bought in the old shop had been placed on top of one of the room's bureaus, while the clothes he had worn, now freshly laundered, hung on the closet door. "What the hell time is it?" he asked the air as he twisted his head to check the clock on the bedside stand. It must have been early evening, for no daylight slipped through the space between the window curtains. Moaning, he sat up with his back to the headboard and ran his hands through his shaggy hair and noticed the black spot on his arm. A knock sounded on his door. Groaning, he pushed out of bed and staggered to the door. A young woman stood staring at him.

"Nesa Katt. You are a dream come to beautify my nightmare."

The girl laughed lightly as she entered the room. "The sun has fallen and starlight awakened. You've slept for some few hours. How do you feel?"

"Okay, I guess. Got this weird black mark on my arm, just over my skin art." He showed her his arm.

"It's treated shoggoth tissue. We use it for wounds. Quite effective. It will dissolve into your flesh eventually, but one portion of its essence will cling to you for eternity." She held his arm with one hand and ran her other hand over the mark. "It's already losing its stickiness." Enoch took hold of her hand and brought it before his eyes. "What?"

With one finger of his free hand, he traced the minute webbing that had formed between her slender fingers. "You're of the Deep. Hell, are you gonna turn into one of those fish-freaks?"

She smiled with her large and liquid eyes. "I am one already. I'm very young; you'll be long dead before I look like Gerhard or Adrianna."

He gazed at her dark beauty, her smooth skin and beauteous round eyes. "That's fucked-up."

"It's glorious. Are those the clothes you're wearing tonight? Get dressed, I have a taxi waiting."

Stepping to the bureau, Enoch unfolded the clothes and wrinkled his nose at their fishy odor. "Pah—that smell! I hate the sea."

"I drink its sweet perfume."

"Yep, you're turning into one of them thar freaks. What's so funny?"

"Your idea that your infant race forms the mold of normality. Your insignificant infant race."

"Say that again and I'll slap you."

"Mmm, I love a bit of brutality. Ah, that's brought some shimmer to your eyes. Need help pulling into those trousers? There, you look authentically Innsmouthian now."

"Smell like it too. Give me that hat." He turned to check himself out in the full-length mirror next to the closet. "Yeah, nice and sexy."

"Let's go, handsome." He reached for his wallet. "You won't need that, come on."

Walking slightly behind her, Enoch admired the girl's figure as it was revealed beneath her simple dress of blue cotton. When he sat next to her in the taxi he touched his hand to her choker and its amulet of white gold. "What is this stuff?"

"What, Innsmouth gold? It's beautiful, isn't it? They bring it to us from the Deep. There are lots of conflicting legends concerning it and its uses in Innsmouth, such as that the townsfolk used it as a form of exchange for productive fishing. That was nonsense. The payment came in worship of the Lord who slumbers in R'lyeh and the surrender of dreaming to His Call. You've read the *Cthaat Aquadingen*, I take it."

"Nope. Heard about it. Like I said, I hate the sea."

"And all her splendid mysteries? Sad. We were told you're well-versed in all matters of the Outside."

"Who the fuck are 'we'?"

"Ah." She pointed out the window as they approached the restored station at the western end of Bank Street south of the river. Lit up, it was a magnificent sight, this Gothic Revival edifice with its marble pillars and clock tower. They stepped out of the vehicle and a sound caught Enoch's attention.

"I hear water on rocks."

Nesa pointed to a nearby barn-like covered railway bridge. "It's one of the waterfalls, beneath the old bridge." Enoch listened to the music that issued from inside the building, which he recognized as a string quartet by Béla Bartók. Nesa linked her arm with Enoch's as they climbed the steps and passed a hunched figure that stood smoking an exotic cigarette. "Good evening, Suresh," she greeted the fellow, who sneered at them and walked away. Following another newly-arrived couple inside, they entered an alien world of golden light and weird allure. The large room was now teeming with people, and Enoch noted that most of the crowd seemed young. He thought it looked an artistic crowd and remembered that those who had helped to rebuild portions of the city had been wealthy young bohemian types. Perhaps they had thought to turn shadowed Innsmouth into an oasis of aesthetic oddness for a very select few. The sight that utterly captured Enoch's attention was a mammoth sculpture composed of Innsmouth gold, a bizarre composition of spires and coils that looked absolutely alien.

"Whoa, that's cool! What is it?"

"It replicates one of the temples of Y'ha-nthlei, the city in the depths beneath Devil Reef, which is one reason why Innsmouth was chosen as our human haunt. Its partial destruction by your government was repaid one million times by squadrons of shoggoths in the 1930s. The damage has since been restored, and this here is a reminder of our eternal glory and providence."

"It's beautiful," he told her as he admired it with his artistic eye, "but it kinda makes you feel lightheaded the longer you look at it. The dimensions are all screwed up. That white gold—it's so alluring, makes you want to enter into it and pray—to gawd knows what."

The music was evocative and its effect dizzying. Some couples moved to it with swoon-like motion that might be mistaken for exotic dancing. The musicians stood on a raised platform: two with violins, one with a viola, and the last with a cello. Enoch noticed that all four were the hairless Innsmouth type, and he liked the way their faces wore fevered expressions as they performed their piece. Indeed, the entire room almost hummed with an undercurrent of eccentric exhilaration. "This crowd overflows with adventurous expectancy."

"Excuse me?"

He waved his comment away as he smiled at his youthful companion. "Nothing. Just nattering to myself."

The music stopped and a young black fellow took to the stage. "Who's that?"

Nesa tilted to his ear and whispered. "Delmore Rahv—he's been selected as this year's Olmstead."

"What the hell is an Olmstead?"

"The One Who Is Pursued."

The young man raised his hands and silenced the crowd. The room stood dead still for some while, and Enoch began to get antsy. He was just about to ask Nesa what was happening when a foghorn sounded from some distant place outside. "The Surge begins," Delmore Rahv whispered. Jumping from the platform, he walked into the crowd, which began to encircle him, and Enoch thought that the black fellow's face wore a smile of perverted pleasure and pride. Someone near Rahv slapped his face and whispered "Traitor." Another pushed him violently so that he stumbled to where Enoch and Nesa stood. The young woman clutched the black man's collar and ran her pointed nails across his cheek. "Judas," was her stern rebuke as she hurled Rahv from them. Enoch sensed an air of fevered playful malevolence that reminded him of his youthful punk-rock days when he thrilled to the violence of the pit. The black lad's mouth smiled as it bled, and then another horn sounded from outside. The crowd stopped their antics as Rahv slipped from them and exited the station. Nesa suddenly grabbed Enoch's shirt and began to rip it off him, and then she lifted and discarded her dress, revealing her shapely breasts and lithe figure. Playfully, Enoch growled at her as he removed the rest of his clothing except for his hat. The girl licked her mouth as she stared at the artist.

"Come to daddy, kitty-kitty."

"Meowrr," she said, and then followed it with her lovely lilting laughter as she spilled into his arms. His hands fondled her breasts as she bit into his shoulder, and then her lips pressed against his ear. "The Surge begins."

The horde of beings oozed from the building as they bayed and barked. Enoch saw that the dark sky was clear, untainted by the storm that he and Speare had earlier evoked. A harvest moon swam within an ocean of starlight, and the crowd continued to bellow as they leapt as if hungry to seize the lunar sphere. And then the multitude moved as one, joined surreptitiously by the more extreme Innsmouth types that crept from out the barn-like bridge and the river that it spanned and joined the Surge, bringing their stench with them. Enoch and his companion flowed with the flopping pack, and the artist stretched his mouth so as to join in with the snarling and croaking emission of inhuman utterance that issued from the rabble all around them. They swelled like some grotesque saraband engaged in fantastic danse beneath a cryptic moon—hopping, leaping, bleating as they pursued the one who fled them. A kind of hypnotic delirium clutched at the crowd, and Enoch found it exhilarating. He raised his hands to the yellow sphere in the sky, leaping in the air as if in an effort to grab the moon and eat it.

He could smell the sea and realized that it spread before him. Wind rushed to him from the water as waves moved toward the sand on which Delmore Rahv danced. Some few muscular figures, all of whom wore bands of white gold around their throats and wrists, approached him and lifted the young black man to the stars, and then they hurled him into the sea, into which they followed. Staring out over the water, Enoch saw the horde of creatures that were climbing onto the dark and distant reef.

Nesa appeared before him and stroked his phallus. He fell with her onto the sand.

V.

It was still dark when he awoke on the beach with Nesa in his arms. Yet, like the ghost of Hamlet's father, he could sense the dawn. Adrianna smiled down on them. The elder woman wore a kind of robe that covered her completely, but she was without her scarf so that the slits that opened and closed at each side of her neck were clearly visible. The wig had been discarded, and Enoch marveled at the shape of the regal head with its inhuman proportions. "How strange," the artist whispered to himself, "to find such ugliness alluring." Nesa stood as Enoch stayed reclined on sand, and Adrianna took the girl's hand and studied the minute webbing between its fingers.

"You've a long wait yet, dear child. But you'll be surprised at how swiftly a century will pass. Millennia await thee." The older woman placed her inhuman hand on the girl's belly and nodded. "Beget, Nesa, and bring forth the children of Cthulhu. We will swim as Nation in the era of His Awakening, and bay with joy at the riot that will devour this doomed world. Breed, child."

"I have made a start, I think," the young one answered, turning to smile at the mortal on the sand.

Adrianna knelt beside the mortal and pressed her monstrous mouth against his forehead. "It has been a pleasure, Mr. Coffin. I hope that you will come often to our shadowed city and breed with abandon."

"I think I'm up for that," he answered as he wore a crooked smile.

He then noticed the craft that sailed toward shore, and Adrianna rose and turned to greet the boat and its navigator. Gerhard Speare lifted his oars out of the water and waited as the first touch of dawn filtered above them.

The ancient woman turned to the couple one last time and nodded, and then she let her robe fall to the sand. Enoch thought there was something majestic about the way the creature walked into the water and moved through it to the boat into which she climbed. Standing, she waved toward shore one final time, and then reached for the fabulous tiara of white gold that her companion held to her. Adrianna placed the strange object on her dome as her boat mate dropped the oars into the water and guided their craft toward the black line of Devil Reef. Enoch smiled wistfully as Adrianna lifted her hands to the sky and then tipped over and into the depths.

Shadow Puppets

I.

Enoch Coffin had met some of these artists before—unfortunately. He even recognized some of the attendees who were not artists, from other exhibitions, including his own. This being the case, he was forced to put up with much small talk before the night's event. Repeatedly he was asked what project or projects he was currently pursuing himself. He fended off most of these questions very quickly, as they were largely just obligatory politeness, though he did converse more at length with a few individuals who seemed to hold a sincere interest in his work.

An aged woman with more paint on her face than some of Enoch's canvases, who had been listening in on his conversation with one of the more tolerable guests, cut in with the admiring comment, "Young man, you put me in mind of that actor ... hm ... he was in Stone's film *Platoon*."

"Gawd, not that Sheen person, I should hope," Enoch said dryly, raising his wine glass to his lips.

"No, no ... another character in that one."

"Must be that scar-faced bastard you're thinking of," said a voice behind Enoch.

He turned toward the speaker, and molded his lips into another of tonight's artificial smiles. "Ah, hello, Dane. The man of the hour."

This evening Dane van der Sloot was artist, gallery owner and host all in one, the venue being his own home in Bar Harbor, Maine. Enoch didn't think Dane's income as an artist could account for the impressive house; he'd heard the man was a widower, his wealthy wife having perished in a freak accident a few years back, her heart apparently having given out when she made the odd decision to swim in the chilly waters off Acadia National Park's Sand Beach, late one summer evening. Odd, because later her family had insisted the woman had never learned to swim.

"Enoch," Dane said with a nod. "Frankly I'm surprised that you accepted my invitation and came all this way. I feared you'd decline, but thought I'd give it a shot anyway. I'm glad I did…thank you."

"Mr. Coffin has traveled the world," said the person he had been conversing with. "Maine isn't all that far from Massachusetts—true?"

It was far enough when one's vehicle—in this case Enoch's battered old pickup—was of dubious reliability, but he didn't care to divulge such personal details. Enoch replied, "It's a beautiful area. I've been to Acadia National Park in the past."

Enoch didn't add, though it might be implied, that he wouldn't have driven six hours (not counting rest stops) for Dane's show alone. September was a lovely time of year in Maine, offering a balance of golden warmth and invigorating chill, and past the high tourist season of summer. Still, even now from the pink granite summit of Cadillac Mountain one could count on spotting some large cruise ship or other prowling amongst the Porcupine Islands, their shaggy humps suggesting the backs of a pod of great aquatic animals. Thus, the streets of quaint Bar Harbor would be filled with tourists from the UK and elsewhere. Enoch had detected a British accent or two amongst tonight's attendees of Dane's art presentation.

"Why do you work from Maine, if I might ask?" the painted grande dame asked Dane, now running her wine-lubricated gaze up and down his tall frame, garbed in a crisp black suit and black turtleneck. "Why not someplace more … sophisticated, like New York?"

"Well, I'm from this state originally, my dear," Dane replied with patient good cheer. "But I did pursue my career in New York for many a year, actually … before they kicked me out." He laughed to show he was joking, though Enoch knew it was not entirely a joke. "I decided to return to my roots. Where else in the world—and I ask you this, Enoch, you being the great world traveler and all—where else can one encounter such a perfect marriage of forest, mountain and ocean? It's like a magnificent nexus point of all the elemental power Nature could devise. The forces of Earth are pure here, resources just waiting to be tapped into. I am here precisely because it is the antithesis of New York, or Mr. Coffin's own Boston."

"But most of the art scene here," the woman continued, with a bright red sneer, "seems to consist mainly of lobsters and lighthouses painted on wooden plaques for tourists in Bermuda shorts."

"All the more reason for me to be here!" Dane exclaimed, clapping his large hands together. "To enlighten!"

"But you're preaching to the choir, aren't you, Dane?" Enoch couldn't resist commenting. "This showing isn't open to the general public. It's by special invitation only. So I'd say you must feel we honored guests are already sufficiently enlightened to appreciate whatever it is you plan to reveal to us tonight."

"Enoch," Dane returned, his eyes glimmering, "there is always room for further enlightenment."

"I see. Very well." Enoch spread his hands. "I await epiphany, then."

"Oh, I think you'll find this right up your dark alley, Enoch. We aren't all that different, you and I, even if I did overhear that you once rather ungenerously referred to me as a 'sad aging goth' and a 'cruel and pretentious boor.'"

The grande dame looked to Enoch with a stifled gasp, as if expecting a fist fight to break out.

Enoch wasn't about to deny or apologize for his words, so he smiled, sipped his wine again, and said, "A boor perhaps, Dane, but never boring."

"I'll accept that as a compliment of sorts, Enoch. But do you still consider me cruel? Isn't Nature itself cruel?"

The man was undoubtedly cruel, even by Enoch's standards, and it was his trouble with animal-rights groups and the law that had chased the artist out of New York state as much as any tree-hugging impulse. Even while in New York, Dane's work had often ostensibly addressed Nature as a theme. The trouble had come from using living things as part of his mixed media. A typical piece would be the *The Game of Life and Death,* a glass labyrinth containing a single white mouse and a large starved rat, an interactive artwork in which two attendees of the exhibit would slide open or lower in place any variety of partitions, as would benefit the animal they had chosen as their avatar. In *Ouroboros,* a snake with a live mouse fastened securely to its tail would thus swallow its own tail, finally expiring as a tightened O. Fish, birds, lobsters, and ultimately cats all factored into his artworks. Those who vehemently protested Dane's work had asked when he would move on to placing human babies in his glass tanks.

"Well," Enoch responded, "it's curious to comment on the suffering to be found in the world, by inflicting suffering yourself."

"Ah, so you came all this way simply to judge me and feel superior. I see. We've had a bit of a competitive relationship, haven't we, you and I? Especially since I began my studies of the occult. I think you felt threatened then, as if you feared I had entered into your own territory ... and might outdo you."

"I understood you were delving into esoteric knowledge, Dane, but I've never seen it manifested in your ... *art*." Enoch placed a derogatory accent on the word "art."

"Ah, but tonight you will see my new body of work." Dane pushed back his sleeve to glance at a wristwatch with a black face. "And I had better get ready ... the show is about to start."

II.

The title of Dane's presentation was *Shadow Play*, and the reference to "play" made Enoch wonder if this were to be a performance art type of thing. So far no physical art was on display other than the house's customary collection. The group of attendees had assembled at the circumference of a large room with not a stick of furniture nor a stitch of rug upon its honey-hued floorboards. It would take up too much space for them all to sit down, so they stood in a tight ring close to the equally barren walls. Enoch thought of the O of the dead snake in *Ouroboros,* and wondered playfully if glass walls might appear out of nowhere as a result of Dane's outré studies, trapping all his guests and making them into the artwork themselves.

At least *that* Enoch might have to applaud.

Dane emerged from a curtained doorway, pushing a wheeled cart covered with a black cloth toward the center of the room. He was not only dressed all in black, but wearing black eyeliner. Enoch muttered to the person beside him, "The eternal goth. Embrace what you are, I guess. Maybe he's finally ready to be honest with himself, and his art."

"Shh!" the person shushed him, watching their host raptly.

"Hmph," Enoch grunted, refocusing on Dane as the man swept the black silk cloth from the cart like a magician unveiling some cheap illusion.

Sitting atop the cart was a good-sized glass fish tank with an open top. Instead of containing water, however, it was filled to the brim with what appeared to be an opaque fluid, black as India ink.

Then Dane swept one hand above the tank, tracing strange symbols in the air. It might seem to the others a theatrical, even ridiculous bit of showmanship, but Enoch recognized one or two of the symbols the artist formed. They were sigils of conjuration ... one of them representing the "Dragon's Head," or "ascending node."

Turning slowly as he spoke, so that his eyes might sweep the faces of all gathered around him, the showman intoned, "Are we ape or apex? We are told we should be humble in the face of the Creator, but the Creator is Nature, and humans are the pinnacle of natural creation. Though we started from humble origins ..."

A flourish of his hand, and the concentrated black fluid resting in the aquarium shot upwards, hovering in the air. In a mere blink, the inky matter spread outward, became a pulsing elongated shape with a single whip-like appendage. Enoch thought of it as a giant protozoan.

Oohs and aahs from the audience. Dane continued. "Nature flexed her muscles, tested new forms, squeezed them from the air with her sheer force of will."

The pulsing shape elongated further, coiled in the air now as a gigantic segmented worm. Around him, Enoch was aware that some people were cringing, recoiling, even shifting behind others in fear. He noted now that the floating, pliable black substance held an iridescence like oil.

"Nature realized she was God," Dane said, "and she found she had a taste for godhood."

The shape altered, took on the appearance of a man-sized fish swimming in place, but remained entirely black. Even its eyes—mere representations. Enoch had recognized this material already for what it was, and knew that its own eyes if they were to manifest would be glowing greenish orbs.

Unconsciously he rubbed at an odd tickling sensation on his right arm, that originated down deep in his nerves.

Dane prattled on, but Enoch doubted the others were listening any more closely than he was. They all watched in awe, confusion and anxiety as the levitating black matter changed form repeatedly. Each time Dane made some odd gestures to command or direct it. The fish developed legs and became an oversized replica of a frog, right down to its throbbing throat sack, though none of these animal manifestations uttered a peep. The frog transformed into a lizard, black as a silhouette or a sharply defined shadow, then the lizard into a rat with a furry coat—each hair an extrusion of that obsidian substance. The rat became a monkey, appearing to sit on its haunches in midair.

It didn't take a genius to see where this was headed.

"Then Nature," said Dane, "made Man in her own image. Because *all* life is her own image. She shaped us...and now with the power she gave us, we shape her. Shape all aspects of this world. We are Nature! We are the Creator!" He wove a mystical sign in the air beside the monkey, like a conductor dramatically orchestrating a crescendo. "*I* am the Creator!"

The strange niggling sensation in Enoch's flesh had become a real distraction, and even as he starting rolling up his right sleeve to reveal the spot he realized what was happening. *Of course!*

Recently he had been to Innsmouth, Massachusetts. There, in an impulsive artistic mood, he had used his switchblade to open an old wound in his arm, a scar that formed a cryptic symbol. One of the locals—her lineage not entirely human, and thus versed in the arcane herself—had used a tiny portion of shoggoth matter to heal the wound, leaving a black mole upon his skin there.

Shoggoth matter. It was reacting to the proximity of Dane's living clay, which was undoubtedly a shoggoth under his enchantment. Shoggoths … the army of the Deep Ones. The servants of the otherworldly Elder Things, servants that Enoch had read had ultimately turned against their masters and annihilated them. And here was Dane, only a fairly recent explorer into esoteric arts, daring to exert his mastery over one of those terrible entities!

By now Enoch had rolled up his sleeve enough to discover more than a mole. The raised black spot had extruded a tiny, thin tendril that wavered in the air, as if reaching out to the levitating, morphing blob.

Dane's gestures caught Enoch's attention, and he looked up to find the artist repeating the same motions again and again. And yet, the shoggoth suddenly seemed disinclined to obey him. The monkey had not become a human, which was obviously the intended climax of the performance. In fact, the monkey's shape was growing unstable, corrupted, as weird and disturbing distortions pulsated across its body. It twitched with terrible spasms, its tail flicking as if it were being electrocuted.

The hair-like growth reaching from Enoch's arm, unnoticed by any but himself, was making similar erratic movements.

On a sudden impulse—an instinctive impulse, as if another force controlled his body—Enoch stepped forward and waved his right arm in the air, tracing a sigil of his own. It was the "Dragon's Tail," or "descending node." A banishment.

Instantly heeding his command, the shoggoth lost its tortured form and dropped down into the glass fish tank from which it had risen. Once more at rest, it again appeared as a benign black fluid.

Dane glared at Enoch, looking ready to burst into convulsions himself as he fought to suppress his rage, but he covered the aquarium with the black silk cloth again, and in a strained voice improvised some concluding words.

"And what is Nature's ultimate form—the apex of her genius? Need I show you, dear friends? You need only turn to look at the person standing beside you. Or you need only look at me. *We* are the climax of this presentation, my friends … you, and I."

With that, he turned to push the wagon toward the curtained doorway, while his audience—freed from their stunned state, and probably relieved that his incomprehensible black putty was being removed—burst into wild applause.

III.

A short time later Dane took Enoch aside in the kitchen, and in a low voice growled, "Were you trying to make me look like a fool? Steal my thunder, Enoch? I wasn't finished ... you cut me off right at my fucking climax! You interfered in my art!"

"Are you mad? You didn't see what was happening? Your pet was rebelling."

"Yes! Because you were commanding it to resist me!"

Not consciously, Enoch wanted to say, but he didn't care to reveal the truth about the shoggoth tissue wed to his own flesh. He only said, "Nonsense—it chose to disobey you. Luckily I've been at this longer and broke down its will. You should thank me for that; there's no telling what that thing might have done in a few minutes more."

"I've never experienced any trouble like this until you came here."

"Per your invitation," Enoch reminded him.

"You were competing with me!" Dane persisted. "Trying to show me up at my own presentation!"

"What are you talking about? It's you who's trying to compete with me—that's why you asked me here. To show off. To show *me* up. Anyway, don't worry; I'm sure no one but you understands what I did, any more than they understand the nature of your parlor tricks. But I'll tell you, Dane ... you might get off on playing God, but you are in way over your head with this creature. Even with my knowledge I'd never try to master a shoggoth!"

Two other guests drifted into the kitchen at that point. In a more composed tone, Dane asked Enoch to stay on after the others had left. Enoch didn't care to be alone in that house with the artist and his familiar, though, so he made excuses about being overtired and needing to get to bed.

"Are you staying here in Bar Harbor?" Dane asked.

"No," Enoch thought it prudent to lie, "I took a motel room in Ellsworth. It was cheaper."

"Meet me for breakfast tomorrow, will you?" Dane persisted, some of his polished charm having returned, at least on the surface.

Enoch consented, curious to understand how Dane had summoned this entity.

And so, as agreed upon, the next morning the two artists sat across from each other in a nice little spot in downtown Bar Harbor, both with blueberry pancakes in front of them. Attired all in black as always, and with his hair gelled into careful disarray, Dane revealed, "I have a friend at the College of the Atlantic here in town. Hurricane Irene didn't do too much damage up this way last month, not like Vermont saw, but after the storm some odd debris had washed ashore on one of the Porcupine Islands. It was spotted from a boat, and so my friend and other researchers from the college went in to investigate. They thought it was going to be a whale carcass. Well, have you ever heard those stories about mysterious 'globsters,' as they're called? Blob-like rotting bodies that wash up and sometimes go unidentified?"

"You mean to suggest those are shoggoths?"

"Well, this one was. It was huge. My friend showed me pictures. You don't think I could manage to control a healthy, full-sized shoggoth, do you? What I have is the living tissue that my friend excised from the hulk before the rest of it decomposed, broke down without leaving a trace. Why it sickened in the first place, we may never know."

"You and your friend are close enough that he knew this thing might appeal to you?"

"*She,*" Dane corrected, "and yes, we are. Close enough that she would accept a generous payment for the sample she salvaged, and for claiming to her superiors that *all* of the mysterious globster disintegrated."

"So it's only been a month since you learned how to command that thing, and devised your performance?"

"Strike while the iron is hot, I say. Who can tell when the fragment of the creature I own might also sicken and die?"

"Or regenerate to full size," Enoch warned.

"Coffin, you're just jealous that I'm doing this and you aren't. Look, I know you despise me. But even you have to admit that I've achieved brilliant results controlling this creature, without the use of telepathy as some of their masters are alleged to have employed."

"I won't say I'm not impressed. And whether I despise you or not, it doesn't mean I want to see that thing twist your head off. I'll have you know that's said to be their signature means of killing."

"Yes, yes," Dane waved at the air, "I've read all that." He sipped his coffee, eyeing Enoch intensely over the rim of his mug. When he set it down, he said, "I still think that you sabotaged my work last night."

Enoch sighed and wagged his head. "Look, as I say, your audience has no idea your performance wasn't meant to end the way it did, and you can always stage more of your … shoggoth art down the road."

"Oh, you can be assured I'm not done with my little pet. But you can also be assured you won't be appearing at any future presentations of mine. You can deny it all you like, but I'm sure you caused the beast to become recalcitrant, and then you made a grand gesture of saving the day by banishing it back to its container. Bravo, Enoch, bravo." He clapped his hands. "Perhaps we should simply become collaborators, hm?"

"Dane, I'm telling you, it's dangerous thinking believing I caused the creature to become uncooperative."

"Of course you'd try to dissuade me, being so afraid that I'll outshine you, and all."

"Gawd, you think you matter so much to me, but I'm done wasting my time on you, believe me. I'm going to enjoy my stay a few days longer and leave you to your own devices. You can take all the chances you like—though I pity the people around you. I hope a week from now I don't see newspaper reports of a whole troop of vengeful protoplasmic monsters emerging from the sea to reclaim their lost sibling." Enoch forked the last bit of pancake into his mouth, washed it down with a final sip of coffee, and dug out his wallet to pay for their meal. "Now, if you'll excuse me I'll take my leave. Good luck to you, Dane. I'd watch out, if I were you."

Dane nodded, smiled, and said, "You might want to watch out, too, Enoch."

IV.

That afternoon Enoch drove his pickup into Acadia National Park and left it in a parking lot, walked down to Jordan Pond with its lovely view of the humped twin mountains called the Bubbles, then went on to the Jordan Pond House restaurant, where he sat out on the lawn drinking more coffee and enjoying the popovers the place was famous for. While partaking of this light lunch he wrote notes to friends on several postcards he'd bought in the restaurant's adjacent gift shop. When he was finished, he decided he'd like to hike some more, so he continued along the trail that looped the water's edge, slouch hat clamped on his head and walking stick in hand.

Afternoon advanced, the lowering light slanting in through the trees in dazzling fragments, the air refreshingly brisk. Enoch had hiked a good distance, and thought it best to pick up the pace so as to return to his vehicle and leave the park for his bed and breakfast in Bar Harbor, not wanting to be out in a pitch-black forest when evening fell. He wasn't sure how prevalent they were or where they were dispersed, but he knew there were black bears and bobcats within the park's limits.

Because day was on the wane he encountered fewer people; now, only one couple walking in the opposite direction, and one pair of bicycles shot past him. Even still, several times he was compelled to stop where the trees thinned at the pond's edge, and admire the thousands of small fish that seemed to hang suspended in the clear, clean water.

On one of these occasions when he turned to gaze into the pond, he caught a glimpse of a larger dark form passing below the surface, but decided it must only be a dense shoal of those little fish, or a distortion of the shifting water. He had had the impression of a shark cruising along, but that was impossible in land-locked Jordan Pond.

The artist had walked a bit further on when a burbling disturbance of the water to his side actually startled him, and caused him to stop and study it again. The splashing eruption quickly subsided, but it left him unsettled ... until he realized that this unsettling feeling also had to do with the tickling sensation deep within his right forearm.

Enoch swiftly rolled back his sleeve to see that the black alien matter fused with his flesh had once again extended a tendril, which wiggled in the air like a hair-thin finger—pointing toward the water of Jordan Pond.

"That bastard," Enoch murmured, turning away and hastening his pace along the trail even more. Black bears and bobcats were now the least of his worries.

Ahead of Enoch, from behind a tree, a man stepped onto the trail directly in his path.

With evening imminent, the figure was merely a silhouette, but Enoch knew that tall frame, the sharp shoulders of its expensive black suit, the post-goth spiky hair.

"Sorry, Dane, but I forgot my six-guns today," Enoch said. "Or do you care to duel with paintbrushes?"

The figure did not answer with words. There was, however, another kind of response. A green orb of light opened in the center of its chest. A moment later, several others surfaced across the shadowy form. More and more followed. And yet the figure had not advanced...yet.

"So Dane wanted me to see the intended ending of his show, eh?" Enoch said to the phantom. "His self-portrait. And it's a fitting one—as black as his tiny soul."

Now, at last, the human-like outline took a step forward, but when Enoch raised his walking stick before him it stopped in its tracks.

"Be gone, poor creature," he commanded, using the walking stick like a sorcerer's staff to draw a series of runes in the air, including that which conveyed the "Dragon's Tail." "You don't really have any beef with me. I'm not the one who's enslaved and degraded you, and you know it."

Enoch was certain that the shoggoth cells wired into his own substance added to the potency he needed. And sure enough, the green eyes glowing like a constellation of fungous stars upon the surface of the figure one by one blinked out of existence. Then the featureless obsidian figure turned and dashed into the forest, rather than return to the water of the pond. In the deepening gloom, it instantly slipped from view.

V.

The following evening, in the *Bangor Daily News,* Enoch read that local artist Dane van der Sloot had been discovered dead in his home by a female friend who worked as a researcher at the College of the Atlantic. Nothing had been stolen, apparently, but the home was found in great disorder as if a desperate struggle had taken place from room to room. The artist had been beheaded, but the details of this matter were not divulged, except to say that his head had not yet been recovered.

"Oh how terribly predictable," Enoch sighed, folding the paper away and reclining on the comfy mattress in his room at the bed and breakfast. "You should have admitted it, you sad fool; you just can't compete with me."

After the threat that Dane had directed at him in the park, he felt no sympathy for the artist's fate. In fact, he would have gladly paid admission to attend Dane's final performance: scurrying about his beautiful house like a small white mouse pursued by a starving rat.

Fearless Symmetry

I.

(From the personal journal of Enoch Donovon Coffin)

I was not at all pleased when the journalist from the monthly Boston arts scene magazine—covering my little exhibition—gave a smarmy smile as he suggested that I was patterning myself after Richard Upton Pickman.

The gallery in question is a wee thing located in the narrow brick chasm that is one-way Prince Street, in Boston's North End... just a few small rooms that were once an apartment, their walls painted cream and the floorboards polished to an amber gloss. The gallery owner also owns the Italian restaurant next door, needless to say one of numerous in this neighborhood. I frequent her eatery and her art showings alike, and she has taken a shine to me; hence the invitation to exhibit my own work. She also offered to hang my paintings on the walls of her restaurant—that is, until she viewed my art for the first time and wisely decided against that concept, lest she discourage her clientele's appetite. She's a cute enough little dumpling, but doesn't stir my own appetites.

The young reporter had given his name as Joel Knox, and in answer to his comment—or accusation—I said, "Certainly I have been *inspired* by that artist. But if I've patterned myself after him, then you must also say I've patterned myself after Bosch, Bruegel, Blake, Dali, Giger, Beksinski, Kahlo, Bacon, Ernst, De Chirico, Escher, Kubin, Topor ..."

When he saw that I had no intention of stopping this litany on my own, and particularly since I'm sure the smug little ass didn't recognize half these names, he regurgitated a name he did know. "I'm partial to Pollock, myself."

"Hm," I grunted, "yes ... perhaps the best of the chimpanzee artists."

"Well, I'm sure you have other favorites, but I mention Pickman because the similarities are obvious. Both of you pursuing your work here in the North End. Both of you seeking to shock your audience with extremely grotesque imagery executed in a highly realistic style ..."

I'm sure I winced. "*Shock.* You trivialize my work."

"Oh, but it isn't your intention to be shocking, Mr. Coffin? To be controversial? I'm reminded of an artist I did an article on who patches together maps of the USA and the American flag from bits of human skin, taken from people who donated their bodies in good faith to *science.* But he only uses white people's skin, because it's a statement, you see, on America's sins. He also claims his work is not meant to be incendiary, or sensationalistic." Knox chuckled. "I've never interviewed such a hypocrite. One can't have their cake and eat it, too. Why not just unapologetically admit, 'Yes, you bet, I want people to feel a thrill of revulsion. I want to shock the living shit out of people.' Isn't there more honor in being truthful to oneself, without any pretentious bullshit?"

"I trust you're speaking of this other fellow ... not me," I said calmly.

"Yes, of course. I'm just making a general observation."

"Hm," I said. "I don't know or care about this person you mention, who does sound more calculating than corpse artists such as Witkin and von Hagens—who are, as you say, honest and up front with their morbid and beautiful work. But at the risk of sounding like I'm spouting 'pretentious bullshit,' those who work from a darker palette are always going to be accused by some as merely attempting to draw attention through offensive effects. Is von Hagens' work merely educational? Of course not. Is it meant to provoke? I should think so. Is he having his cake and eating it, too? Maybe. Is that dishonest, or is the work simply functioning on multiple levels? Why not stop putting the artist on trial and focus on the art itself, and what it's saying?"

"Aren't the art and the artist one and the same?"

"Now that's a more provocative question than I might have given you credit for, young man."

"So what is your art saying, Mr. Coffin? Tell me."

"Ask my art, is what I'm telling you. Go on ... commune with it." I waved my arm toward the paintings framed upon the walls around us.

"Are you afraid to just tell me straight what your themes are? Your aesthetic, your motivations and and intentions and inspirations?"

"Ahh," I sighed, "you want me to encapsulate all that into one or two facile lines you can use as a caption beneath a photo of one of my paintings?"

"If I can find a painting of yours the magazine won't be afraid to publish a photograph of." He smirked.

"Well, let's just say I'm a reporter—like you. Does a reporter only impart, 'Today I saw a puppy frolicking in the summer sun?' No. Reporters tell us that blood gurgles in the gutter. That brains slide down the windshield ..."

"No, no, no," Knox cut me off, waving a hand. "We may need to hear that dark events have happened, but we don't always need someone holding those bits of brain under our nose, and then on top of that trying to convince us there's a *beauty* in those brains."

"Well as you can see, I sometimes achieve a visceral effect, though I should hope not even you would dismiss me as a gore-hound. But to me, there is undeniable beauty in the knotted form of the human brain."

"But it's how that brain came to be exposed ... how it's presented ..."

"How indeed. I suppose one is either attuned to terrible beauty or one isn't. Though I should hope you would try to *open* yourself to such beauty."

"I'm open enough to appreciate that your technique is beautiful. Just as Pickman described himself, primarily you're a *realist*. Or at least, you pretend you've seen some of these things you portray."

Now it was my turn to smile. "What makes you think any of these images are pretend?"

For a beat or two the journalist almost looked afraid, as if he were willing to open himself just a little more and believe me, but then up came the protective screen of his grin. "Anyway, so you're sensitive to the comparison with Pickman. It hit a nerve. You want to be known as an individual. Well, not to offend, but I still say it's plain to see. Look at these, for instance!"

He pointed to a nearby pair of oils. The painting on the left was rendered during a trip to Vietnam, extrapolated from a battered old photograph I was shown. It portrays three Viet Cong soldiers glaring back at the viewer, behind them an opening into a tunnel network of the type employed throughout the war. Lying at their feet is a nude albino carcass, shot a number of times. With its canine aspect the corpse suggests a large hairless baboon, and yet the feet appear to be oddly hoof-like. The gallery card accompanying this piece gave its title: *The Tunnel Rat*.

On the right, a painting entitled *The Dig*. The name refers to Boston's disastrous "Big Dig," the costliest highway project in the history of this country, which even resulted in a number of well-publicized deaths. Less well known is that one worker vanished during the project, leaving his family to wonder if he was accidentally buried alive, or if he ran away to start a new life somewhere. My painting depicts a terrified worker in a hardhat being pulled into a rough opening in exposed ancient masonry by several pairs of unnaturally white, simian arms. The faces of his attackers are mostly obscured in the shadows, but their eyes glow like those of hyenas caught in infrared light.

One of the visitors to my exhibition had praised me for my political metaphor … he seemed quite proud that he had gleaned a statement in my painting about the whole Big Dig debacle; its consumption of time, money and blood. I have been accused of cruelty by more than one acquaintance, certainly by more than one lover, but I could not divest this poor chap of his satisfaction, and so I'd thanked him for his insightfulness.

But my current and less enthusiastic companion asked, "These paintings in particular aren't influenced by Pickman?"

Perhaps out of mounting defensiveness I spoke too freely. "They are influenced by my living across the street from Copp's Hill Burying Ground. By living above a system of obsolete tunnels that most people in this city would never suspect the existence of. Pickman did not invent those tunnels, and they and their inhabitants are not his alone to represent."

"*Inhabitants?*" The fellow wagged his head. "Mr. Coffin … I'm not trying to be antagonistic, here, but the similarities between you and Pickman can *not* be denied! Come on now, what else do you have in common with him? I heard he had a strained relationship with his father, who lived in Salem. What was your upbringing like?"

"I can't vouch for what you say about Pickman and his father," I replied evasively. "Of course the father might have been disturbed by his son's art—but then, why would he take possession of such infamous pieces as *Ghoul Feeding* after his son's disappearance? Perhaps you're only speculating unfairly about Mr. Pickman." I took a step closer to the man, and he took a step back, his shoulder nearly brushing one of my framed works. "And it would be unfair, and unwise, to speculate on my own family matters."

"Sorry," Knox stammered, "I didn't mean …" But his words trailed off when he looked over his shoulder, saw the frightful visage of one of my typically outré portraits only inches from his nose, and jerked away from it with a little gasp.

I snorted with amusement. Yes, I had to admit, if only to myself … there is something to be said for the shocking.

That evening when I returned to my nearby house on Charter Street, my encounter with young Joel Knox stuck with me. As if still debating with him in my mind, I thought of Blake's words: "*What immortal hand or eye/Dare frame thy fearful symmetry?*"

If one believes in a Creator, then one must recognize Him as an artist of many terrifying works. Fearful things that one would think He created quite fearlessly.

My young critic was blinded by morals, I felt, and morality has no place in art. Would he object to a painting of a tiger, tiger, burning bright, in the forests of the night? Ah, but a tiger has no morals. A tiger is a work of terrible beauty. Should other creatures that rend and feast on flesh not be considered manifestations of terrible beauty, just because they are more obscure?

The little puke did hit a nerve with me. But not so much about Pickman, as about my own father.

II.

(From the article "Ghoulish Legacies:
The Art of Donovon and Enoch Coffin," by Joel Knox)

I'm sure I never would have been driven to investigate the matter of Enoch Coffin's family had it not been for his hostility about the subject, at the scene of his exhibition. The next day I returned to Prince Street, but this time to interview the gallery's owner, Marie Lavoria. I met her over espresso in her small but noteworthy restaurant, Ristorante Lavoria, next door to the gallery. Owing to the shocking (yes, I said it, *shocking*) quality of Coffin's work, I was curious as to why this wholesome-seeming woman should be such a supporter. When she spoke of him in glowing—bordering on gushing—terms, I suspected that the attraction might extend beyond the art to the artist himself. Ms. Lavoria didn't seem to be so intimate with Coffin as to possess great detail on his upbringing, but there were a few tantalizing tidbits she had learned in conversation with her newfound friend, and in her enthusiasm she innocently gave them up to this fellow "fan" of her hero's work.

She said, "When I told Enoch my father was a mason who dabbled in sculpture, thus inspiring my own interest in art, he told me his father Donovon Coffin was a very gifted stained-glass artisan, whose work could be found in churches and private homes throughout New England. He also crafted beautiful glass lampshades in the fluid Art Nouveau style, but also the more linear and symmetrical Art Deco style. He was a great admirer of the stained-glass work of Frank Lloyd Wright. Enoch said his father was always experimenting with style and technique, and achieved some very striking and original effects."

"How fascinating that the senior Coffin was also an artist, then,"

I replied, "but one who pursued more beautiful modes of expression. I wonder what went wrong with the son that he took on such a darker outlook."

"Well," said Ms. Lavoria, as if hesitating to add to her revelation, "Donovon's church work was always praised for its execution, but there was some controversy about the subject matter he chose, which was apparently often a bit gruesome. John the Baptist's severed head presented to Herod on a platter ... St. Bartholomew flayed alive, with his own skin draped over his arm ... St. Sebastian almost erotically pierced with arrows ... and of course, explicitly bloody depictions of the Savior in His sufferings. Enoch said that children looking up at some of these artworks burst into tears and thereafter refused to return to church, and even some adults complained at being unnerved the way light would glow weirdly in the eyes of various figures. There were even complaints, maybe unfounded but maybe not, that there was hidden imagery—I guess you might compare it to subliminal imagery—such as demonic faces leering from seemingly innocent designs. More than once Donovon was asked to remove and substitute one of his creations, and as his reputation started to become tainted, increasingly his artworks were outright refused. Finally, he stopped getting church commissions, making just enough of a living off his other work."

"How fascinating. I guess the apple didn't fall far from the tree, after all. So where did the elder Coffin grow up and ply his trade?"

"Oh—in the very same house on Charter Street that Enoch lives in today."

III.

(From the personal journal of Donovon Abraham Coffin)

I am home again, after my demeaning incarceration. If there were any chances of me fashioning windows for a church in Massachusetts again, my arrest has exploded them.

Fools. They of course thought I meant to rob that grave in the Copp's Hill Burying Ground, across the street from my own abode. Rob it! Rob it of what? A handful of dust? But I couldn't tell them the truth, could I? That there are tunnels below the graveyard, a whole ant's nest of tunnels through this area of the city, in which those hungry *others* dwell. I couldn't reveal the truth about that old blue slate, with its image of a winged angel of death seated on a block bearing the words *Memento Mori,* a scythe

166

in one hand and the other pointing downwards. Yes, pointing down *there*—a hidden sign, like those I incorporate in my own glasswork, so as to communicate with the perceptive and sensitive explorers of this world who are not satisfied by the spiritual pabulum they feed the sheep, those sheep I terrify with their own blood-drenched faith! No, I knew that figure pointing at the earth was a signpost left by a kindred soul. I knew that there was no body in that plot to be robbed! Had they not interrupted me, I would have revealed a hidden trapdoor, perhaps taking me into a section of the tunnels walled off from the rest, with steps leading down further … maybe even leading me to what I seek!

A door into the Dreamlands.

No, I had to lie, of course. I told them I sought a skull to use as a model in my art, for a piece portraying Mary Magdalene contemplating a skull after the manner of Gustave Doré. Ha. They seemed to buy my explanation, though it didn't enhance their feelings toward me, and they warned that if I were caught at such activities again I'd be shipped off to Danvers State Hospital.

This is why I must resist my compulsion to locate a secret passage in the cemetery again. I must at least wait until a sufficient period of time has passed, as frustrating as that may be.

But ah! I am making progress with my very own Dream Lens, I feel, and may not need a prosaic trapdoor at all. If my efforts are rewarded, I will be able to see into the Dreamlands at will!

And not only see, but in seeing, part the veils and open a portal—so that I might pass bodily into that other realm as the Ghouls themselves do.

IV.

(From the personal journal of Enoch Donovon Coffin)

It was a beautiful afternoon for a stroll in the graveyard, with the lowering sun glowing through the overhanging autumnal foliage, painted leaves scuffed up by our feet and swirling about our shoulders like fiery infernal ash. Marie Lavoria must have felt it was quite the romantic setting indeed. I kept my paws in the pockets of my suede jacket lest she try to hold my hand.

We stopped every now and then to read the inscription on this or that slate, tilting in their rows in the Copp's Hill Burying Ground. Marie smiled and reached up to me, and I nearly flinched away, but she merely plucked a leaf that had alighted on the brim of my slouch hat. She then squatted down before a headstone so as to read its engraved script.

"*Sacred to the memory of Miss Mercy Jones ... Aged 20 and 6 months.*"

"How specific. But when you die at so young an age, I suppose one need be grateful for a few extra months."

"Yes—so young. I wonder if she ever got to experience love." Marie rose and again smiled up into my face. "How about you, Enoch? Have you ever experienced love?"

"I experience love every day."

She raised her eyebrows.

"The love of my art," I went on. "I'm afraid it leaves me little room for other forms."

She looked a bit crestfallen, and said, "But I've seen you in the company of a number of different people in my restaurant." She was polite enough not to mention she had observed me in the company of both genders, and then some.

"My name is Enoch, not Eunuch, my dear." I winked. "When one is hungry, one must dine. A restaurateur must understand that."

Marie blushed a little and looked away, but she was also smiling again. "I understand that hunger," she admitted, no doubt still holding on to the hope that she and I might share a special feast of our own one of these days.

We continued strolling, and she asked, "What about your parents? You never felt the urge to marry, as they did? Surely your father loved your mother."

"He did indeed. He loved her so that it split his heart."

"Really?" My companion came to a halt again, intrigued. "Is that why you're afraid to love?"

"I said nothing of fear. But perhaps I'm reluctant to be distracted by the pain or pleasure of such conventional pursuits, when I have my calling to attend to."

"But how was your father hurt? Did your mother pass away at a young age?"

"Lebanah Coffin was a beautiful creature. He portrayed her in his glasswork numerous times, and she even graces a few churches ... as an angel. She was an albino, with flowing white hair and skin white as a blank canvas, and uncanny eyes with pink irises. Her feet were deformed, however. They could be said to have resembled the feet of Chinese women who had bound their feet tightly for too many years. One might say they were even ... hoof-like."

"Oh! From an injury?"

"A congenital deformity," I replied. "Yes ... something in her *genes.*" Ah, if only my innocent friend understood the full ramifications of such a genetic lineage!

"So what happened? Did she leave him for another man?"

"She did leave him, yes, but to follow her destiny. It was time for her to *change.*"

"Change? You mean, she felt she needed to discover herself?"

"Something like that."

"But she left you, too! Her only child!"

"She had no choice. She didn't want to hurt me, or my father."

"I don't understand."

I began walking again, and Marie was forced to hurry to catch up to me. "I suppose I seek her in my art at times," I mumbled. More to myself, really. "But it wasn't enough for my father to immortalize her beauty in his own art. He sought to find her again. His dream was that he might join her somehow."

The key word—the word that surely escaped poor mystified Marie—being *dream* ...

V.

(From the article "Ghoulish Legacies:
The Art of Donovon and Enoch Coffin," by Joel Knox)

I was very happy that I returned to Ristorante Lavoria for lunch after another visit to Enoch Coffin's latest exhibition, in the course of researching this article. Not only was the fare excellent, but I met Marie Lavoria again and she had some fresh material to share regarding her favorite artist's childhood. The sad matter of his abandonment by his mother when he was just a wee sprout, and the father's apparent obsession with her.

"Sounds like maybe she had some issues," Ms. Lavoria confided in a whisper, tapping her temple with a finger. "Oh, but please, don't quote me on that ... I wouldn't want to hurt Enoch."

"Of course," I assured her.

I was more intrigued than ever, and now determined to interview Coffin again before I put this piece together. To that end, I phoned the man via the number Ms. Lavoria provided. Even though she cautioned that the artist shunned the telephone, he picked up when he heard my voice. I asked him if I might interview him in his own home, so as to view his studio and more examples of his art.

"Of course," Coffin said. "When would you like?"

"Well, you live on Charter Street, correct? I'm just a short ways away, here on Prince Street. I could walk right on over if you're available."

"Certainly, please do. I'll put a pot of coffee on."

VI.

(From the personal journal of Donovon Abraham Coffin)

Many have fleetingly and flittingly visited the realm called the Dreamlands—naturally, in dream—but did not remember afterwards, or did not appreciate what they had experienced if they did retain a fragment of remembrance. But there are those adepts who have reached the Dreamlands purposely, intentionally questing, by projecting their essence while in a hypnotic state or meditative self-entrancement. They descended the seventy steps to the cavern of flame. And I have tried to find those steps … oh yes, I've tried. Yet my talent doesn't lie in lucid dreaming, or astral projection. My talent lies in my love of art, a love I have sought to instill in the mind of my young son. He is all I have left of my darling wife. I will not be content with that, however, so long as my art might serve me.

My Lebanah was more knowledgeable in arcane matters than I, more attuned to them, but we had learned some things together, and since her departure I have furthered those studies on my own. Driven no longer merely by a sense of curiosity as an artist—an artistic curiosity as scientific as it was mystical—but now by a desperation of the spirit. So I have learned what I could, wherever and however I could, with a kind of *violence* of need.

Oh, I would be lying if I said I only want to find my way again to my beloved's side. I am forever an artist-seeker. How could I not dream of creating artworks modeled—from *life*—after the blank-faced wheeling Night-gaunts … the strangely leaping Ghasts? And in the background, the looming Tower of Koth? Those oversensitive hypocrites who no longer want my work casting its multi-hued light into their silly hovels of worship have no idea that if I had my way, those windows would not portray tortured saints but Gugs with fanged vertical grins! Titanic, winged Shantaks!

Yes, as a pilgrim of the Dreamlands I know my Lebanah has changed … transformed as does the butterfly to fulfill her true nature. But though her beauty has altered, I am sure it has altered to a beauty of another sort. A terrible beauty.

Yet I have not sought her by literally venturing into the tunnels below these streets, where the dangers are too acute and the rewards too limited. That nesting place is only the intermediary zone between here and the Ghouls' true home. And it is *that* place of wonders I seek.

In my seeking, I had encountered rumors that in the Sesqua Valley, in the Pacific Northwest, there was a Dream Lens secreted in the basement of an old home, a lens that had been guarded by generations of one family. A great lens that allowed one to peer directly into the Dreamlands. Yes! This I must see, and duplicate with all my skills! So I ventured to that strange valley, to the town situated in the shadows of twin-peaked Mount Selta, a town where the veils are thin the way they are in a place like Arkham or Dunwich. But my quest proved fruitless. The weird locals with their silvery eyes and, often, suggestively deformed countenances mistrusted me … professed to know nothing of any such Dream Lens. I begged, bribed, even threatened, all to no avail.

I did not return to Massachusetts with a sense of defeat, however, but only a new determination.

If I could not copy the alleged Sesquan Dream Lens, then I would design one all my own.

VII.

(From the article "Ghoulish Legacies:
The Art of Donovon and Enoch Coffin," by Joel Knox)

Coffin greeted me quite cordially at his door facing onto the old North End street, and admitted me into his narrow little home. Not unexpectedly, I was immediately struck by the décor, though to go into it at length would require another article all its own. Suffice it to say I was surprised to find that the grotesque—though certainly in evidence, and very grotesque—did not outweigh the beautiful, and he really does seem to be a man of diverse, eclectic tastes. Though how much of the décor could be credited to him, as opposed to the parents who owned the house before him, I couldn't then gauge.

Noting my fascination and occasional revulsion as I took in my surroundings, he proceeded to conduct a little tour for me. In the comfortable parlor with its leather furniture and overflowing bookshelves, amongst his own paintings hanging on the walls—some of which I can't imagine any gallery in the city would consent to display, nor any sane person wish to purchase—I spotted a painting that was unmistakably the work of Richard Upton Pickman. Unsurprisingly, it presented a number of ghastly nude figures with distended dog-like features, white-skinned and blotchy with greenish mold or infection, clambering out of a freshly dug grave in what was clearly the Copp's Hill Burying Ground. The title, I read, was *A New Doorway.* I grinned at Coffin. "I see a Pickman here, but nothing by any of those other heroes you listed for me at the gallery."

"Actually, it was my father who acquired that piece," Coffin revealed.

"And he must have done these, himself," I observed, sweeping my arm toward the room's two windows, both of which were of brilliantly colored stained glass. For the first time I focused my full attention on them, and was quite frankly stunned when I did. Perhaps I'm not sufficiently familiar with this craft, but I didn't know such complex work was possible. One of them was so intricately ordered and symmetrical I was put in mind of the mirrored view through a kaleidoscope. The other was a swirling chaos like thorny nebulae that reminded me somehow of a fractal image. Looking too long at either one of them brought on a kind of dizziness, or vertigo, as if I might plunge through them into a cosmic void from which I might not return. At last I had to look away, muttering inarticulately, "Remarkable."

A circuit of the ground floor alone was already too much to take in, but my host let me catch my breath by inviting me to sit at a dining room table for coffee. I asked him, "Do you live here alone?"

"Except for my friends." He waved at a nearby credenza, on the marble top of which stood a bizarre array of objects, including a limbless anatomical model made of wax with intricately painted internal organs, a pallid heart (dog? pig? human?) preserved in a block of Lucite with a tangle of long black worms emerging from its split sides, a deformed human fetus with strangely fish-like features crammed in a bottle of alcohol, and a coiled snake rearing its head inside a bottle of yellowish fluid.

I pointed to the last item. "Is that drinkable?" I asked.

"That's a matter of opinion. It's a cobra preserved in rice wine. I picked it up in Vietnam."

"What does it taste like?"

"It tastes like a cobra preserved in rice wine. Care for a glass?"

"I'll stick to the coffee, thanks." I watched the artist dump spoonful after spoonful of sugar into his own cup. "Have a little coffee with your sugar," I joked.

Coffin smiled at me oddly. "Amusing. I've never heard that joke before."

"Sorry," I chuckled. "I'm sure you haven't."

"I see you brought your laptop."

"I had it with me earlier; I like to write on the run. In coffee shops and so forth."

"And in Italian restaurants?"

"Hm?"

"After you called, our mutual friend Marie Lavoria rang me and admitted rather sheepishly that you had been interviewing her about my family. Silly girl even gave you my phone number and precise street address." Coffin had been stirring his coffee now for an unusually long time, though maybe it was just to dissolve the unusual quantity of sugar. "I can't be angry with her ... she's innocent to the point of ignorance ... though I did gently suggest that she should be less free with information I might share with her, in the future."

"Well, I know you sort of suggested at the gallery that you would rather I didn't speculate on your family ..."

"I don't think I 'sort of' suggested that; I thought I was quite clear."

"But I'm not speculating, Mr. Coffin. I'm here to ask you straight out. Tell me about your father, Donovon Coffin. Tell me about his art, and how it influenced you. You can deny Pickman all you want, but denying your father's hand in what you do—"

"Would you like to see?" he cut me off.

"Hm?"

"See his art studio for yourself. My own studio is in the attic, and we can look at that, too, of course. But since you're unrelenting on this topic, I'd rather tell you about him myself than have you pry around clumsily and assemble an inaccurate or unbalanced story. Thus, if you are so determined, let me show you what remains of my father's workplace." Coffin drained his coffee, including the sugary sludge at the bottom, and clinked the cup down in its saucer. "His studio was in the basement."

VIII.

(From the personal journal of Enoch Donovon Coffin)

I led my guest to the door to the cellar, but with my hand on the knob I turned to face him. "Before I show you my father's workplace, and the culmination of all his skills and efforts—a caveat."

"Which is?"

"You're on a path to investigate my father, and so it's inevitable that in digging deeper you'll uncover certain facts. Certain ... unsavory, scandalous stories. As I say, I fear that in focusing on these details in your article— taking them out of context, exhibiting them in unfair proportion—you'll besmirch my father's name. And, by extension, my own. But it's more a matter of a son's loyalty than an artist's pride. Otherwise I might not share with you the thing that I've decided to reveal. I entrust this experience to you so that you might see my father less as a madman, and more as the tainted genius he truly was."

"I appreciate that you're willing to give me a broader understanding of your father, so I agree to treat him fairly in my article."

What a sincere look he gave me. Did I believe him? Not fully, I'm afraid, but all I could do was try to impress upon him my strongly-felt desires. If I couldn't stop him, I must at least try to educate him. But this family matter touched a vulnerable place in me, one I do not easily share, and I'm not sure if he understood the level of anger I was forcing myself to restrain. I do not like feeling vulnerable or angry, emotions that amount to a loss of self control, and yet I felt myself holding back growling fury like a dog straining at its leash.

"Before we descend, I'll tell you what you'd soon enough discover on your own. My father, for all his brilliant efforts, wasn't satisfied with the outcome of his experiments. One night he stole into the Copp's Hill Burying Ground, to a plot he felt bore a secret message inscribed in its slate, and began digging in the earth there. Despite the late hour, he was spotted and arrested. He had been arrested briefly for the same crime, once before. This time he was incarcerated at that sprawling monstrosity, the Danvers State Hospital. Father suffered a complete breakdown there. He began to only eat meat … and then, begged for only uncooked meat. He stopped communicating with words, just howled and growled like a wild beast."

"Oh my … well, uh, I'm sorry," my guest stammered uncomfortably.

"On one occasion he attacked an orderly, biting him quite badly on the face and neck. They put him on certain antipsychotic drugs, and eventually these seemed to be effective. Maybe that caused the staff to become lax in their attention, because ultimately my father escaped from the hospital … and disappeared. There is no official record of his fate beyond that."

"Oh! My God, that's … wow." Then the word "official" obviously sank in. "The authorities never learned his fate, but do *you* know where he ended up? What happened to him?"

I turned the knob, and opened the basement door on its old squealing hinges. "This way," I instructed, starting down the stairs.

I led Knox into the basement of my little house, the former house of my parents, with its ceiling of old exposed beams and walls of red brick squeezing out a cake frosting of crumbling mortar. Immediately his attention became focused on the bizarre display featured at the center of the largest room. Overlooked were the various sturdy wooden tables, and the large light table with its milky glass top, upon which my father had worked his craft. The young man also seemed to overlook my own spare easel, which I had left set up here, for I did not exclusively work within my studio in the attic. He was so distracted, he didn't even acknowledge the unfinished painting propped upon that easel.

He also didn't appear to notice the axe leaning against one brick wall, in case of emergencies. I abhor guns.

"What was this thing originally ... a well?" Knox asked, walking tentatively around the low stone base rising from the cement floor.

"While other families in this neighborhood long ago paid people to cover over the openings in their basements—especially after strange rumors of attacks and disappearances—my father actually paid workmen to remove the heavy cap from this ancient well. He had already built his Dream Lens, as he called this construction, so he and the workmen then fastened it in place over the opening." I didn't add that my father had directed the operation to take place quickly, before anything below might come through.

Knox was in the process of taking in the construction that I had called the Dream Lens. It was a convex hemisphere, a web of lead that held in place many individual sections of glass of various sizes and colors, in totality forming no obvious pattern. The hues were subdued, however, not bright primary colors as one would expect in a stained glass composition. Faint, sickly-looking tints of gray and amber and sepia, absinthe green and urine yellow and ghostly blue.

In addition, around the perimeter of the lens were a number of apparatuses on hinged arms. Some looked like magnifying glasses, others like telescopes. Several were strong lamps, with differently colored filters over them to change the tincture of their beams, though presently none of them were turned on.

"Father tried various combinations of color ... of magnification. Different types of crystal for the lenses. And of course, different sorts of spells to imbue the device with outré potency."

Knox looked up at me, his expression torn between admiration for my father's craftsmanship and revulsion at this seeming monument to his insanity. "To achieve *what*?"

"Enoch? Enoch, are you down there?" called a familiar voice from the head of the stairs.

Oh Gawd, when would I learn to lock my front door?

"Is that Marie Lavoria?" the journalist asked.

"Yes," I sighed. "Let me go up there and see what the silly wench wants."

"Mind if I stay here and get down some impressions while they're fresh?" The man had carried his precious laptop downstairs with him, under his arm. He placed it on one of the work benches and opened it.

"Yes, go ahead. I'll explain the Dream Lens … perhaps … when I return. I may even let you look through it, on one more condition. That you do not report what you see through it."

"What?"

"If I should permit you to experience my father's achievements, you must swear to me on your word of honor you will not reveal what the Dream Lens can do, nor what you see."

"But … I don't understand."

"Enoch? I hear you down there!" Marie called, sounding agitated. "Please!"

I groaned, and gestured at Knox's portable contraption. "Just play with your toy and I'll be back in two shakes of a Night-gaunt's tail."

"A … what?"

But I left him to attend to my other unwanted guest.

Apparently not content with having admitted to me over the phone that she had spoken with Joel Knox about my parents, Marie had come to apologize in person, bearing the gifts of a bottle of Pinot Noir and a box of the Sicilian cannoli she knew I adored. And no doubt, she hoped, the gift of her own voluptuous self. To spare her further guilt, or perhaps out of some vague premonition, I didn't reveal to her that the writer was at that moment tapping away at his computer in my very own cellar. I sent her away as quickly as I was able to extricate myself from her moist eyes and babbled apologies, which wasn't quickly enough to suit me. Naturally I accepted the wine and cannoli, to placate her, and with thoughts of sharing them politely with the arrogant brat in my basement—to which I finally returned.

IX.

(From the personal journal of Donovon Abraham Coffin)

I have failed in parting the veils, but not utterly. That is to say, I have not opened a gash through which my embodied consciousness might enter into the Dreamlands—the realm of my beloved. But with my sleeve, so to speak, I have cleaned dirt from the windowpanes of reality. I am sure I have peered into the Dreamlands, but into other planes as well, which I had not intended to gaze upon. Different panels of glass, in conjunction with a variety of incantations and sigils traced in the air, have yielded different results. They are but murky, fleeting visions. One might think they had only imagined they'd seen something, or misinterpreted what they did see. The additional instruments help focus the images somewhat, enlarge or clarify them. I have to angle the lamps just so. And then, if the fates are kind, I am peeping through a keyhole …

Who could consider this a failure? I will admit with all humility it is brilliance, even when it is accidental brilliance (for what artist isn't well acquainted with, and reliant upon, pure serendipity?). But it is not the goal I seek.

… Even as I marvel at the barely discernible yet heart-clenching sight of a prowling shape tall as a mountain, a silhouette against the stars, its twin dog-like heads surmounted by headgear like a bishop's miter—surely a scene of the Dreamlands.

… Even as, holding my breath lest I jiggle the scope just a fraction and banish the image, I spy upon a herd of amorphous black hulks congregated about an underground lake, constellations of green eyes blinking in and out of existence across their heaving, pulsing forms.

… Even when, through another of the colored windows, acting like a television screen receiving transmissions from some other dimension, I watch a swarm of arthropod beings glide through the infinity of space, their ribbed wings spread wide like sails.

The cosmos itself taunts me, as if to say: "You think the matters of your puny human heart have any significance in the face of *all this?*"

But more men than I have suffered under the magnificence of the stars, for there is a cosmos just as vast inside our puny human hearts!

These glimpses of alien vistas are failures, I say. Magical, miraculous failures the likes of which other men would sell their souls to achieve. But these visions do not put me in my lover's arms!

There has been one serendipitous outcome, however, that granted me an especially remarkable gift. It may be the closest I come to my goal. It may have to suffice … oh, though the word "suffice" rakes its claws through my soul!

I was gazing through the hexagonal green pane, as viewed through the brass spyglass and with the pale green filter fitted on the nearest lamp. And down there in the tunnel, three figures scuttled into view. Pale as creatures that had never known the light. Naked and furtive, and gazing back at me with wary curiosity. But they were beautiful! They were humans! They were more beautiful than humans … beautiful as *gods!* And one of them—yes!—one of them was my very own Lebanah!

They peered up at me only a few moments, then shifted position as they meant to scurry away into the tunnel again. I shifted, too, before they could flee. I wanted to call out to her! Tears welled in my eyes!

It wasn't the tears distorting my vision, though, that accounted for the change in what I saw. It was moving to another panel of glass that did it—this one the amber octagon. Through this pane, the effect was entirely different.

Before they disappeared into the darkness of their honeycomb beneath the city, I saw the three figures in their true form. This time, the green blotches of mold on their white flesh. Their animal-like countenances. Their glowing feral eyes.

I fell against the Dream Lens, embracing it with my spread arms, wracked with sobs.

"Come back!" I sobbed. "Come back! Let me see you a minute longer!"

Why didn't she stay, so that I might gaze upon her at greater length? Does she love her tribe more than me, now?

No, I don't think that's it. The thing is, she doesn't realize I unwittingly imparted this occult attribute to one section of glass. She doesn't realize that through it, I can see her and her fellows as they once were.

She is ashamed that I should see her as she is now.

But she must come back—she must! For I am a failure … a failure … and a view of my darling through the keyhole is all that I have left of her. This illusion, this lie, this teasing memory.

No! I will not let that suffice.

Even if I have to return to Copp's Hill with my shovel, and again seek my path through the realm of the worms.

X.

(From the personal journal of Enoch Donovon Coffin)

When I reentered my basement, it was to be confronted with a tableau that was for a moment too much to process. Multiple details clamored for my attention. There was Joel Knox's laptop computer, open on one of the work tables with its screen glowing and covered in text: his article in progress. Not far from that, also open upon the same table, was my father's journal, and I cursed myself for forgetting that I had left it there.

I had left the Dream Lens' lamps turned off, but I saw that one of them had been switched on … the one with a green filter, positioned above one particular panel of glass that was also tinted pale green, and hexagonal in shape.

When he had first circled the Dream Lens, examining it, Knox must have noticed that at its base the dome was hinged on one side, and locked in place with two bolts on the other. I knew he had noted this feature, because the Dream Lens now stood open like a large hatch. Knox had undone its bolts, which I myself had never dared attempt.

Finally, there was Knox himself, standing before the opened hatch defiantly and gripping the long handle of my axe.

"You evil son of a bitch!" he spat.

"I am something of a son of a bitch, in ways you may not know, but I'd advise you to clear away from that hatch and let me lock it again."

"The hell I will, you bastard!"

"What are you saying, Knox? I tell you, move away from that opening!"

"I read a little of your father's diary. All insanity. There, I said it—*insanity!* An insanity you've clearly inherited. But I thought I'd have a look anyway … and that's when I saw your prisoner!"

"My … prisoner?"

"How long have you had that poor girl in that pit, you psychopath? I'm going to call the police down here and get that wretched creature out of there!"

Terrible awareness had dawned, and I took a step toward the young journalist. "Knox, get away from there!"

"No!" He brandished the axe threateningly. "One more step and I'll put this in your skull!" His eyes were wild. "You imprisoned her so she could model for you, huh?" He nodded toward my painting on its easel. At some point he had noticed it, after all. But one thing he hadn't done was call the police already. His cell phone was still in the pocket of his jacket, which he had left upstairs in my parlor.

"Knox!" I shouted.

"All your noble talk about art," he raged. "Now I understand you, and your sick father, too!" He demanded: "What did you intend to do to her when the painting was complete? Kill her? Chop her up with this axe? *Eat* her, you monster?"

I lunged forward then, in an attempt to seize the axe's handle and grapple for it.

I was too late. I don't know if the creature sprang upward on its own, or if another one or two of its kind gave it a boost, but I saw a pair of unnaturally white, simian arms like those I had rendered in my painting *The Dig* reach up from below and grasp Knox's ankles. He was wrenched off his feet, falling in such a way that his belly slammed hard against the rim of the hatchway. The force of impact caused him to let go of the axe, which clattered to the floor. He scrabbled to hold on to the rim, and for a moment his eyes locked on mine in a horror so profound I wish I had captured it in a photograph. I would have loved to paint it.

Then, he was dragged below, and I heard a frenzy of high-pitched screaming, and the deeper tones of savage snarling. Finally, the shrieks gave way to a ghastly gurgling, as one hears from a man choking on his own blood.

I scooped up the axe, dreading that I might have to use it, but the beast below was satisfied with its prey and didn't make a second leap. I took hold of the lifted hatchway and eased it back down to its base, then shoved the two strong bolts in place.

I fell away from the Dream Lens, panting. As infuriated as I had been with my guest, I hadn't wanted *this* to happen. If he had sworn himself to secrecy, I had thought to tantalize the writer with a glimpse into the Dreamlands, or one of the other alien worlds my father's device could penetrate, but I hadn't planned on showing him the creatures that dwell below these streets. Perhaps the familiar, tinted light of the lamp had attracted them. Attracted *her*.

Having regained my composure, I went to bend over the fellow's computer and read the last words he had written:

'… *if you are so determined, let me show you what remains of my father's workplace." Coffin drained his coffee, including the sugary sludge at the bottom, and clinked the cup down in its saucer. "His studio was in the basement."*'

"Sugary sludge," I muttered. "Ever the disapproving wretch, this one."

I turned from the device, and went to the Dream Lens. I reached out to switch off the lamp with the green filter over its bulb, but I could not resist the imp of the perverse and brought my eye close to the spyglass on its jointed arm. Through its quartz lens, I gazed through the green-tinted hexagonal panel and thus into the ancient brick tunnel below.

She was still there, her slender nude figure crouched over a torn scarecrow that had once been a man. Thankfully, in this light the blood appeared black, but there was much black. Sensing me above, she tilted up her face to peer back at me. I was struck, as always, by the impossibly beautiful face that my father had long ago fallen in love with. The face he had given to angels in the stained glass windows of churches throughout New England. Her long white hair wild in her face, and her lips and chin smeared with glistening blackness.

Minus the blood, it was identical to the face of my oil portrait in progress.

"Oh, Mother," I admonished her sadly.

XI.

(From the personal journal of Donovon Abraham Coffin)

Failure, and failure again. But I have succeeded, at least, in escaping from their madhouse and returning here. Yet how much longer can I evade them? They may have already come here looking for me, and will no doubt do so again. Therefore, I haven't much time.

My dear son Enoch has been in the care of his aunts. I trust those spinster sisters will raise him well. They love art, and books, and I'm sure they will nurture him. I hope they will see that this journal reaches his hands.

Yes, I hope you are reading this, my beloved son.

I am proud of you. The proudest moment of my life, apart from my wedding day and the day you were born, was when I came down into the basement and found you had switched on one of the lamps of the Dream Lens. With a pad and pencil, you were sketching a flock of weird, crab-like beings with membranous wings soaring through the place between stars. You looked startled and ashamed, but I reassured you. Of course, I forbade you from looking into the Dream Lens unattended again—until you were ready—but my praise for your drawing was sincere. It was remarkable! You will be the artist I wish I had been. You will succeed where I could not.

Forgive me for abandoning you, my son, but I hope you understand my love for your mother. If I cannot use the Dream Lens to join her in the Dreamlands as a fellow citizen of that realm, then I will lift the Lens aside and descend bodily into the brick and mortar labyrinth below.

If I cannot join your mother's pack, then what I want is for her to dismantle me with her own hands ... consume me with her own teeth ... digest me in her own belly until we are conjoined. Until I am part of her ... one with her ... forever.

(Note: Joel Knox's proposed magazine article, "Ghoulish Legacies: The Art of Donovon and Enoch Coffin," remains unfinished and unpublished. —EC)

Unto the Child of Woman

"By faith Enoch was translated that he should not see death;
And was not found, because God had translated him …"
—HEBREWS 11:5

The New England artist considered the sun over Sesqua Valley with an artist's eye, astonished that he had never witnessed such a sun, its radiance so soft yet compelling, its warmth so gentle. He didn't feel the need to squint his eyes as he regarded it and half-fancied that he was seeing something new or alien, an antique globe of fire observed through a different kind of atmosphere than he had ever known. He sucked in the sweetly-scented air of the valley, the air that was another new sensation. Never had sun and aether seemed so seductive. Never had the verdant shade of woodland felt so cool and soothing on his eyes. He sat upon a boulder, his shirt removed so that his torso could bathe in balmy breeze, and sketched onto the pad that rested on his knee. Examining once more the twin-peaked mountain of white stone, he was astonished by its eerie sentience; for it struck his imagination that the titan of rock was more than mountain, that it was some slumbering god that would eventually reawaken so as to stretch its wings over the valley and darken the realm with magnificent unholy shadow.

"What are you doing there?"

"What does it look like? I'm sketching," was the abrupt reply, for the artist did not like to be interrupted as he worked. A figure moved before him and blocked his view of Mount Selta. "Move your ass."

"I think not, sirrah." Although the figure faced the sun, the artist could not see its face, which was hidden beneath a hat's wide rim; but then the gentleman lifted his head a little and smiled at the expression of horror on the other fellow's face. Simon Gregory Williams never tired of the effect that his bestial countenance had on those humans who first glimpsed it.

But then his smile faded, replaced by a look of sudden interest. He sniffed. "You have been tainted by the Outside."

"What?" Simon pointed to the large black mole on the artist's arm. "Oh, that. Yeah, remnant of shoggoth tissue. I guess I'm stuck with it for life."

Simon snuffled a second time. "It has altered your corporeal components. You may be surprised at how long a life you live."

"You're a poet, right? No? Your speech has a lyrical ring. Well, I'd like to return to my sketch, if that's okay with you."

"It is not. Selta does not like to have her image reproduced. I must ask you to desist, Mr.—"

"Enoch Coffin, how d'ya do?"

"Coffin? The son of Donovon Abraham Coffin? Well, how fascinating. Truly, you follow in your sire's footsteps. And you're an artist as well. Well."

"Well what, buddy? Yeah, he was my father."

"He came here asking some rather curious questions—about an antique lens that was a doorway to the Dreamlands. Rather ironic."

Enoch bent to place his pen and pad into his leather satchel, and then he grabbed his shirt and stood. "How was it ironic, mister?"

"Ah—Simon Gregory Williams, your servant." He bowed slightly. "Yes, quite incongruous. He wouldn't tell us where he had garnered his information concerning certain aspects of this valley—we like to know such things and murther the source, you see; and so, naturally, we told him nothing. I could ascertain, from things he spilled in frustrated babbling, that he was a keen student of arcane matters, and yet he was so absorbed by his obsession that he could not detect the gateway beneath his very nose! Are you an adept as well?"

"Proficient in alchemy? Yep."

"Then perhaps you have read that there are two earthly spots at which the world of mortality touches the realm of dream? No? Again, so like your sire; for there is indeed a gateway unto the Dreamlands, sequestered within our woodland divine. You're from Boston, as was he? Well, there is more irony yet; for it was another artist from your region who found our local gateway and thus entered into the Dreamlands in years bygone." The tall man moved at last, walking slowly away as he muttered in an offhand fashion, "I have a window by your father at my hut."

"You *what?* Show it to me immediately!"

"Sirrah, you are presumptuous. I never shew anyone my home." He then lifted his head a little to observe the sun. "And yet—and yet, when the sun is at this height, and its beams pierce through the trees and alight on the window just at this hour—oh, the fantastic array! Ah, the fairy colors!"

Enoch clamped his satchel between his knees and put on his shirt. "Please show me. You cannot know what it means to me." He straightened up, and the beast of Sesqua Valley saw the way the mortal's eyes were glistening.

"How long are you in town?"

"Until Marceline tires of me."

"Marceline Dubois? Ah, she has engaged you in sexual rites. Excellent, in this season of the Black Goat with a Thousand Young. You are a singular young fellow. I shall make you a proposition, as I presume that you paint as well as sketch. I shall allow you to enter my abode, and you will paint my portrait. Agreed? Excellent. Come, follow me."

"Lead me where thou wilt, O Lord."

Cynically, Simon curled his lips. "How perspicacious of you, for I *am* the lord of this realm. Come, sirrah, before we lose this light."

The artist followed the beast down a road, across a small meadow and into the woods, and then things got a little weird. Enoch's senses became overloaded with sensations, and he had to pause one moment and get his bearings. Simon's soft laughter floated to him. "You are indeed in tune with supernatural forces. I can see in your eyes that they have consumed of weird words, and that awful tissue on your arm has mutated a portion of your essence in a wonderful way. You have a singular future ahead of you, long and adventurous. Did your father work in glass only?"

"Yes."

"And where is he now, your sire?"

"Don't know." This was not entirely a lie.

"I imagine he found a way into the Dreamlands, as some rare mortals do. It must be a fascinating adaptation, for human blood and breath are alien elements there and need transmogrification—just as wandering this woodland requires a subtle alteration in the few mortals that are allowed to walk within it. You can probably feel the change on your eyes and in your flow of blood. We are almost there."

They came at last on a place where the trees were not so thick, thus allowing the sun to shine on the circle of bare earth on which a small cottage sat. Enoch observed the few painted stones that were grouped suggestively at one place and was reminded of a similar group of stones he had seen in a yard in Kingsport. He walked up to a small stained-glass window and touched his hand to its surface.

"Nay, come inside, lad—'tis more effective when viewed with the sun shining through it. Come." Simon entered the cottage and left its slim door open, and his new acquaintance finally followed him inside. "There, you see how the easy sunlight illuminates the whole of the thing and how its fantastic colors swim on floor and walls. And here and there one can just make out the queer sigils that have been subtly planted within the various colored shapes. I had a friend in Salem commission the work for me; your father became, at the end of his stay here, so hostile that I don't think he would have composed the piece had he known its eventual destination. We were adamant in our denial of his request, you see, but he, in his emotional state, was easily played with and spilled forth significant personal information. After he departed the valley I went on a small exploration of the churches and whatnot that wore his windows, and I was quite impressed. This small thing is wonderful indeed, but it cannot compare to the other."

"The other what?"

"The other thing that I required of your sire, the magnificent arched sheet of stained glass that has been affixed to its especial erection. Perhaps Marceline will shew it to you anon. How odd, your pensive expression. You seem disappointed in your sire's work."

"No—no; I was expecting another facet of it that isn't there."

"The pale portrait of an albinic phantom? No, she is not featured in this small thing. I noticed her repeated representation in those works that I examined when I journeyed hither and yon. She was …"

"My mother." The saying of those words caused the artist's voice to choke. "May I have some water or something?" And then, as he was looking around for a kitchen or sink, he saw the painting on the wall and began to shout and sputter.

"Pray stop making that grotesque noise. Whatever has clutched you? Ah—the Pickman. Yes, it is admirable."

"But it's of *you!*" Enoch exclaimed as he strode toward the painting and examined signature and date. "1926!"

"Merely yesterday. It's a playful portrait, of course, as you can see how he enhanced the sallow texture of my temporary flesh. And the eyes are too bright, they contain too much white, whereas you can see my eyes are in fact the shade of polished nickel." At this the beast removed his hat and fully revealed his fantastic face. "The face, of course, is perfection—for portraiture was his forte."

"You look exactly the same!"

"The same yesterday, today and tomorrow."

"What the hell are you, an Immortal?"

186

"I am a child of Sesqua Valley."

Enoch peered at Simon's face, with its grotesque combination of wolf and frog features, and suddenly grew afraid. Taking one last look at his father's work, he backed out of the cottage and hurried through the woodland, confused as to direction and destination. But at last he came upon the clearing where he saw the small lake, the two-story house and totem poles. He stopped to catch his breath and ease his sense of panic, now aware of the way in which the valley and its elements had indeed altered his perception of things, if not his actual physicality. He breathed differently, and his eyes saw in a dissimilar manner. Those eyes now watched the black woman who moved within the depths of the lake, accompanied by a strange white thing. Enoch watched as both figures submerged and escaped his view for a few moments, and then the pale entity bubbled onto the water's surface as the woman's hand reached out of the water and entered into the creature's substance. The white thing spread what might have been three wings and drifted lazily into the sky as Marceline swam toward land and crawled onto the earth, where she watched the uncanny being divide into particles that split apart and melted from view. Enoch walked along the lake's edge and approached the woman as she lay on her back and smiled into the sunlight.

"What was that thing with you just now?"

"Hmm? Oh, an aspect of the Thousand Young," came her nonchalant reply. "I was wondering where you went. Did you return to your little room above the store? I told you to stay here with me."

"These woods freak me out."

"You're safe with me. Your body and mind will adapt. I thought you liked the region's beauty, the soft green shade on your eyes, the sugary essence of our air."

"Yeah, it intoxicates; but there is something sick here, something untoward. I experienced a similar disquiet in Dunwich, which is also a land of primeval beauty. I encountered Simon Gregory Williams."

Marceline laughed. "Ho, no wonder you're distraught! The beast has that effect."

"He's a devil."

"That and more. You'd be amazed at his occult library, which he keeps in an ancient tower in the woodland. Really, Enoch, this isn't like you. Part of what attracted me to you is your propensity for wickedness, your lack of anything angelic. You have your fiendish qualities, as Simon has. No, this is something more. Some weird thing has touched you, deeply."

"His house has a window by my father."

"Yes, and there is another work by your father on a hill, before an altar. That is where we shall frolic tonight. Is that what has so affected you, seeing your father's art so unexpectedly? It's amazing that Simon allowed you to see his home at all—quite an honor, that."

The artist shrugged. "It got me thinking about my mother." He shrugged again, but the deepening sorrow on his face was palpable. "You didn't prepare me for any of this, cruel wench."

"This is your first mention of your mother. What sort of woman was she?"

"No, I'm not talking about her in this place. I don't belong here. I'm leaving tomorrow."

"Fie, wretch. You belong here more than most. That aspect of you that is other than human makes you most welcome in this valley. No, I'm not speaking of the tissue that has been grafted onto your mortal flesh. I refer to that part of your heritage that is other than human. I smelled it on you from the first. What is your heritage, Enoch? Are you the child of a changeling?"

He raised his hands in protest and shook his head. "No—nope, we're not playing this game. I came here to fuck you during the season of Shub-Niggurath. My magick phallus is all yours, but leave my soul alone."

How smoothly she rose before him, with what uncanny motion, as if she were some phantom come to haunt him. There was fire in her eyes and annoyance in the sound of her deep breathing. "You would do well to consider how you converse with me. Were you an ordinary mortal I would have my brother reduce you to rubble for speaking to me as you have."

"Your brother …?

"The Strange Dark One beyond the Rim." Enoch's sense of unease escalated as she approached him, her dark body moving with a panther's deadly grace. "No, you cannot move a muscle. The pain will be severe for but a moment as I plant my talons into your brow and read your memory. Yes, you would scream if I allowed it; you would clamp shut your eyes so as not to look into mine own. Ah, my necromantic nails elongate and pierce your little brain. What was your mother's name?"

Enoch's mouth barely moved as he whispered, "Lebanah."

"Ah—a Hebrew name, that potent alchemical language. Its meaning is linked to whiteness, to the moon. And she is an embodiment of all that is pallid, bleached—beautiful as smooth polished bone. Her hair is like spun milk, and silky. Do you recall her kiss? How strange, when you contemplate her mouth you see naught but teeth. Let me give you my sharp kiss then, in memory of your daemon-dam."

The temptress allowed him to wince as she bit into his mouth, and she laughed as, freed at last from her spell, his muscles worked again and allowed his prick to rise. She moved seductively and clamped him with her loins.

"I don't remember my mother ever kissing me," he confessed, as tears dropped from his little-boy eyes. Beneath them, the buried thing that was the valley's heart shook the ground with deep-rooted rhythm.

Removing him from within her, Marceline gazed into the artist's eyes. "Poor soul, I have never seen such sadness. It is the thing you never allow others to witness. You keep it locked in a secret chamber of your little heart. And yet it is enormous, and rules you utterly. Poor lamb."

"I want to see my father's other window, the one on the hill."

"You will see it in moonlight. Come now, your sadness had exhausted us both. Let us sleep the day away. I have a dream I want to share with you, an ecstasy of vision. You have shown me your soul, Enoch. Now I shall show you mine."

He barely heard her, for his senses had been thoroughly debauched by Sesqua Valley's lunacy. Enoch could feel the valley's pulse in his flow of blood and smell its essence in his nostrils, a fragrance that coiled to his brain and frolicked there. He did not understand where he was, or why he was reclining onto such a soft surface. He felt the hot tongue that licked his throat and then his face; he felt that muscle stroke his eye with a serpent's kiss and seem to splice into the tissue of his orb so as to lap his brain. He witnessed eyes that multiplied into one million stars set deep within a black face that expanded as some gulf of night, which he crossed into another pocket of undreamt-of galaxies. He learned how to kneel before a throne of fire as gremlins with outrageous faces pressed flutes to amorphous mouths, and their music was a malfunction in the maneuverings of ordered time and space.

Enoch opened his eyes and found himself wrapped within Marceline's embrace. From somewhere in the room, a devil played his pipe. Marceline arose and smiled. "Simon—is it time?"

The beast removed the pan-pipe from his mouth. "The moon has risen, but she hides behind a bank of clouds. Perhaps your magick can free her from that prison. I shall meet you there, anon."

"Meet us where?" Enoch queried as the beast exited and the woman wrapped herself into a robe of black silk that was open at her bosom.

"I want to show you your father's other piece. It's quite majestic."

She held her hand to him; pushing off the bed, he clasped it and allowed himself to be guided from the house and into the weird woodland.

Patches of night wore starlight, but the moon was indeed concealed and the woods drank darkness. Enoch saw, for a moment, the shadowed stone of the twin-peaked mountain, and then there was nothing but trees that watched them on their way over the earthen pathway. He lifted his eyes to watch the trees as the woman held his hand and pulled him through the gloom, and then the trees ended and they climbed a low hill to its summit. The artist marveled at the sight that greeted him, the stone arch that rose twenty feet above the ground and into which had been fitted a massive sheet of murky glass. He moved to the length of altar slab that had been positioned before the arch and sat as he continued to study his father's work. Even without the air of moonlight he could ascertain the various muted colors with which the glass was subtly enhanced—deep reds and blues and purples. And there, at one specific point, was the blur of pale whiteness, the features of which were not discernible because of the lack of light. That did not matter, for he knew instinctively what those features would portray.

Marceline sat beside him on the slab and kissed the back of his neck. "Come, recline. No, don't undress. We've paid enough homage to the Great Old Ones. We've had enough of sex. Now I want to help you conjure something far more potent—deep and everlasting love. Come, Enoch Coffin, stretch onto this bed of stone, with your head toward the archway. See there, the coiling clouds that conceal our lunar sister. Raise you white hand and move it with mine own as we make the Elder Sign. Yes! Excellent. See how the clouds move away, more and more—and there our sister unfolds her radiance unto us, her cold refracted glow. See how she enhances the sigils that your clever father, that sorcerer *par excellence,* had secreted into the glass. Look here, Enoch Coffin, at how those emblems enhance the beauty of my breasts on which they swim." Fluted music issued from some distant place, and the artist shuddered because he knew what beast haunted the woodland.

Stems of black cloud oozed away from the satellite that hung over the valley. Enoch turned his eyes away from the moon and its enhancement of the stained glass and watched as Marceline slipped out of her robe and let the fabric fall onto the ground. He watched, as the lunar light, revealed more and more as the clouds continued their dissipation, reflected the hidden symbols onto his companion's black flesh. And then he moaned as the moon, now fully freed from cloud, pierced its brilliance through that portion of the glass that was pale and oval; and he watched as the witch's dusky countenance turned white and became familiar. He watched her flowing pallid hair move about the visage that was as white as a blank canvas; and when the sorceress opened her eyes more widely he sighed at the beauty of their pink irises.

The woman's phantom face smiled down on him with a love that he had ached for; and then it lowered to him so as to grant one last compelling gift—a mother's kiss.

About the Authors

WILUM HOPFROG PUGMIRE has been writing Lovecraftian weird fiction since he was a young girl in the 1970s. His first American collection was published by Jeffrey Thomas, through his Necropolitan Press, in 1997. Pugmire's books include *The Tangled Muse, Some Unknown Gulf of Night, The Strange Dark One, Uncommon Places, The Fungal Stain,* and *Gathered Dust and Others.* In April of this year Arcane Wisdom Press will publish a new collection, *Bohemians of Sesqua Valley.* Wilum is currently writing his first novel, inspired by Derleth's *The Lurker at the Threshold,* and he will be working on an Enoch Coffin novel with Jeff in some dim future aeon.

JEFFREY THOMAS is the author of such novels as *Deadstock, Blue War, Letters from Hades,* and *The Fall of Hades,* and such short story collections as *Punktown, Nocturnal Emissions, Thirteen Specimens,* and *Unholy Dimensions.* His stories have appeared in the anthologies *The Year's Best Fantasy and Horror, The Year's Best Horror Stories, Leviathan 3, The Thackery T. Lambshead Pocket Guide to Eccentric & Discredited Diseases,* and *The Solaris Book of New Science Fiction.* Forthcoming from Miskatonic River Press is a role-playing game

based upon Thomas' universe of Punktown. Thomas is also an artist, and lives in Massachusetts.

Colophon

The text of this book was set in Adobe Garamond, designed by Robert Slimbach. Windsor Bold and Bold Elongated were used for titling.

81497739R00121

Made in the USA
Columbia, SC
01 December 2017